A Life Spent Looking

Liza Drozdov

Toronto 2023

ISBN: 978-1-7776142-2-5
eBook ISBN: 978-1-7776142-3-2

Cover design by Damonza

ACKNOWLEDGEMENTS

I was a child of the 70's and I thought of little else but music, rock concerts, music festivals, drinking, dancing and drugs and all manner of bad behaviour—basically all of things that can—and do—go terribly wrong for naive young women. Those young women now fill my thoughts: Women who are healing, rediscovering themselves, women finding what they lost, women who can't hold on but won't let go.

The characters and situations in this novel are my own invention and any mistakes in the book are my own.

As always, thank you to my dear friend Martha Mason who first introduced me to PoCo and to the Damonza team for their fabulous cover design and formatting.

Most of all, I'm grateful to my mother for inspiring me with a love of reading and of books, and to my children for their love and support.

A Life Spent Looking

ONE

OLD SINS CAST long shadows I've often been told and I can tell you it's true. Those sins may be dead and buried, but their shadows live forever. And they have claws that will tear the heart right out of you.

When I walked into the fire I knew it was dangerous, but I hoped I wouldn't be burned. After all, when you sell your soul, after you've made a deal with the devil, the flames might not set you ablaze. But there's always a cost. I knew it would have to be paid at some point, but I didn't know the price. And it didn't matter. I had no choice.

When Pandora opened the box she released all the evils upon the world. Her curiosity brought misfortune. But I didn't open the box because I was curious. I already knew what I'd find there. I knew exactly what it would unleash but I hoped I could handle it. I still hope so.

At least tonight I won't have to think about it. Nothing is going to happen, not yet. I've got two chilled bottles of wine in the backseat calling my name and the bag of takeout Thai food I place carefully into the hatch smells so delicious I'm tempted to grab a spring roll right now, but I resist.

I slam the door shut and I'm going around the back of the car when pair of strong hands grabs me. A black hood is pulled over my head and I put up a good fight until a second pair of hands restrains me and I'm thrown into the back of a car. There's no point in fighting two assailants I can't even see.

My heart is pounding and my mind racing. *Keep it together. Stay calm.* I guess they aren't going to kill me—they could easily have done that by now. So this is something else. The devil wants his due.

TWO

Two weeks ago

"It won't take long. The bank's closing in fifteen minutes," I say as I push open the door.

"Promise?" I hear Maja ask as I end the call and realize I've made a liar out of myself. There's a long line inside the bank and single flustered teller is serving customers while the head teller is on the phone at the back of the room. I can see the manager is in his office with some clients.

From the sighs of frustration I can hear and the tense body language of everyone ahead of me, it's clear they've all been waiting a while. At the front of the line, an old guy with his long grey hair in a ponytail is leaning on the counter, monopolizing the teller. His leather jacket and very expensive hand tooled cowboy boots indicate he's wealthy and his body language and attitude speak of entitlement. I'm sure we'll be waiting a long time.

I take a deep breath and scan the line, trying to be patient. Ahead of me is a frail elderly couple both sitting on their walkers, a young mother with a toddler in a stroller and a fussy infant on her hip, and the usual guys in hoodies and businessmen in suits. Just behind the guy at the counter I recognize my friend Rachel. As usual, she's impossible to miss. Rachel's plus-sized and doesn't try to hide it—the purple highlights in her grey hair perfectly match the woven lavender and purple cape she's wearing. I'm sure it's something she's woven herself; Rachel's a textile artist who lives and teaches at the feminist collective outside town.

To pass the time I distract myself by glancing around the bank's interior. Built over a hundred years ago, it's a beautiful old limestone building and a symbol of our town's earlier prosperity, especially compared to the shuttered factories and boarded up shops currently lining Main Street. Most of the bank's original architecture was lost when they renovated and carved up the interior space. I bet there are carved mouldings and ceiling medallions behind the modern drop ceiling that's been hung a few feet below the original one. The ugly speckled foam boards are stained and water damaged, thanks to the flood last week that forced the bank to close for repairs. Scaffolding is still set up along one wall and there are sections of ceiling still exposed, revealing wiring, and plumbing and sprinkler lines.

Another impatient glance at my watch tells me it's five minutes to closing. Just as the security guard is about to lock the main entrance, a man wearing a baseball cap slips in. The guard turns the lock and pulls the metal security grill partway across the glass doors then turns the sign to Closed and stands ready to let customers out as they've finished their business. Then the man in the baseball cap yanks a neck warmer up over his face and pulls a gun out of his jacket pocket.

"Move," he says, motioning the guard away from the door as three guys in hoodies step out of line ahead of me, pulling balaclavas over their faces and shouting "*Get down! Everybody down on the floor!*"

Within a minute they've cleared the offices and start herding all of us into one of the back rooms.

"Drop your cell phones and wallets here," one of the robbers shouts, kicking a blue recycling bin in front of the door the room. One by one we're quickly searched then sent inside. Before he locks us in, he tears out the phone on the desk so we can't call for help. They take the manager with them and I can see the look of terror on his face as the door closes. He knows he's going to die.

Nobody says a word as we're all straining to hear what the robbers are doing. At least they've kept the lights on and I'm able to quickly scan the room. There are no windows and the only way out is the locked door.

"Did you hit the alarm?" I ask the teller. He drops his head, embarrassed. I feel the tension flare in the room when everyone realizes the police aren't already on the way. "Are they going to kill us?" someone whimpers.

"I doubt it." I have no idea, but I try to sound as if everything is under control, even though it makes no sense. Most bank robbers are in and out in a couple of minutes. This looks like they are planning on a longer stay. Why lock us up? Are we hostages?

"Please, try to stay calm," I say. "We all need to sit down, especially you two." I push the two office chairs over to the elderly couple who gratefully collapse into them, their arms around one another. "The rest of you, just sit on the floor, behind the desk. It'll be safer there." I'm thinking of gunfire. The walls are just thin partitions—a bullet would go through them like cardboard, in case either the robbers or the police decide to start shooting.

"Who the fuck put you in charge?" The old guy with the ponytail barks, crossing his arms and looking for a fight. I may be only five foot five inches tall, but I could take him down in a heartbeat if it came to it.

"She's a police detective," Rachel snaps before I can reply. "*Asshole.*"

He glares at her and it looks like he's thinking about starting something with her, then sits on the edge of one of the desks, either unable to get down on the floor or unwilling to look like he's complying. I no longer care.

The baby starts to snuffle and cry and my heart falls. The last thing we need in here is a screaming baby. The mother slips it out of the sling and quickly lifts her shirt. An audible sigh of relief goes through the room as the baby starts nursing. The only sound is the embarrassed laugh of the man in the suit. I recognize his face from ads plastered all over the town's buses and transit shelters. He's a local realtor: Joe Rossi.

Rachel sidles up next to me. "Lucy, do you have your gun?"

"It's my day off." I shrug. It wouldn't have done any good since they'd just have taken it from me anyway. God only knows how much trouble that would have created for me at the station and I'm already in for it with Maja at home: I'm definitely going to be late for dinner.

I perch on the edge of the desk next to the security guard. "Are there other alarms?" I keep my voice low.

"Sure," he says, shooting a glance at the trainee teller. "But someone has to trip them."

"What about cameras?" He nods. "Oh yeah, all over the place." Okay, so at least we may have a shot at identifying them after the fact. Something doesn't fit though. They didn't pull up their masks until after they'd begun the robbery. Maybe the cameras aren't working after all, and they knew it.

I keep my ear to the door and can clearly hear the sound of machinery.

"Are they cutting the vault door?" someone asks. "Isn't that where all the money is?"

"I doubt we even have 30K on reserve in the vault," the head teller says. "This is just a small local branch."

Not that thirty thousand dollars isn't a lot of money, but I don't think it's enough for four robbers, two with guns, to risk holding up a bank for. Robbing a teller at gunpoint for the contents of a cash drawer is typically the work of a lone robber. This is something else.

"I think they may be after the safety deposit boxes," the teller says in response to my look. "They must be drilling out the locks."

I feel my anxiety building and know I need to do something, soon. Sitting in here, waiting for something to happen and being unable to do anything about it is not something I'm able to handle.

A glance up at the dropped ceiling tiles overhead gives me an idea. If I can just get up there the noise of their drills will mask what I'm doing.

"Did they count us when we came in here?" I ask the security guard.

"I don't think so." He looks confused. "Why?"

"I need you to boost me up there." I point at the ceiling. "Everyone else—stay quiet."

We both climb onto the desk and I push up against a ceiling tile. It pops up easily and he heaves me up high enough that I can pull myself up above the suspended panels, ignoring the pain in my shoulder.

"You're going into the ventilation duct?!" The trainee teller says. "Awesome!"

"No. Just the ceiling. This isn't Die Hard."

"Still very cool." He gives me the thumbs up.

"I'm going to drop down on the other side and unlock the door," I whisper. "When I do, you're all going to run out down the hall to the back of the building and out the emergency exit. Help each other," I point to the elderly couple who are already getting up and clutching their walkers. "Understood?"

"But when we open the emergency exit the alarm will sound," the head teller says.

"I'm counting on it. Count to fifty before you go out that back door. And when you do, keep running—all the way up the street, okay? Get as far away from the building as you can."

I carefully keep my weight over the steel ceiling supports as I slide the tile back into place behind me. "If anyone comes in, I was never here, okay?"

I creep along the inner ceiling, hearing ominous creaking every time I shift myself to crawl forward, but the structure seems stable so I keep going, wondering the entire time what the hell I'm doing this for. We could have all just stayed locked in the room. The robbers would have finished what they're doing and left the way they'd come. But that's not me. Feeling vulnerable and exposed, just waiting around and hoping for the best isn't something I'm capable of doing. I know from painful experience; I tried for years and it ended badly.

Once I've moved about ten feet along, I carefully pop up one of the ceiling tiles and take a peek below to make sure none of the robbers are in sight. I don't see anyone so I take a deep breath, slide the tile over and I'm about to drop down the nine feet to the stone floor, then I hesitate. What if I turn my ankle or break my leg? That wouldn't be helpful and I don't need another injury; I've barely recovered from my last one. So I shuffle a little further along, planning to drop down onto one of the sofas that line the wall outside the meeting room, when suddenly one of the robbers appears below me. He's looking up, curious about the noise and I freeze, holding my breath. I see he has his weapon tucked into his belt, like an idiot. He'll shoot his balls off one day.

He goes over to the door and tests it, making sure it's still locked. Satisfied everything is under control he turns to leave as I allow myself to fall through the ceiling, right on top of him. He's not as soft a landing as the sofa would have been, but he still breaks my fall. It may also have broken his neck, but I don't bother to check. I'm not that interested in his well being.

I run to the door and start to hustle everyone out. Two by two they creep out of the room and head down the hallway, leaving me with the security guard.

"I'll just take out the trash," the guard says as he picks the limp body and tosses him like a rag doll into the office, then gives me a wink as he closes the door.

First I take the robber's gun—a 9mm Glock semi-automatic pistol, exactly like my police weapon.

"Thanks," I whisper. "Now go. When you're all there, count to fifty and head out the door."

"You aren't coming?"

I hold my finger to my lips and shake my head, then give him a little shove to get him going as I creep back down the hall and wait for the alarm to ring. When it does the robbers will come running and I'll be ready for them. I count to fifty, but no alarm goes off. I wait another ten. Is the alarm silent? Is it even working? Were they not able to get out?

I can't risk waiting any longer so I creep up to the end of the hall and look toward the bank vault. I can still hear sound of drilling and metal being smashed and I can just get a glimpse of the men pulling jewellery and cash out of the safety deposit boxes and dropping it all into a bag. A glance behind the counter tells me the teller's cash drawers have already been emptied.

How much time has passed? It feels like ages, but I know that's just the adrenaline rushing through me. They're working fast and should be done in a few minutes by the look of things. As I watch one of the robbers comes out of the vault carrying a bag that he leaves by the front door. Then he slides something into the inner pocket of his jacket, unlocks the front door, slips past the metal security grill and heads down the sidewalk. He must he going for the getaway vehicle.

I see two other robbers still in the vault, filling another bag. The bank manager is cringing in the corner of the vault, clearly terrified, but there's nothing I can do to help him. They still have another gun, and I'm not about to risk endangering the manager by attempting an arrest now. As I turn to head out the back door I see the second gun, just lying on a desk behind the teller station. They must have felt so confident once they'd locked us all in they thought they wouldn't need it.

I draw the Glock from my belt and check the magazine. It's loaded. One of the guys in a hoodie carries a bag out to the front door and puts it down, then peers through the glass, checking for the driver. While his back is turned I creep up to the vault, picking up the second gun on the way.

I knock on the metal bars of the vault with my weapon and the robber turns, thinking it's his partner. He goes for his weapon, but remembers too late that he's left it lying on the counter. He freezes, staring at my gun.

"Raise your hands." I see his eyes behind the balaclava, desperately calculating what to do as the bank manager takes the advantage, runs out of the vault and cowers behind me. Then I slam the metal gate shut, locking the robber inside.

At the sound of the vault slamming shut the last robber comes running and I turn to meet him. He's already standing in the middle of the bank, eyes wide in astonishment before he even notices me pointing the gun at him. I see his eyes dart toward where the gun had been lying on the counter.

"Too late," I shake my head. "Now, lie on your stomach, hands above your head," I shout over the sound of sirens outside in the street. He panics and starts to run toward the back exit, but I fire a shot that gets him in the leg. That puts him down and as the police rush through the door I lay down both weapons and raise my hands in the air.

"Hi Detective Gauthier." One of the Constables recognizes me and grins. "Are you working today?"

"Funny," I smirk. Two more patrol officers come in, weapons drawn. They look disappointed when there's nothing to do but clean up and they holster their guns and head over to the man lying on the floor. He's moaning in pain from the bullet in his knee.

"There's another one in the back office," I say. "And one locked in the vault." I look around for the manager, who's now peeking over the top of the courtesy desk. "Maybe he can help you get him out."

"Did you get the driver?" I call after them as they spread out to get to work. They look baffled and stop short.

"What driver?"

"There was another guy. He went out the front door just a minute ago." They shake their heads.

"Dammit!" I pull out my phone to call Maja. I'm going to be late.

"Looks like I'm going to be stuck at work," I say when she picks up.

"You weren't at work Lucy," she sighs. "You went to the bank." She pauses for a moment. "You did go to the bank, right?"

"Yeah…Something came up. Now I've got paperwork to do."

"But Abby and Chantal are coming for dinner! I don't understand…"

"Save some for me. I'll be late."

THREE

WHEN I WALK into the station Monday morning I'm greeted by all the administrative staff and duty constables whistling and clapping in applause. I take an awkward bow, flushed in embarrassment. The hostages made a meal of the story and it was splashed across media, though I never gave a statement. Let the police department's PR division do that if they want. I can't think of anything worse than being the center of attention, for lots of reasons.

There's a lush flower arrangement on my desk, fragrant with roses, freesia and even some early sweet peas. The card is unsigned, apart from a large heart and a lipstick kiss, but I know it's from Rachel. The women at the collective make crafts and sell flowers to provide employment training and income for the women they shelter, and their arrangements are beautiful—too good to waste on the station. I'll definitely bring it home at the end of the day; I'm sure Maja will love it.

It might help appease her. She was furious with me when I got home on Saturday night. They were just finishing dinner but at least I was able to join them for dessert and a few glasses of wine. Maja managed to smile and pretend to be calm when I shared the story of the bank robbery with Abby and Chantal, who were maybe a little more excited than I was able to cope with. It must have been the wine they'd drunk with dinner; they were asking a million questions and praising me extravagantly while Maja sat with a frozen smile. I know that smile. And I knew I was in trouble.

She brought me out an ice pack, anticipating I needed it. "I'm sure your arm must be aching," she said. And it was. I just had a cast off two weeks ago and my forearm was tender and weak. Not to mention my old rotator cuff injury in my shoulder was throbbing. She opened her hand, revealing two ibuprophen capsules.

"Thank you," I whispered. She just sighed heavily.

The minute our guests left she gave me a dressing down as she slammed around the kitchen and cleared away the dirty dishes. "*Why would you take that risk? You could have been killed. Again. Haven't you learned your lesson yet? Not even after last time?*"

She barely spoke to me on Sunday morning and it was only after she got back from her shift at the walk-in clinic that she seemed to be back to normal. At least I got a hug and a smile when she walked in the door.

I've just got my coat off and my feet under the desk when DS Agu calls me into the meeting room. I'm sure it's the bollocking I've been dreading. I know exactly what he'll say: I risked the safety of the bank customers. I should not have escaped through the ceiling. I should have gone out the door with them and not gone after the robbers. I shouldn't have shot one of them. And I definitely shouldn't have put the one guy in hospital with a broken neck.

There's another man in the office and Agu introduces him as DS Dudek then invites me to sit down. If I'm getting a reprimand—official or informal—it doesn't look like it's happening immediately.

"DS Dudek is in CID out of District 2," Agu says. "He's leading the investigation into Saturday's robbery attempt." District 2 is one of the largest divisions in the Niagara Regional Police Force, thanks to the fact that more people live there, more businesses operate in the area including a casino and an indoor theme park, and millions of tourists flock to Niagara Falls every year. District 6, where I'm posted, is small by comparison. We don't even have our own Criminal Investigation Division, which is why District 2 is taking over.

"I just want to take your statement," Dudek says, pulling out his notebook and I go over the story again, with him interrupting for clarification a few times. But my story is the same as it was when I gave my first statement after the robbery. Nothing has changed. I've never managed to change the past yet, even though I often wish I could.

"Have you caught the driver?" I ask when Dudek's finished.

"No," he says, with a glance at DS Agu, who looks uncomfortable. "According to the men we've got in custody there was no other robber."

"Of course there was! There were four of them. I saw one slip out the door."

I try not to get defensive, and fail. "Why would I make it up? There was a fourth man. He came out of the vault, dropped a bag by the door then snuck out. He was wearing a baseball cap. You must have seen him on camera. Check the CCTV."

"There's no footage," Dudek sighs. "The cameras weren't working."

"So that's why the robbers weren't concerned about their faces being seen when they were waiting in line at the bank," I'm thinking out loud. "Convenient."

He grimaces. "It appears the flood at the bank last week wasn't an accident. The necessary repairs gave the contractors a way in to turn off the CCTV cameras and the alarms. We've got nothing on video for eighteen hours before the robbery."

Which explains why I didn't hear the alarm go off when everyone ran out the back emergency exit. "So someone at the bank set this up?"

"We're checking into it," he nods.

"There would have been a lot of workers there," Agu adds. "Plumbers, electricians, flooring guys, painters, not to mention insurance adjusters and God knows who else. It wouldn't have been difficult to get in."

"How much money did they get away with? Anything?" It can't be much, since the bags were all retrieved when the last three robbers were arrested. Apart from whatever it was I saw the fourth man slip into his pocket.

"It's impossible to say," Dudek admits. "We know how much cash there was in the tellers' drawers, but whatever was in the safety deposit boxes is unknown at this time."

"People use them to protect valuables," Agu adds. "Important documents like Wills or whatever. But they're also good for hiding things you don't want anyone to find."

"Because no-one's going to admit to having them," I say as it dawns on me.

"You're technically *not allowed* to keep dangerous or illegal items in safety deposit boxes," Agu says. "Like guns or drugs or stolen items. But people do all the time. There's no way to know."

"Doesn't the bank need to know for insurance purposes?"

"Nothing left in a safety deposit box is insured by the bank. Whoever owns the box would need to insure the contents themselves—on a special rider on their home insurance policy."

Safety deposit boxes suddenly don't seem all that safe after all.

"Were specific boxes targeted?" I ask after a moment. "Or did it seem random, like they were just smashing and grabbing?"

"The manager said it looked like they were working from a list. We'll know who the boxes belonged to by the end of the day. And the owners will tell us something, but who knows if it'll be true?"

"They're not likely to admit to anything incriminating," I say. "If I was hiding something from the law, you'd be the last person I'd tell."

Dudek looks uncomfortable. "The only question mark is this fourth robber you claim was there…"

"I saw him," I insist, trying to stay calm. "And he put something in his pocket before he left."

Dudek raises his hand to forestall me. "DC Gauthier, let's be clear. I believe your word over that of the bank robbers we've got in custody." I'm relieved to hear it. "But why they deny his existence is interesting. And unfortunately we have no proof. Nothing on camera…"

"The security guard will remember him. He was the guy who slipped in at the last minute, just as the bank was closing. He pulled a gun on him—just before he pulled up the balaclava. You'd think he'd remember his face." Dudek thinks for a moment.

"We'll speak with him again. Get him to give us a description, maybe do a sketch. Release it to the media." He turns a fresh page in his notebook. "This item you saw him put into his pocket. Did you get a look at it? What size was it?"

I think back to Saturday afternoon, trying to call up the mental image of the man as he went out the door. "I saw him from the side. Three quarter view, maybe. He was wearing jeans, and a long olive green jacket. And a baseball cap. The logo on the front… was a sports team." I'm thinking hard. "It was the Blue Jays. Definitely." Dudek writes notes as I recall the details. "He was maybe in his late forties. Clean-shaven, round face. About five foot eight inches tall. Slightly overweight—he had a beer belly hanging over the front of his jeans."

"Good, thanks. And the item?" Dudek prompts me. "It must have been small, since he put it into his pocket.

"It was long, white, in an envelope."

"You're sure it was an envelope? Not a jewellery case, maybe? Like for a necklace?"

"I'm not sure," I admit. "It was definitely white. About four inches wide, maybe eight inches long. He put it into the inside pocket of his jacket."

"Okay, that's good. We're checking other CCTV cameras in the area to see if we can pick anything up. This description will help."

Dudek thanks me again and gets up to leave, but DS Agu keeps me back. Great. Here comes the bollocking.

FOUR

"Gauthier," Agu begins once the door is closed. "I need to review something with you."

"Sir?" I brace myself for what's coming. His use of the word *review* brings others to mind, like *disciplinary* and *misconduct* and *neglect of duty.*

"One of the bog bodies has been positively identified," he begins. "From last summer?" he reminds me when he sees the stunned expression on my face.

"Bog bodies?" I echo, not quite on the same page as he is. Then it clicks. I'm not in trouble. DS Agu hasn't brought me in here to reprimand me.

"Yes. The remains of a female have been identified from her dental records. She went missing in 1990, when she was fifteen years old. Her name is Ella Weaver. Maybe you remember the case?"

"1990? Sir, I was born in 1992. Before my time, literally."

Agu laughs. "I realize that. I meant, maybe you've heard of the case, or read up on it at some point."

I shake my head. "Sorry, Sir. No."

"Ella Weaver went with a friend to see a band perform at a concert at the Buffalo Auditorium. Her friend was found two days later, in bad shape, with no recollection of what happened. Ella Weaver was never seen again."

I make a note to read up on the file when I get a minute. "Why did you want to speak to me, Sir?" I assume it has something to do with the bog case, which I'd been involved in last summer. In the process of solving another homicide I discovered dozens of decomposed bodies buried deep in Wainfleet bog, bodies we're still in the process of identifying, without much success.

"I'm assigning this cold case to you," Agu says. "You'll be the lead on the investigation."

"Sir?! Really?" I can barely keep the grin off my face.

"You've earned it," he says as he sits behind his desk. "You may still be new on the team, but you've shown me—several times already—that you're an excellent investigator with great instincts." He slides a file folder across the desk to me. "Read up on it. You'll have a lot of catching up to do."

Taking the folder I thank Agu and head back to my desk. What a great turnaround. I thought I was in for it and it just proves how things can change in a heartbeat.

I turn to Vogel's desk, eager to share my news, then my heart sinks when I see his empty desk. He's away on vacation, at his sister's wedding in the Rockies. DC Vogel gets me. He's the one person who wouldn't make a big noise about what happened at the bank, but he'd totally support my being assigned this cold case. He's the closest I've ever had to a friend, and he's become my emotional support here at the station, almost against my will. I miss him, not that I'd ever let him know it.

I feel a stab of regret admitting that to myself. Before he went away we hadn't been getting along. I know it's my fault; I'm not great with people and I like my boundaries. Vogel tries to get close and he pushes too hard.

The last time we worked together he just wouldn't let up.

"You never talk about your childhood Gauthier," he'd said with a forced laugh. "Why not? Are you hiding something?"

I started to panic as adrenaline flooded through me. My heart was pounding and I swear I saw red.

"Why would you think I'm *hiding* something?" I'd snapped at him, my voice shrill. "What would I be hiding?"

Vogel had recoiled in surprise. "Nothing. I'm just…joking." After that I made a point of avoiding him until he left on vacation. My past is my own business and I'm not about to share it with anyone, not even Vogel.

I flip through the file Agu gave me. There's not a lot in it. Many of the pages are brittle and yellowed with age and none of them will have any digital support either, given their vintage. They are thirty years old after all, and I bet most of the investigating officers on the case are retired, or dead. So no help there, but there are also probably boxes archived in storage that I'll need to requisition.

How did this fifteen-year old girl end up dead and buried in Wainfleet bog? We still have very little information about any of the bodies that were found buried there; forensic investigation has been slow, given the age of the bodies, the amount of decomposition and lack of resources. All we know for certain is they were buried by a man named Louis Zappa, who had mob connections going back decades. But he'd died before we got a chance to interview him.

It's going to be a challenge to go back thirty years and untangle the threads of this girl's story to find out what happened to her. Having a positive ID is a start anyway. Her dental records and the distinctive belt and earrings found with the body are a match to those in the missing person's report her mother filed thirty years ago.

Not much else was found with her body. I glance through the photos of the evidence. There was a tube of lip gloss and some breath mints found in the pocket of her pants. Luckily the pants were polyester so they hadn't decayed. There were two photographs but they were completely ruined, the images faded to nothing. There was also a folded piece of paper, with some words printed on paper in black pen. The paper was badly degraded when it was found in her pocket, so it's difficult to figure out what the words mean. They seem random, like some kind of a list, or maybe a poem. I make a note to see if the original can be restored in some way. Forensic technology has progressed a lot in thirty years; it might be possible to use Infrared Luminescence and photography to help restore the missing words and letters. Then I can work on deciphering their meaning.

From the papers in the file I read that Ella Weaver was born in 1975, she lived in town, had attended the local high school, and was fifteen when she disappeared. She'd lived with her mother, a single parent.

My heart skips a beat as just like that the day goes to hell. Her mother is Rachel Weaver. Rachel, my friend from Womyn Collective. I stare at the bouquet of flowers on my desk and wonder how I'm supposed to manage this.

I quickly review all the material in the folder to make sure I know all there is to know, then I requisition the cold case files. They'll be pulled out of storage this afternoon and with any luck I'll have them by end of day. Now I have to go speak with Rachel. I've delivered several death notifications to family members in my police career, but never one to anyone I consider a friend. I'm not sure I know how to handle it. I push out my chair and slowly pull on my coat. If I could walk any slower as I head out to my car, I would.

I pull into the Womyn Collective Farm driveway and park close to the shop where they sell lotions, oils and their signature textiles and weaving. That's Rachel's contribution to the success of the enterprise. She's a talented textile artist whose work has been displayed in museums and galleries around the world. She's also helped create a profitable business for Womyn's owner, Sophie. The abused women who come to Sophie for shelter are trained by Rachel to dye and spin yarn, to weave and to sew and to create unique table linens, quilts, soft toys, clothing and rugs that they sell at the farm, at markets, and online.

I find Rachel where she usually is, inside the Womyn shop. She's sitting in a circle of women who are attempting to learn knitting. Rachel is laughing with them as they struggle with these traditional female crafts, the sort of thing our great-grandmothers all knew how to do blindfolded.

As usual, Rachel is wearing layers of colourful printed scarves, over a woven tunic and pants, no doubt her own design. The purple streaks in her long grey hair have been enhanced with several new ones in fuchsia since I saw her on Saturday, and they match the chunky bead necklace she's wearing. Rachel is heavy-breasted and very overweight and her hips and thighs hang over the sides of her stool. She reminds me of an ancient fertility goddess, mystical and radiating power and love. I feel sick at the thought of what I have to tell her.

"Lucy!" she laughs when she notices me. "My hero!" She shakes the shoulder of the woman next to her. "This is Detective Gauthier," she says as she gets up and comes around to meet me. "She's the one who foiled the bank robbers." All of the women in the circle turn to me and I flush with embarrassment.

"Thank you for the flowers," I say. "They're beautiful."

"And so are you, my dear," she says giving me a big hug. "So are you." I hug her back, as hard as I can, lingering for a moment before I break it off.

"I have to talk to you."

A slight frown creases her forehead. "What's wrong Lucy?" She studies my face for a moment. "Your aura is cloudy."

"Yeah, I guess it probably is. I have some news."

"Is it about the bank robbery?" she asks, once we're sitting at a table across the room, out of earshot of the other women.

I shake my head. "I don't even know how to tell you this." Now she looks really worried and I know I'm just making it worse by dragging it out. "We've identified one of the victims found in the bog last summer." I'm trying to be sensitive, not saying *body* or *remains*, but really, who am I kidding?

Rachel just looks blank.

"It's Ella Weaver," I say, my voice catching. "Your daughter." Rachel doesn't move, but I know she heard me. She just can't process what I said. I reach over and take her hands in mine. "I'm so sorry."

"Ella," she whispers after a moment. "She's dead." It's not a question.

"The police said she'd run away. I knew it wasn't true." Rachel looks into my eyes, willing me to believe her. I can't explain whatever the investigating officers said or did all those years ago, but I fear I won't like what I find out when I go through the files. They'd probably discounted much of what Rachel had said during the initial interviews, putting it down to maternal hysteria.

"Ella was a beautiful soul," Rachel says. "A Libra."

I pat her hand, but there's nothing I can say. "I've spent my life looking for her," she says. "And she's been here all along." After a minute Rachel pushes herself up from her seat. "Please come with me Lucy. There's something I want to show you."

I follow her past the now empty knitting circle, the women all discreetly gone, into Rachel's studio. It's an open well-lit space at one end of the barn, with her loom set up next to a spinning wheel. An easel stands in the far corner, with an unfinished painting on it, and a collection of canvases are stacked next to it on the floor. On the far wall is a massive textile piece, almost a sculpture. It's a work in progress, destined no doubt for some prestigious exhibition halfway around the world. It's abstract, but reminds me of a dream landscape, with trees and grasses, moss and lichen and bark, all woven from yarn.

I sit on a worn sofa while she rummages around her things for a while, then she extracts a photo album. She lays it open on the table, pulls her chair up next to mine and starts to go through the pages. Before my eyes I see Ella's life pass by, from her baby pictures, held swaddled by a Rachel so young I don't recognize her, to a toddler and a beautiful blond little girl riding a bike, climbing aboard a school bus, and finally a Ella as a teenager. The last photos in the album were taken on the same day in summer, in a garden full of flowers. Ella is laughing and standing next to her mother, enduring a hug and rolling her eyes like a typical teenager. Both of them are wearing long, flowery and layered dresses with ruffled hems, along with cowboy boots and fringed vests—the height of hippie grunge fashion.

"These were taken on Ella's birthday. Her last one," Rachel's voice breaks. Ella's thick hair is almost waist long and wavy, a blonde version of Rachel's sea of grey waves. "She hated her hair," Rachel whispers. "Always wished it was straight."

"She looks a lot like you. And not just the hair." It's true. Rachel is so young and slender she could be taken for Ella's sister.

Rachel smiles her thanks. "She was a golden child. Her name means light." She strokes the photo, then glances up at me. "So does yours, Lucy. From Lucia."

"Can you tell me anything about when she went missing?" I change the subject. Rachel doesn't know Lucy isn't my real name, and I'm not going to tell her.

"I know it's been a long time, but anything you can remember might help."

"Even after all this time?" She sighs heavily. "Whoever did this to her is probably dead himself."

"Maybe, maybe not," I say. "But let's find out."

Rachel thinks for a moment. "You know, when I read my chart this morning, I knew something would be revealed. My moon's in Scorpio, with Neptune and Pluto."

"Okay…" I suppose Rachel's belief in Astrology isn't so different from most religions. It's her way of making sense of the world, and her world has just been turned upside down and shaken hard.

"When Ella first went missing," Rachel says. "I spent every minute looking for her." She looks at me intently. "I used divination. I scried crystal balls, threw I Ching, studied astrology and my crystals, consulted various mystics and psychics and healers, all of it. I left the mundane searching, the tangible kind of investigation, to the police and focussed on the ineffable.

"But none of it worked. Not my seeking and not what the police did. In the end I decided she wasn't lost after all. That's why we couldn't find her. It's the only thing that made sense to me. The only thing I could accept."

She pulls a photo of Ella out of the album and hands it to me. "You'll need this," she says. "For your investigation. I never liked the school photo the police used last time. I wasn't the real Ella."

Rachel sighs and studies her hands for a moment. "The day she disappeared, Ella and I weren't getting along. We'd had a big argument. The last words I said to her weren't…kind."

"What was the argument about?"

"Typical mother-daughter stuff. Nothing important." I feel like she's evading the question but don't see the point in pressing her.

"What can you tell me about her friend? The one she was with the night she went missing."

"Kim Parsons. Her best friend for years."

"Is she still in town?"

"She went away for a while, after it happened. But then I heard she came back a few years ago, with a daughter of her own." I hear Rachel's voice break. Ella might even have had kids by now too, if she'd lived. "She's living on her mother's goat farm, out by Stevensville." I make a note of what she tells me and give her time to collect herself.

"Do you ever see Kim Parsons? Speak with her?"

Rachel shakes her head. "She avoids me. I'm sure it's too painful for her. For me too, so I'm grateful for that." She exhales deeply and stands up. "I'm going to have to call my son."

"Your *son*?" I'm not up to another surprise today. "I didn't know you had a son."

"He's Ella's half-brother, born after she disappeared. He's grown, of course. Lives in town. "

"What's he do?"

"Nothing, really." Rachel shrugs. "He was born with his moon void of course. And his Mars in retrograde, among other things. Destined to spend his life ambling around…amounting to nothing."

"We all amount to something, Rachel." I shouldn't correct her, but I don't want her to say something she'll regret.

"Okay," she says. "Aimless, then? Yes, I'd say that's fair: aimless. No real direction or focus. He gets along. Takes what comes."

"What's his name?"

"Dillon. My ray of hope." I suppose that's what his name means, but I somehow doubt he's lived up to it.

"What does Dillon do?"

Rachel puffs out her cheeks, thinking of an acceptable answer.

"You could say he's a petty criminal I suppose. He has lots of friends and acquaintances from all walks of life…"

If this weren't so tragic I'd have to laugh at Rachel's delivery. How was this woman coping with the train wreck of her life? And how did I not know about any of it before now?

"What's Dillon's last name? Weaver, like yours?" I'm definitely going to look for his police record the minute I'm back in the station.

"Byrne. My ex-husband's name is Sean. We divorced years ago, when Dillon was just a boy."

I have one more difficult question for Rachel then I'm going to leave her in peace.

"Who's Ella's father, Rachel? Is this something I should be telling him?"

"Her father," Rachel muses, shaking her head. "You've just seen him, actually. On Saturday."

"I did? Where?"

"He was in the bank with us. The guy wearing the leather jacket?" I think back to the other customers who were there. And remember the hostility Rachel had for the guy in the leather jacket and cowboy boots. I'd just put it down to our having been in the middle of a bank robbery.

"The old guy who thinks he's a rock star?! Are you serious?"

"He wasn't always old," she says with a smile. "Not when he fathered Ella anyway. And he actually is one. A rock star, I mean."

"What are you talking about?" *Rachel? A rock star?*

"Haven't you heard of Running Deep?" I shake my head. "They were a big deal in the 80's and 90's, touring the world, their music all over the radio. Ella's father is Stan Price, the bass player."

"How'd you meet?"

"He grew up here, over in Ridgeway. My friends and I'd sneak into bars to watch his band play. I lied about my age, had some fake

ID. We had such fun in those days. Running Deep was really good. They had this country rock sound, kind of like the Eagles."

"Stan was a Leo, and his Mars was in Scorpio." A slow smile spreads as she meets my eye. "I was crazy about him. Over the moon. We had a volcanic sexual connection." She shrugs, and as her smile fades I can't help but think of her animosity toward him during the bank robbery. Where does that kind of love go?

"He wrote Star Queen for me, because I was always doing our astrological charts. It was one of their early hits," she adds in response to my blank look. "Then he ran off to become a rock and roll star…"

"Leaving you pregnant?"

She nods. "I was just eighteen when Ella was born."

"And he's back in town?"

"Years ago now," Rachel waves it off. "He opened a vanity winery, over near Pelham. I've heard he buys a lot of art and antiques. Just what you'd expect from a guy with too much money."

Money that Rachel clearly doesn't have now and didn't have when she a single parent, struggling to raise Ella. "Does anybody else know about the two of you? About your connection?"

"You're asking me if I told him, right? If Stan Price knew?" It's the obvious question, especially given how wealthy he became. If he'd denied it, she could have forced him to take a paternity test.

"Who's going to believe me?" Rachel laughs bitterly, avoiding the question. "I know what people would say. They'd all think I'm a fantasist, because he's *famous*." She makes a face as she says the word.

"It's not like he's Mick Jagger," I say and she nods in agreement. People are cruel and petty and I'm sure they'd doubt her story. Not that it matters at this point. Ella has been dead a long time.

"So you've never told anyone the story." She shakes her head.

"I couldn't bear to see the look on their faces. I have a mirror, Lucy. I know what I look like."

FIVE

KIM PARSONS IS living back on the family farm in Stevensville near the Safari Park. It's a real working goat farm, not a trendy place where you do goat yoga or have a *goat experience*. We have two of those on the other side of the escarpment, doing their best to capitalize on the summer tourist trade. They give tours and have petting zoos, provide a tasty lunch and the chance to purchase souvenirs and goat products all from their Pinterest-ready rustic shops.

The Parsons' farm is rustic, but definitely not picturesque. The barn and outbuildings all look like they could use repair and some boards replaced. But the fencing is all in good shape and I can see dozens of goats charging toward me from across the field as soon as I climb out of the car.

Within a minute they're all pressing their soft noses through the fence, hoping for cuddles or treats, or maybe just curious about what my business is. Most are white and brown with long, floppy ears and they are up on their hind legs, standing tall to look over the top of the fence.

Rachel had told me the Parsons had gone *back to the land* in the seventies, after their stay in the commune where they'd met.

"They bought that small farm and tried to be self-sufficient, growing their own food, living off the grid. They needed to make

29

some money so they started a market garden and sold produce at the local fresh market. Then when Kim was born that was all too much work so they turned to goats.

"Eleanor runs the farm on her own," Rachel had said. "Ever since George had a stroke years ago. She reduced the size of her herd but her goats still produce plenty of milk for her to sell. I guess she makes enough money to get by.

"She sells to artisanal goat cheese makers in the area. Womyn buys a lot from her too, to make the raw milk soaps and lotions we sell. Definitely have to put a lot of fragrance into it, to mask that goaty aroma."

"Doesn't her daughter help out? Since she's living there now?"

Rachel gave me a look. "I hear Kim's not up to much."

"Do you ever see them? Kim or Eleanor?"

"No." Rachel looks away. "We haven't spoken since Ella disappeared."

I find Eleanor Parsons in the barn. The sinews and tendons in her hands and wrists stand out as she milks a goat, the thick white liquid streaming into a large stainless steel bucket. The goat is up on an elevated wooden stand, with its head stuck through a hole into a manger and it's contentedly munching away, seemingly oblivious to the fact that someone's pulling on her teats.

Eleanor Parsons is probably in her late sixties like Rachel, but she looks much older. Her skin is tanned and leathery, thanks to a lifetime spent working on the farm. She's singing in a deep contralto voice, a beautiful melody that feels somehow deeply familiar. I don't know it, but at the same time I feel like I've heard it forever.

She stops singing when she sees me standing there. "The singing helps them produce more milk," she says, embarrassed. "It relaxes them."

"She doesn't mind?" I point to the goat, still chewing the grain.

"They barely notice, as long as they have their grain. And my singing, of course." She chuckles, then she finishes milking, plunges the steel bucket into an ice bath and leads the goat away.

"Can I help you?" she asks when she returns. Her tone is neutral. Not unfriendly, but careful.

I introduce myself, tell her I'm here to speak to her daughter and see a look of disappointment wash over her face. I'm used to it; the police are seldom welcome. She nods in resignation. "I'm just finishing up," she says. "I've got to give my husband lunch." Then she heads toward the house and I follow her, assuming I'm invited.

"What song was that?" I ask as we walk toward the house. I watch her shoulders rise in a shrug.

"I sing them folk songs from when I was young. The ones I can remember the words to—not too many of those anymore. But I'm partial to Gordon Lightfoot and Joni Mitchell myself."

We pass by the herd, still nosing through the fence.

"Those are Nubians," Eleanor says as she reaches through the gate to stroke a few noses. Their milk is high in butterfat, so it's good for cheese."

"They're certainly curious."

"Smarter than dogs," she laughs. "I have to make sure my back is turned whenever I open a gate latch or the feed bin. Otherwise they'll do it themselves the minute they get a chance. More trouble than a bag of cats."

From where I sit at the kitchen table I can see through to what was once the dining room of the farmhouse, which has now been converted into a bedroom for Eleanor's invalid husband. A hospital bed dominates the room. Mounted to the ceiling is a hoist that she must use to lift him out of bed and into a wheelchair. The mechanism looks like some kind of do-it-yourself contraption a resourceful woman might have adapted from a piece of farm machinery. Hospital equipment is expensive and I doubt the Parsons have a lot of money.

I try not to watch as Eleanor first changes her husband's diaper. Years of practice have made her efficient and she first rolls him to one side, then the other. He's compliant, like a big pale doll with floppy limbs and wasted muscles. Once he's clean she dresses him in fresh clothes and hoists him into the wheelchair, then pushes him into the kitchen and parks him next to me. George Parsons' eyes are closed. I can't tell if he's awake, or even if he's alive.

Eleanor puts a pot on the stove to heat then sits at the table. "It'll be ready in a minute." I'm not sure who she's speaking to.

"What happened to your husband Mrs. Parsons?" I hesitate at first, feeling awkward speaking in front of him, unsure if he even hears me.

"A stroke, ten years ago."

"And you look after him? Yourself?" George Parsons absolutely should be in care somewhere.

She gives me a tired smile. "We made a solemn promise to each other, years ago, that neither would be put into a nursing home." There's nothing for me to say. People make those promises all the time. But they're usually broken when they come up against the hard reality of what caring for an elderly sick person really means, and understandably so. But not Eleanor Parsons.

"Community Care sends a PSW comes in three times a week to bathe him and help out for a few hours," she continues. "But yes, I do it all. Lucky I'm healthy as a horse."

I look around the gloomy kitchen. The floor is dirty and there are piles of dishes in the sink and empty tins of soup left out on the counter. A load of laundry is hanging to dry on a folding rack next to the radiator and an ironing board is set up in the corner next to an overflowing basket of clothes. "I'm no expert, but it seems to me you should qualify for more than three visits a week."

"I would…but my daughter lives with me. So, they consider she's support for me."

"And she's not?"

Her silence speaks volumes.

"Kim has to look after her daughter Jade. She's only five. Just started full day school last September." It seems to me that when the daughter's in school all day, Kim should be able to help out, but I don't say anything.

"Does Kim work? I mean, does she have a job outside the home?" That earns me another weak smile from Eleanor. So Kim Parsons doesn't work, doesn't help out with her father's care or on the goat farm. What's her story? "Is Kim home now? I need to speak with her."

Eleanor goes to bottom of stairs and shouts up. "Kim! Someone's here to see you."

"She'll be a while," she says to me before she heads over to the stove and ladles out a bowl of soup for her husband. "What's this about?" she asks as she sets down the bowl and starts to feed George.

"Ella Weaver."

Eleanor looks more irritated than surprised. "I thought that was all put to bed thirty years ago."

"I'm sorry to tell you that we've now found her remains."

Someone behind me shrieks and I look to see a woman at the door into the kitchen. It must be Kim Parsons. Her face is white and she looks like she's about to pass out.

Eleanor leaps up and supports her daughter to a chair at the table. She gives me a sharp look then pours Kim a glass of water. It's not the ideal way to give someone bad news, but I didn't realize Kim Parsons was eavesdropping, or that she would take it so badly.

A quick glance at Kim tells me she's a wreck. She's wearing a soiled bathrobe over her pyjamas and her long hair is oily and tangled. She looks like a heavy drinker, possibly an addict and I doubt she's the one who'd gotten her daughter off to school this morning. As she raises the glass to drink her bathrobe sleeve slides down, giving me a good look at the marks and discoloration on her inner elbow. She catches my look and pulls her sleeve down to cover the raised scars and dark red trail of old injections sites.

I wonder how serious a user she was, or possibly still is. If there are noticeable old track marks on her forearms, it's as likely she's got others, like in her groin or between her toes-places she could more easily hide the signs of shooting up. Her pupils are normal and her eyes aren't red or bloodshot so I don't think she's high at the moment. Kim Parson's neglect in personal hygiene might be depression, or maybe she's in recovery, or at some point her life broke and she hasn't managed to put it back together again.

She's in her mid-forties, around the same age Ella would be if she'd lived. Her daughter is only five. So what did Kim Parsons get up to between the ages of 15 and 40 when she had daughter? Apart from a lot of drinking and drugs, that is.

Kim clears her throat but doesn't look at me. "You found Ella," she says, her voice a croak. "Where?"

"Her remains were buried in Wainfleet Bog."

"She's been there...all this time?"

I nod. "We believe so, yes."

"Why are you here?" She glares at me, her eyes narrow with suspicion. "It has nothing to do with me."

"We thought you should know, directly from us, rather than learning about it in the media," I stumble, surprised at her hostility. "And, since you were with her the night she disappeared..."

"...I already told you people everything I know," she interrupts me.

"It was thirty years ago!" Eleanor says at the same time.

"We're reopening the investigation," I say when they've quieted down. "As a cold case, given this discovery."

"Reopening the case! Haven't I been punished enough?" Kim's voice is rising and she looks desperate. "Why can't you just leave me alone?"

I put up my hand to try and calm her down, so I can try to explain why I'm here. "We got separated at the concert," she shrieks and she starts to pound her hand down on the table, punctuating every sentence. "I never saw her again. I think she must have hitched home. Ella was my best friend and I never saw her again." She jumps up and runs out of the room. I hear her feet pounding up the stairs then a door slams.

The room feels like the air has been sucked out of it. Eleanor Parsons looks embarrassed for a moment then she picks up a spoon and starts to feed her husband. He hasn't moved.

"Her friend died," Eleanor says, wiping George's chin before inserting another spoonful of soup. "She never got over it. People around here blamed her for everything. Why did she leave her friend behind? What did she have to do with it? What isn't she saying about what happened that night?

"Kim tried to stay in town after that but there was so much anger, everyone blamed her." Eleanor shakes her head. "She went bad. Because everyone thought she already was, so that's who she became. Hanging out with that crowd in the East Village. All those lowlifes and druggies." She pauses for a moment, staring into the middle distance. "That Melnyk girl and her boyfriend McAlpine. A bad lot."

My heart leaps into my throat when she says those names. The blood rushing in my ears is so loud I can barely hear what Eleanor is saying. I'm being haunted by them, by the secrets from my past that just won't stay buried. And now I learn that Kim Parsons was in their crowd?

"Kim never finished high school. Dropped out, then she ran off and went out west. George finally tracked her down in Vancouver. She was living on the East Side, doing drugs. He brought her back. She stayed a few months, then she was off again." She shrugs. "Did that a few times over the years. We finally gave up. *It's her life*, George said. He was right."

"When did she come home?" I force myself to ask as she's putting the empty soup bowl into the sink with the rest of the dirty dishes.

"She just showed up five years ago, with her baby girl. Clean and sober. Had been for over a year. Of course we took her in." She includes George in the decision, even though I can't see how he had any input into it.

"Of course," I echo. "How could you not?"

"It hasn't been easy. She's not strong. Honestly, I think just being back here has brought up a lot of stuff. But she has Jade now and she's been doing okay." If what I just saw of Kim Parsons is *okay*, I hate to think what a bad day looks like. "She helps out as much as she can."

"Does she have any friends? Does she see anyone in town?"

Eleanor looks away. "Kim never leaves the farm," she says in a quiet voice. "The last thing she wants is to talk to anyone from town, or to have anyone recognize her."

"The town's changed a lot in thirty years," I say, doubting that's likely. "I'm sure it's all forgotten."

Eleanor laughs. "People never forget. I don't like to think what your visit today is going to cause. This bringing up the past isn't a good thing."

SIX

THAT MELNYK GIRL and her boyfriend McAlpine. It was all I could do to not run out of that terrible kitchen, get into my car, drive straight out of town and never look back. But what I did was go into my pocket and open the vial of my rescue medication and slip an Ativan under my tongue. Afterwards I sat in the car, taking deep breaths and counting slowing to ten over and over until I felt the wave of panic begin to abate. *A bad lot. That Melnyk girl and her boyfriend McAlpine.*

I've spent the past fifteen years trying to put that past behind me, to forget it, to obliterate it completely, but every time I think I've succeeded it sneaks up and bites me, hard. All the times when I was a patrol officer, getting called out to yet another domestic or arrest in the East Village and working to make sure I never showed a reaction, keeping my face a mask of indifference and hiding the turmoil and shame roiling inside me.

Faces I thought I recognized, people I knew, kids I grew up with and their parents—all painfully familiar to me. When I'd get called out to one of their houses I'd hide behind my uniform and my badge with the new name the Crown had given me after my life all went so horribly wrong. Most of those kids were already on the local police radar; it's just the usual East Village crap. I'd go into their houses and have flashbacks to that time and to the house I used to live in with my mother before she died.

The house with the dirty linoleum tiles in the hallway, the cracked plaster ceilings and the nicotine stained curtains in the windows. The house full of people drinking and smoking every day when I'd come home from school; some people I didn't know and the rest I wish I didn't. My druggy uncles and their girlfriends, my stepfather and his friends, my beautiful sad mother Helena Melnyk.

How did Kim Parsons even know my mother and their East Village crowd? She'd grown up on a goat farm out in the country and did well in school, according to the case files. Kim was a good girl—or she was until after Ella's disappearance. She'd found her way to the East Village through the choices she made. Eleanor talked of the blame and cloud of suspicion Kim was under after it happened. Was it shame that drove her? Or maybe she was she guilty of something.

The drive back from the Parson farm in Stevensville is slower than usual, and the traffic gets heavy as I get closer to town. I've got no choice but to stay on the road though; out here in the country you don't have a lot of options since there's only one two-lane highway between the farm and Highway 3. By the time I'm getting close to the station I can see clouds of black smoke billowing into the sky. I have a good idea of what's causing the slow down.

There's a large fire downtown just on the east side of the Main Street bridge and fire engines, patrol cars and paramedic vehicles are blocking the road in both directions. Luckily the main fire department building is literally around the corner, so I guess they were able to arrive on the scene quickly, but from what I can see it's burning out of control.

There's smoke billowing out of second floor windows along

the block and it looks like the offices and apartments above the stores are already gone. The roof is in open flame and even though both pumpers are spraying it with jets of water it doesn't seem to be slowing the spread.

Traffic is being diverted along several side streets and I pull over to offer assistance.

"It's been burning hot like this for at least two hours already," the constable on duty tells me. "It took off really fast." That's suspicious. Fires don't usually engulf entire buildings in such a short time, not without a little help. I guess the CID team now has another case to deal with.

When I get back to the station I find a message from DS Dudek. I'd like him to tell me they've caught up with the fourth robber—the one everyone believes is a figment of my imagination, but I'm not holding my breath. Even though CID has gone through all of the available CCTV and traffic cam footage in the area around the bank, nothing turned up that even remotely matched my description of the man. It's not entirely surprising, given that we only have a few cameras in the entire block around the bank, but still. Some validation would have been nice.

"DC Gauthier," he says when I call him back. "I think we might have found your guy." So the fourth robber is now *my guy*. Well, at least maybe Dudek now believes he's real. Unfortunately, from his tone I think *my guy* may be dead.

"Meet me behind the new restaurant next to the Canal. The one in they've built in the abandoned railway station." I head back out the door; I can be there in five minutes.

I leave my car out front and head past the patrol cars and two constables posted to keep everyone out. My instincts are good; it's clearly a crime scene. Just past the large green dumpster I see Dudek, standing a safe distance behind Dr. Vijay Singh, one of our local Coroners, while he observes the initial post mortem investigation.

A white pop up tent has been erected over the scene, both to protect any evidence and to discourage onlookers. Given the fact there's a four-story apartment building within sight and people are already out on their balconies, holding their cell phones and posting live feeds to social media, that was a good call. This way the most they'll see is the tent and some police officers coming and going. If they're lucky they'll get a shot of the body bag being wheeled away into the mortuary van when we're done.

The back door of the restaurant is cracked open a few inches and I can see the white uniform of one of the kitchen staff, trying to get a look at what's going on. Dudek reaches out and slams the door shut, hitting the guy's nose. We exchange grins and the guy behind the door yelps in pain as Dr. Singh finishes his exam and backs out of the tent, carrying his medical bag.

"Single gunshot, close range, to the chest," he says. "Death would have been immediate."

"Time?"

Dr. Singh pauses to calculate as he's peeling off his nitrile gloves. "Rigor has passed. Liver temp suggests he could have been dead forty-eight to seventy-two hours."

"Two or three days?!" Dudek says. "How's that possible? This is a busy restaurant. People come and go all the time."

"It's been closed for repairs, Sir," one of the constables nearby says quietly. "Since last week. Just re-opened today."

I shake my head. "I wouldn't be too sure about that," I tell her. "Please find the manager or owner or whoever's in charge. They aren't going to be allowed open today, not until we're done here." She heads off around to the front of the restaurant, to deliver the bad news. I hope SIU won't be too long, but it's going to be a few hours at least. Maybe they'll be able to open for dinner.

"May we?" Dudek asks Dr. Singh for permission to approach the body.

"Be my guest," Singh says, then he turns to the mortuary attendant who's just arrived on the scene. "When they're done you can remove the body." With a wave he's gone.

I follow Dudek into the tent and look over his shoulder. The body is that of a middle-aged man, wearing jeans, a dark olive green jacket and a Blue Jays baseball cap. He's slumped half-behind the dumpster, lying onto a pile of cardboard boxes that have been broken down and neatly bundled for recycling. Anyone passing by the back of the restaurant wouldn't have seen him lying there. Only when the kitchen staff had come out through the back door to toss some garbage was he noticed.

"Is this your guy?" Dudek asks.

"The clothes are the same," I tell him. But there's nothing especially distinguishing about the dead man's features, especially now that they're flattened out in death. His eyes are closed, so that's no help. "It's probably him," I say. "I don't suppose you found a mysterious white package in his pocket?"

Dudek shakes his head. "Nothing."

"Any ID on the him?" Dudek shrugs. That would be too easy.

We leave the tent, giving them the okay to remove the body and let SIU begin their investigation. Dudek and I stand together watching, far enough away that we can speak without being overheard.

"I figure he leaves the bank," Dudek is thinking out loud. "Leaving the other three robbers behind. Maybe he's going to get the getaway car but takes off when he sees the police cars pulling up in front of the bank..."

"Or," I interrupt him. "He slips out the front door, never intending to come back at all. He takes whatever it was he was after—that mystery item I saw him slip into his pocket—and walks out, never to be seen again."

"You think he just left the other guys to finish the robbery? Whatever cash and valuables they managed to steal weren't important to him?"

I nod. "Or he knew he'd get his share at some later time. He was the one who knew how to reach them."

"Possibly," Dudek concedes my point. "And then sometime later on Saturday he meets up with his contact, maybe whoever he was selling the item to—and gets shot for his trouble."

"So you think it's about this item? The other stuff they tried to take was just gravy?"

Dudek shrugs. "Maybe this guy, whoever he is, was hired to steal that thing specifically. That's why he left the scene."

"And that's why he was killed. He's the only one who knew the buyer."

"That fits," Dudek says. "The other guys are dummies. Smash and grab. They wouldn't have the brains to set up the robbery."

"Have the other three said anything?"

"They aren't talking and I doubt they know. When I said they're dummies, I meant it."

"Could they ID him? He's the one who brought them into the plan."

"If they'll talk. I'll bring a photo around later. They're all due in court today for a bail hearing. Except the guy who's still in hospital," he laughs. "You really stuck that landing—on his head."

SEVEN

THE FIRE DOWNTOWN burned all day, thanks to the fact that it spread quickly along the row of storefronts along the block. They were all built before fire and building code required separation walls between structures so there was nothing stopping the flames from jumping from one unit to the next. And most had wooden lean-to garages and storage sheds on the back, which burned like kindling once the sparks hit. By the time firefighters put the fire out, a Chinese restaurant, a thrift store, a butcher and a gluten-free bakery on the main street were smouldering ruins and the two apartments and the lawyers office above were completely gutted. But nobody died and even the pet cockatoo and two cats that'd lived above were safely rescued.

The fire had started in the lawyer's office and as I suspected it was clearly arson, given the multiple points of origin, burn patterns and evidence of an accelerant having been used. Investigators are still on the scene, and will be combing through the site for weeks, looking for evidence.

The air smells scorched all over town and the streets in the area are still closed off as contractors board up the buildings to prevent anyone entering the scene. It doesn't look as though anything is salvageable and the buildings will have to be torn down, which is a shame since they are heritage properties dating back to the 1800's.

I'm not surprised someone would want to burn down a lawyer's office, but this isn't one of the Niagara Region's high-profile firms. It's a small practice that deals in Trusts, Estates and Wills, as well as some Family Law divorce and custody cases. They don't even do criminal law and apart from the fact that some divorce cases do get ugly and violent, nothing about the sort of cases they took on makes them the likely target of an arson attack, or at least not that I'd have thought. Just shows what I know.

I'm on my way out to Womyn Collective to speak with Rachel again. I haven't given her any sort of an update since I told her we were re-opening the case, mostly because I haven't had anything to report. I've spent all my time going through all the files, and my desk and the floor around my desk is covered with boxes that have been delivered from the archives. It's laborious work, going through pages and pages of witness statements and notes made by the investigating officers, and none of it has been especially illuminating.

One thing I'd come across in files was a clear unwillingness to believe anything Rachel said. It was obvious the investigating officers didn't have any respect for her. Most of what she'd said at the time was put down to hysteria, attention-seeking or even suspected drug abuse. It seems that a single mother, and an artist or a mystic or a psychic or whatever she identified as, automatically discredited her. There are a couple of photos of a younger, and very beautiful, Rachel in the file, with those of Ella and one of Kim. She was big, but not morbidly obese like she is today. The loss of Ella—her grief, looking for comfort, must have caused the weight gain. It's no wonder she's so sensitive about her appearance now.

It feels as if Ella's disappearance was not a very high-priority case at the time. Several comments I read indicated she was a runaway, or even that she was possibly a groupie who'd run off with the band, despite several people's statements to the contrary. By all accounts, Ella was a good kid who was into music and did well at school, who'd just happened to go to a concert at the Buffalo Auditorium and was never seen again. The media and police statements feel like a whitewash, as if Ella could do no wrong. But maybe that's not the full story. I need to have Rachel explain to me what I'm missing, if she knows. And if she's willing to tell me.

I have no clue how Ella ended up buried in Wainfleet Bog—only a straight forty-minute drive along Highway 3, but in another country entirely from the Buffalo Auditorium. She'd have to have been brought across the US/Canada border from where she was last seen in Buffalo NY, either alive as a passenger or already dead.

When I step into the shop at Womyn, it's heavily fragrant with lavender, to the point of giving me a headache. They must be distilling some essence for some of the lotions and potions they are famous for.

Sophie emerges from the back room when the door chimes, and her face lights up when she sees me. Sophie's the owner of the Womyn Collective Farm. She manages all of the production and oversees the various money-making enterprises that help provide the financial support that keeps the women's shelter afloat.

"Hey stranger! Good to see you." She gives me a hug and brings me over to a table. "Can I get you a coffee? A glass of water?" I accept the offer of coffee, even though I've just finished one in the car and watch as she busies herself making it.

"I'm here to speak to Rachel." I see her back tense.

"About Ella," she says. "Rachel's having a really hard time, ever since…"

"Since I brought it all up again?"

She shrugs and puts down my coffee. "I know you're just

doing your job, believe me. It's just…I don't know. Dredging up the past…"

"Nobody likes to revisit bad times," I say. Especially me, but I don't say that aloud.

"Anyway, Rachel's not here. She's out picking up a shipment at UPS. Some alpaca wool from Peru, and I think some mohair from Turkey."

"Exotic," I smile. "She's going to love working with that."

"She's been invited to exhibit at some museum." Rachel's textile art is brilliant and it's been displayed—and sold—at galleries around the world.

"So she's pretty inspired right now," Sophie continues. "I think it's helping her, especially…" I don't need to ask what she means.

Sophie smiles and sips her coffee. I'm relaxed sitting with her and I don't feel the need to chat and fill the silence with conversation, which for me is rare. I'm socially awkward and my default is usually uncomfortable silence and a quick exit.

I catch a glimpse of a new painting on an easel in Rachel's studio space. I can see it's a portrait of a young woman, looking off into the distance. She is remote, detached, as if her mind is far away. I go over for a closer look.

"Is that one of Rachel's?"

Sophie nods and follows me. "Good, isn't it?"

I don't know if *good* is the right word to describe the painting. It feels sad, and empty. "It's Ella."

Sophie nods. "Rachel goes through bad times, when she'll get into a dark place. She paints Ella, over and over. When she's not walking the fields for hours, day and night." She points to the canvases stacked against the wall and I flip through them. Every one is a portrait of her missing daughter.

"Any idea where she goes?"

"None. She's always bringing back bits of rock and moss, flowers and broken twigs."

"Why does she do it?"

"Who knows?" Sophie shrugs. "Looking for inspiration for her textiles? She told me once artists must develop *the habit of looking*, of seeing."

Rachel has probably spent her life looking at faces, searching for signs of her daughter. For the tilt of her nose, the curve of her cheek. Looking eagerly at any young woman who could be her daughter's age, followed by the crushing realization that her daughter would be over forty years old now. If she were alive.

"I met Kim Parsons the other day," I say as we go back to the table. "Did you ever know her?"

Sophie shakes her head. "Not really. I mean I knew *of* her, especially when it all happened and was all over the news. But she's a few years older than me. Different crowds." She thinks for a moment. "Maybe not so different, really. But she was already gone by the time I started hanging out with that crowd, if you get my meaning." I'd heard Sophie had some druggie boyfriends, one of whom did time in prison.

"What did you hear about Kim?" Kim Parsons isn't the focus of the investigation into Ella's death. But the more I know about her, and how she ended up like she did, the more insight I may get into Ella's story.

Sophie looks uncomfortable. She's one of the most discreet people I know. Many abused women come to her for help and she's heard and seen it all, but she never speaks of it—unless she's asked to testify in court on behalf of one of the women she shelters.

"Do you remember high school Lucy?" Sophie asks, studying my face. "The cliques, the cool kids, the popular kids, the nerds, the losers. The sluts. The druggies."

I nod. "Sure, of course." I remember it very well; mostly how hard I worked to erase who I was and where I'd come from. To keep my past a secret buried as deeply as I can.

"Kim was one of the good kids. The ones who never made much of an impression, who did well in school, but weren't outstanding in any way. Not particularly creative or sporty or anything. Just… ordinary." She pauses, looking into her coffee cup. "Then, after it happened, she started hanging around the East Village, skipping school, experimenting with drugs…"

"Sex?"

"Lots of that." She sips her coffee. "The guys passed her around. Then they dropped her, of course. It was a big joke to them."

"Poor Kim," I say. "I can't imagine what that was like for her, being used like that, then laughed at. Slut-shamed."

"That's the patriarchy for you," Sophie scoffs. "Still going strong even in a welfare-class backwater like the East Village. A girl puts out and they never forget."

I shake my head. No wonder she's a recluse, staying out at the farm.

"She worked for a while as a stripper," Sophie says. "Or tried to anyway. One of the girls she hung out with got her into it." My heart starts to pound. "Apparently she wasn't very good at it. Too shy." One of the girls she hung out with. *That Melnyk girl and her boyfriend McAlpine.* She means my mother. *A bad lot.*

"How did you hear this?" I ask. My mouth is so dry I can barely speak.

"Maggie," Sophie says. "We lived in the East Village then, when I was young. Until she inherited this farm, didn't you know that?" I think I knew this information, but somehow I'd misfiled it in my memory. I hadn't placed Sophie and her mother Maggie into the *avoid at all cost* file, into the *danger do not open* file, the ones I've avoided at all costs for years. Now my anxiety is blossoming in my chest and I reach into my pocket for a rescue Ativan.

"Headache?" Sophie asks. I nod and slip the tablet under my tongue.

"It's this weather," I lie. "Low pressure system moving in."

Did Maggie recognize me? Did she remember that time, all those years ago? Did Sophie? Did they know me as the girl who'd killed someone? As the one who'd been sent away and changed her name? I breathe a sigh of relief that Maggie is dead now. She was so sharp; she'd have recognized me, I know it.

I hear the doorbell ring and Rachel bustles in, pushing a handcart loaded with boxes of yarn. "There's a whole van full outside," she calls out. "If anyone wants…" She stops short when she sees me. "Lucy! How are you?"

Her smile fades as she takes in Sophie and I sitting at the table. Why that should make her nervous I don't know, but I see her tense. "What's going on?" she asks. "You two look…muddy. Your energy is off." Auras again.

"I came by to talk with you," I say.

Sophie gets up and heads for the back room with a wave. "I'll get someone to unload the rest of the van."

"What is it?" Rachel says. "Did you find something? Already?"

"Sorry, not yet. I've been going through the files. There's a lot to review." She nods. "I just have a couple of quick questions."

"Okay, let's have it."

"Ella and Kim were going to a concert that night—at the Buffalo Auditorium, right?" Rachel nods. "Do you remember who they were going to see?" I'm disappointed to see Rachel shake her head. I know she's lying.

"It was Running Deep," I say. Rachel looks away and I know I'm right. "Her father's band." Why didn't Rachel want me to know? Was she hoping I wouldn't find out?

"You said you'd had an argument the night she left. That the last words you said weren't kind." Rachel nods and looks down at her hands. Her eyes are welling with tears. "Did you tell Ella the truth about her father? Is that what your argument was about? You didn't want her to meet up with him?"

Rachel sighs and wipes her eyes. "Yes. You're right," she whispers. "I'd told her about a month before she…died," she hesitates before she can say the word. "Who her father was, how we'd met and how she'd been conceived. Not all of it." She meets my eye. "I gave her the nice, romantic version of the story. I didn't want her to know what an asshole he'd been."

"Then, when she heard on the radio that they were playing in Buffalo, she wouldn't let it go. She wanted to go to the concert, to meet him, to talk to him. She thought we could go together, that he'd recognize me. God," she whispers, wiping her eyes. "I honestly think she believed we'd get together and be a happy family."

"And you gave her a reality check."

"I tried! She wasn't listening. I told her there was no way. That's what caused the fight."

"And she went to the concert anyway. With Kim."

Rachel nods. "I've been to plenty of concerts," she says. "I knew there was no way she'd ever get backstage or even close to him or the band. I wasn't worried. It never occurred to me that anything would happen."

"And you never told the police any of this at the time?"

She shakes her head. "What was the point? I knew she hadn't gotten past the security detail. The police looked into that. And I didn't want to see the faces on those cops when I told them my story about who Ella's father was. I knew they wouldn't believe me."

EIGHT

I NEED TO speak to Kim Parsons again, and maybe this time she'll stay calm enough to tell me something helpful. Did Ella say anything to her about Stan Price being her father? Did they discuss trying to meet the band, try to get backstage at the Running Deep concert? According to her original statement, she and Ella had taken a bus into Buffalo and walked the few blocks over to the Auditorium, stopping at McDonald's for a burger and fries on the way. They did not drink any alcohol—they were underage. They did not do drugs—neither of them was into them. Kim says she wasn't even especially a fan of Running Deep, but that Ella wanted to go. Kim thought they were *an old man's group*, like Styx or Journey. She preferred The Tragically Hip but Ella convinced her. They bought tickets—last minute, way up in the nosebleeds.

They went to the concert, and got into their seats. Then, midway through the show, Ella wanted to sneak up to the front, so she could get close to the band. Kim didn't want to. She'd done it at lots of other concerts, but it was a different crowd at the Aud—everyone was older. She'd stayed in her seat and Ella pushed her way up to the front of the hall. The agreement was that Ella would return at the end of the show. Kim suspected she'd be back sooner, that security would ask to check her ticket and send her back up to their seats in the rafters.

Then Kim's memory fails. She doesn't remember what happened after. She doesn't remember anything until she woke up two days later in hospital. She had been found, after a two-day search, asleep on a park bench on Crystal Beach. She had no idea how she'd ended up on the bench, or what had happened to Ella.

They had tested her blood for drugs and found nothing to explain her memory loss. I now know there are several pharmaceuticals that would have explained what happened to Kim. She may have been given Rohypnol, or GHB or ketamine or even something else, but at that time they weren't yet able to test for those drugs. They'd found trace alcohol in her blood that she didn't remember drinking. No one remembered seeing her, or Ella, either at the concert or after it, apart from the staff at McDonald's. Ella had simply disappeared, leaving no trace.

As soon as I get out of the car at Parsons' farm I hear the loud bleating of the goats. They're all huddled near the fence that leads to the barn. I'm not a farmer, but something about the goats looks desperate and their odd behaviour is making me nervous. What do they want? They are thrusting their noses through and constantly crying. I can see their udders are huge and look like they might burst.

There's no singing coming out of the milking parlour. I see a pail of milk has been kicked over and spilled across the milking stand and a bag of feed tipped over in a corner. I head toward the house and knock on the kitchen door. There's no answer, so I raise my voice and call her.

"Eleanor? Hello?" I push the door open and step inside. "It's Detective Constable Gauthier!" Nothing.

There's nobody in the kitchen, but it's a mess. There are spills all over the floor, badly wiped up with tea towels that are tossed into the sink. There's an open box of cereal on the kitchen table next to a half glass of milk. I don't like this. Eleanor may not have been the tidiest housekeeper, but this mess was next-level stuff.

I brace myself and push open the door to the dining room. The smell knocks me back and I have to force myself to go in and check on George Parsons. He smells awful. *Is he dead?* He smells very dead. I check for a pulse and find a faint one in his neck, so I pull out my radio and call for help. An ambulance is on the way.

I know I should wait for backup, but I need to know what happened to Eleanor. And Kim. And Jade—she should be home from school by now, but there's no sign of her or her mother and grandmother.

"Eleanor?" I call in a loud voice as I head for the stairs. "Are you okay? It's Detective Gauthier. I'm coming up!" No response.

There are four doors at the top of the stairs, all closed. I push open the first on the left. It's a little girl's room and Jade isn't in it. The next one to it is a depressing mess, with the bedding rumpled in a heap, clothes tossed on a chair and the curtains drawn. It must be Kim's room. The next room is the bathroom, and it's empty. My heart's in my throat as I push open the last door, which must be Eleanor's.

The windows are open and the curtains are fluttering in the spring breeze. The bed is made, and there's a little mound in the middle of it, as if a small animal had burrowed under the duvet and gone to sleep. Eleanor is sitting up in an upholstered wing chair, next to the bed. Her eyes are open and her mouth agape. She's dead. A little girl is sitting on her lap, hugging her. Jade.

I have no idea how to handle the situation but instinctively I crouch down, thinking maybe talking to frightened children— even those who are sitting on their dead grandmother's laps—is like approaching new pets. You've got to stay small and unthreatening.

"Where's your mommy?" Jade shakes her head and looks away. Is she mute? Does she not speak at all or is this the result of trauma?

"Are you hungry?" She nods. I reach out my hand to her. "Let's go downstairs, okay? I'll make you something." Jade slides off Eleanor's lap, takes my hand and I lead her downstairs.

She sits at the table while I go through the fridge, blindly looking for things that go together and that a child might like. I have no idea. Then I open the freezer and find the answer.

"Would you like some ice cream?" She nods.

"With chocolate sauce. Please." She points to the cupboard next to the stove. Inside is a plastic bottle of chocolate syrup and I quickly scoop her some ice cream and squeeze a dollop on top. "Aren't you having any?" she asks when I hand her a spoon.

"No, thanks. It's too close to my dinner." She nods. I think it's probably something she's heard before.

George moans in the next room and Jade's shoulders hunch in fright. No wonder she's afraid of the old man. He scares me too. "It's okay," I say. "Your grandfather is going to be fine. An ambulance is coming to help him." I check my watch, wondering how much longer they'll be when I hear the siren coming down the road.

"Was your mother here today?" Somehow I doubt it, based on state of the kitchen. Jade shakes her head and swirls more chocolate syrup onto her spoon.

I was last here on Tuesday, two days ago. I can't tell how long Eleanor has been dead, but for all I know I was the last person to see her alive. It's obvious no one has tended to George in a couple of days at least.

"Did your mama get you off to school today?" A head shake. "Yesterday?" Another no.

So Kim Parsons wasn't around today, or possibly yesterday by the looks of it. She left her daughter and took off, God knows where. I just hope her mother was still alive when she did it.

"I'll be right back," I tell her when the paramedics come

through the door. "Eat your ice cream." I lead them through to the dining room and brief them on what little I know about George Parsons, then leave them to it. They'll need to remove him to hospital once he's stable. After that I have no idea what'll happen to him, but he's definitely never coming back to this house.

Two patrol officers enter the house and I direct them upstairs to Eleanor's room. "There's an elderly woman up there. She's dead. You'll need to call the Coroner."

"How did she die?" I see one of the Constable's eyes dart around and his hand reflexively goes for his weapon.

"Looks like natural causes, but who knows?" I leave them to it and head out onto the porch. Eleanor was old. She may have been healthy as a horse, but her heart could have finally given out. It's not surprising, with all the hard work of running the farm and looking after her husband. The stress from Kim and Jade would have added a load as well.

The goats are bleating even louder now, in pain from their swollen udders. It's probably been a couple of days since they've been milked.

I approach one of the Constables. "What do you know about goats? Is there some kind of Goat Rescue Society we can call to take care of them?"

"A vet, maybe?" she suggests, pulling up her radio.

"Sure. That's a good start." She calls it in while I go back to Jade.

She's just eating her ice cream, as if nothing's going on around her, as if her world hasn't just come crashing down. A little child alone, waiting for her mama to come home. Sleeping in her grandmother's bed, next to her dead body, for two nights. Drinking goat milk and eating dry cereal from a box.

"I tried to milk the goats, the way Nana showed me," she whispers. "But I didn't know the song."

Tears stream down her cheeks and she shoves the empty ice cream bowl away. So that's what happened in the milking shed. She tried to feed them too, by the look of it, and ended up dumping the grain all over the floor.

"And your grandfather?" Jade's eyes flick toward the next room. She's terrified of what's lying in there. "Did you think he was dead too?"

"Yes," she whispers.

I sit down to wait with her until someone from Family and Child Services shows up to take over. Jade will be taken into care, certainly until her mother is found and possibly longer, depending on why Kim disappeared. I haven't allowed myself to consider the possibility that she's dead, but why else would a mother abandon her child for two days? My rational mind argues that she didn't know Eleanor would die. She probably felt safe leaving Jade in her care. Possibly she even thought her little girl was safer that way. Was that why she had to get away?

A police cruiser pulls up and a constable gets out, followed by a woman who I assume is the social worker. Jade's eyes widen with fear. I'm sure they've had visits from Child Services before.

"Jade," I begin. Tears stream down her face and she starts to shake her head violently. "These people are going to look after you."

"No! No!" She's clinging to my arm like she's drowning.

"It's just for now. Until your mother comes back." I'm lying to her. I have no idea how long she'll be in care, or if her mother will ever come back.

"I'm waiting for mama," Jade screams, then she gets up and runs back upstairs with the social worker and police constable following her. My stomach turns over and I'm afraid I'm going to vomit. The scene is so familiar to the one I've worked my whole life trying to forget, to when I was taken into care after the death of my mother.

I hear her screaming but then it's no longer Jade I hear, it's me. I'm screaming as they take me away, as they pull me away from my mother's dead body. I'm covered in blood. In her blood.

After it happened, after Ray died, I sat next to my mother all day. *Catatonic*, the report said. That's how they'd found me. Catatonic. Until they pulled me away, to get me to the hospital. Then I started screaming and screaming until they sedated me. And I'm still screaming, but no one can hear me.

For weeks after it was like I was stuck in a huge, incomprehensible machine, where everyone was talking at the same time, at cross-purposes, in languages I didn't understand. I was just a cog, just a spoke in the wheel, a problem to be solved, something to be dealt with. Not even a person, much less a child. Poor Lucy. Poor Jade.

Thankfully a pick up truck pulls up and two men get out so I have an excuse to walk away.

"We're from Lewis Dairy, in Ridgeway," the younger one says, first pulling off his baseball cap. "We heard what happened…"

"To Eleanor," the other one interrupts. "We're here to help."

"With the goats…"

It takes a minute but I finally understand. "Yes! Thank you. Please, have at it!"

They head over to the fence and start leading the goats into the milking barn. I follow, not because I can help in any way, but I need to get away from the sound of Jade's wailing. I don't want to be there when they bring her out of the house and put her into the back of the police car. I don't think I could stand it. I don't want to bring back the pain or the memories. Much better to keep that box closed tight.

The two men work efficiently and quickly start to milk the goats and fill the feed mangers. To my surprise they dump the milk as soon as the pails are full.

"You just…waste it? You aren't going to take it away?"

"No, ma'am," says the older one. "These goats haven't been milked in at least two, maybe three days from what I can see. Probably have mastitis. Their milk's tainted."

"Will they be okay?"

He nods. "Vet will be here before we leave. Probably put them on antibiotics."

"We'll come back again every day," he says. "Keep milking them so they don't dry off." I wonder what will happen to the farm now that Eleanor's gone. If we can find Kim will she be in any state to keep it running?

"We'll help out anyway we can. Maybe find a buyer for the herd, if it comes to that." It's like he's reading my mind.

"Okay, thanks. I'll leave it in your capable hands." By the time I leave the barn the police cruiser is gone, taking Jade with it.

NINE

WHEN I GET into the station in the morning there's a large Americano sitting on my desk, next to an almond croissant. Hallelujah. Vogel's back from vacation.

As I'm hanging my jacket on the back of my chair I hear him heading my way, his loud laugh echoing through the room.

"Hey Gauthier," he says. "Did you miss me?"

"I did," I admit, toasting him with the coffee. "This is a nice surprise."

"I knew you'd have been slumming it with station coffee. Since I'm always the one who brings you one in the morning." He's right. Even though Vogel is slightly senior to me on the Homicide team, and even though we have the same rank, he's comfortably fallen into a supportive role, and we're both fine with that.

"How was the skiing?" No doubt perfect, as you'd expect from a week in the Rockies for his sister's destination wedding, held at the lavish Banff Springs Hotel. Nothing is too good for her and Vogel's family has the means to indulge her.

Vogel shrugs. "Spring skiing is always a crapshoot," he says as if I have any idea what he's talking about. I've never been on skis in my life, let alone heli-skiing in Banff. "The snow was a bit soft and it got a bit slushy by the end of the day…" he breaks off

59

when he sees the glazed look in my eye. "Sorry. Forgot you don't ski." I don't like anything that involves sliding out of control—like skiing, tobogganing, and especially skating. I fail to see the point of an activity that puts me at peak anxiety, especially in the cold.

"And the ceremony? How'd that work out?" Vogel's sister had wanted to exchange their vows at the top of the hill then the married couple would ski down, holding hands, while the rest of the party followed them. She'd even bought a new white ski suit for the occasion.

Vogel rolls his eyes. "Fine. Nobody broke an ankle. She got lots of photos for her Instagram." I understand; that's what mattered most to her.

He downs the rest of his coffee. "It appears that when I was skiing down Mt. Norquay, you were foiling a bank robbery. What else have I missed?"

I fill him in on the cold case DS Agu assigned me, and Vogel is suitably impressed. "In fact, I'm on my way to interview someone for the case now. Want to come along?"

Vogel looks doubtful. "Maybe I should stick around here for a bit. See what Agu has for me. Who are you going to interview?"

"Stan Price."

Vogel's eyes light up. "Are you serious?" he says. "*The* Stan Price? From Running Deep?"

"You know them? I must be the only person in town who hasn't heard of Stan Price or his band."

"You're kidding, right?" he laughs. "Running Deep were *huge.* They opened for Led Zeppelin! They toured with Aerosmith and Journey. And Rush!" I pretend to be impressed.

I pull on my coat and start walking out the door. "Guess you're coming along then. I may need you to bring me up to speed."

All the way out of town and up the escarpment Vogel pesters me with versions of Running Deep's hit songs, none of which sound familiar.

"Here, take a look through this," I say handing him the case file. I'm hoping it will distract him and stop the melody of top ten hits. Vogel stops singing and flips open the file, but as he starts to go through the various interviews and statements, he starts singing again. I just grit my teeth and drive.

"Wow!" Vogel whistles. "This is amazing." I slow down and glance over at Vogel.

"What's amazing? Wow what?" I can't imagine what he's seen that warrants that amount of excitement.

Vogel is holding out the copy of the indecipherable paper, the one with the random words on it that I thought might be a poem.

"*This!*" Vogel says.

I pull over and stop the car. "You know what that is? Are you sure?"

"It's a set list. From the concert."

"I have no idea what you're talking about."

He shakes his head in disbelief. "I can't believe you're from this planet Gauthier. Do you not have any cultural references? Have you never been to a concert?" I'm unsure where this is going. "Didn't you try to get one of these, after the show?" I shake my head and Vogel laughs, pointing at the page. "Look, these are the song titles—what they played that night. *Arcadia. Beyond the Dream. Star Queen.* They are all Running Deep songs."

"Okay…so these are the songs the band played. And somehow Ella ended up with that list in her pocket, after the concert?"

"Yes! The roadies tape the set list down on the stage, so the band can see it through the concert—in case they forget what's up next I suppose. After the show's over, fans will try to get the set lists, get them autographed by the band. It's a huge prize."

I take the document from Vogel and study it. Now that he's explained it to me, I can more or less make out some of the words myself. And I can clearly see there are a few marks made in different ink. "Do you think these might be autographs? Of some band members?"

"Sure, it's possible." Vogel continues to study the list. "It must have been a great concert."

I pull back onto the road. I'm still going to have the document analysed, but this time to see whose signatures those are. This set list, if it's genuine, proves Ella got at least as far as the stage. And the autographs could put her backstage, meeting the band.

"C'mon Gauthier. You must have heard this one." He starts to sing and play air guitar then stops when he sees my eyes roll. "Seriously? You don't know that song?"

"Maybe it's your singing."

Vogel sighs and pulls out his phone, quickly scrolls through his playlist and presses play, then turns up the volume. The car is filled with music and in fact, this time I do recognize the song.

"Isn't that one recorded for charity?" I vaguely remember it from my childhood. "Like, twenty years ago?"

Vogel nods. "Yes! It was a huge international hit. Running Deep must have made a small fortune off of it." As we crest a hill a turret comes into view. Then we see the rest of the house: It's a sprawling mansion, three stories tall, built with two wings that we can see, though I expect there are more out back. A house for a king. Or a rock star.

Vogel whistles in admiration. "I'd say that maybe it was a big fortune, based on that house."

"I'd have thought all the money would have gone to charity."

"Off that song, maybe," he shrugs. "But I'm sure the CD sales and the exposure for their other songs would have made them all really rich."

"I imagine you're right," I say as we pull up in front of a set of iron gates. Down a curving driveway I can just glimpse the house, nestled by a private lake. I roll down the window and press the button for the intercom. "Funny how even an act of charity seems to pay off for some people."

After I've identified myself to a voice over the speaker, the gates slowly swing open and we're able to drive up to the front of the house. By the time we get there, Stan Price is already waiting under the portico. His skin is leathery and tanned, as if he's spent far too much time in the sun, smoking cigarettes and drinking. I know he's in his early seventies, but Price looks older, almost cadaverous. Clearly the sex, drugs and rock and roll lifestyle really takes a toll on your complexion. He's wearing jeans, a leather jacket and cowboy boots, exactly like he was at the bank. It must be his signature look but honestly if I didn't know he was a rich rock star I'd take him for another old drunk.

"What's this about?" he demands as we approach. Then he recognizes me. "I told everything I know about the robbery to that other detective. I don't have anything else to say."

"Yes, Sir. I appreciate that." I give him my sweetest smile. "We're here on a different case." Price's eyes narrow in suspicion, then he grudgingly gestures for us to follow him inside.

I immediately dislike like Stan Price. He's an arrogant prick, which I guess is to be expected of a hugely rich rock star. Maybe it goes with the territory—you've got to be arrogant to make it in that world, to hold a crowd of thousands of screaming fans in your palm as you perform in a packed stadium.

The heels of his boots echo as he leads us through a vast marble foyer, down a hall and into an enormous room overlooking the endless expanse of lawn, his vineyards, and the rolling hills of the escarpment.

"Fantastic house Mr. Price," Vogel gushes. "Did you build it yourself?"

I know Vogel doesn't mean that Price actually had a hand in

any physical work. He means Price paid the bills to the designer and architect and any contractors who had a hand in the construction. But as is always the case with these massive ego-built houses, Price takes full credit.

"Yes, I did," he grins. "I was involved in every element of the design and construction. I'm very proud of it."

"I can see why," Vogel says, stroking the wall. "Is this sandstone?"

"Good eye," Price says. "Yes. Everything in the house is natural and organic material. There's nothing artificial here. No plastics or adhesives or anything that off-gasses. It's all stone and wood."

"Why is that?" I insert myself, if only to interrupt the sausage party.

Price shoots me a look designed to put me back in my place. "Toxins, man. I don't want any carcinogenic materials and chemicals and VOCs off-gassing into my home." I imagine he's taken in more than enough toxins his entire rock and roll life, so he's hedging his bets now. And he can afford to.

We've made it into a wide hallway with a stairway leading to the upper floor. There's art on all the walls all the way up to the roof; a mix of wall hangings, sculpture, quilts, and paintings, all of which I am sure cost a great deal. A Navaho rug on the wall, next to a 17th century tapestry of animals and big cabbage leaves. Some Indian weaving incorporating a sacred mandala next to a Persian rug. It looks like an art gallery, but one without a skilled curator.

"Great place to display the art, don't you think?" Price beams with pride. "I'm a big collector." I catch a glimpse of a large textile piece that looks somehow familiar hanging on the back wall. I walk over to get a better look and when I get close enough I can see it's unquestionably one of Rachel's. How ironic that Stan Price has one of her pieces hanging in his collection and I'm sure he has absolutely no idea.

I hear a noise as we turn into the main living room and turn to see a young woman in the kitchen. She looks to be around thirty years old, far too young for Stan Price. There's a laptop open on the kitchen island and several boxes open next to it. She's eyeing me warily and as I watch she gets up and closes the door without a word. I guess Price's girlfriend doesn't want to get involved with the police.

Suddenly there's a ringing that sounds like a school bell, echoing off the marble tile and so loudly it fills the room. Price heads across to a desk in the hall, leaving us standing as he answers an antique rotary telephone, so ornate I'd thought it was a piece of art.

"That's the loudest ring tone I've ever heard," I whisper to Vogel.

"I bet he's got hearing damage from being in the band," Vogel says. "And you've got to admit, it is kind of cool. Vintage."

We pretend not to listen as Stan Price starts shouting into the mouthpiece.

"Fuck you!" he shouts, his face dark red with anger. "No way, I'm not waiting another day, or week, or month, or minute. *Fuck you Rossi*, I've had it with your bullshit excuses. You'll be hearing from my lawyer, you limp prick." He slams down the handset so hard the telephone rattles. The name Rossi rings a bell, but I can't recall why.

"Can't do that with a cell phone," Stan Price says. He's wearing a wide grin as he rejoins us. It looks as if he's baring his teeth in rage. "Very satisfying, slamming down a good solid phone, don't you think?" I turn away so he can't see my eye roll and leave the conversation to Vogel until I can get my neutral expression back on.

"Guess he deserved it?"

"You'd better believe it," Price mutters. "Useless little shit."

Price goes over to a sideboard and pours a large whisky, downs it in one, then tops up his glass. The natural colour starts to return to his face.

"Beautiful view," Vogel says, trying to charm Price. "How many acres of vines do you have?" I wouldn't be surprised if he already knows the answer.

"Just over thirty hectares. Mostly Sauvignon Blanc. Some Riesling." Vogel nods, encouraging him. "We hand craft each of our vintages. It's a real passion project of mine." It takes all I have not to roll my eyes again. He's clearly caught up in the glamour of owning his own winery, like so many other celebrities with their own labels.

As he talks I do the math. A hectare is about two and a half acres. Land around here is at least fifty thousand an acre. Thirty hectares probably set him back one and a half million dollars. Then he'd have to prepare and level the land, plant the vines, wait at least five years before a harvest. Not to mention whatever staff he has on the payroll to run the operation, equipment and buildings. Passion project indeed.

Eventually he gets fed up with Vogel's chat. He sits down and puts his feet up on the table and eyes us. He looks equally wary and bored. "What can I do for you, Detectives?"

I sit across from him while Vogel admires the gold and platinum records on the wall. It's not difficult to figure out where Stan Price got all his money. Vogel pulls out his notebook.

"It's a cold case," I begin. "A girl disappeared in 1990," Price looks irritated. "After one of your concerts at the Buffalo Auditorium."

"And?"

"And I'm wondering if you remember meeting her?" I slide a photo of Ella Weaver across the table to him. He doesn't even look at it.

"Is this a joke?" He laughs. "You expect me to remember anything from thirty years ago? Especially some random girl?"

"Can you tell us, was there a party after the concert? Maybe some fans came backstage after, or up to your hotel for drinks?"

He shakes his head in disbelief at the questions. "I couldn't possibly tell you. Sure, we'd usually have drinks after our shows: Backstage, on the bus or at the hotel, wherever, to unwind. But I can't tell you anything for sure. It was a long time ago."

"It was the last time you played Buffalo," I say. "Your band never came back again."

Price looks puzzled. "Was it?" He brow furrows in concentration then I see a light come into his eyes. He's remembered something.

"Mr. Price?" I prompt him, but he shuts down.

"The manager handled all of that," he waves me off. "If tickets didn't sell, we wouldn't have come back to town."

"The show was sold out," I say. "Two nights. And, you'd played in Buffalo every one of your tours before that one, as well as an opening act for Boston." I glance over at Vogel, who's staring at me in surprise. I may not know who Running Deep is, but I can use the internet.

"I guess it's a bit of a hometown crowd, right?" Vogel chimes in. "Local boy made good and all that? Surprised your manager wouldn't have booked you back again."

"Not my department, not my decision." He glares at me. "Anyway my manager had to do something to earn his percentage."

I see we aren't going to get anywhere with this line of inquiry, so I change the subject. "Were you interviewed at the time this young woman disappeared? Back in 1990?"

I know the answer is no. There are no statements from anyone in the band or crew in the file. The police also hadn't thought to speak with the roadies or any personnel from the Buffalo Auditorium, beyond the head of the security team, who remembered nothing. I'm sure the band had already moved onto the next city on their tour by the time Kim Parsons was found, but it wouldn't have been impossible to make the trip to Toronto, the next stop. Especially since there was speculation at the time Ella had gone with them, like a groupie.

"Who is this girl?"

"Her name was Ella Weaver." I study his face for a reaction. There isn't one. The name means nothing to him. No doubt he's slept with so many women since Rachel he has no memory of her.

Price shakes his head. "No idea."

"She was your daughter. By Rachel Weaver."

He stares at me, speechless for a long moment. "My *daughter*!? What the fuck are you talking about? Who's Rachel Weaver?"

I pass him a recent photo of Rachel.

"Her?! That crazy bitch." He tosses the photo back at me. "I've seen her around town. She's a loony." He thinks for a moment then his head snaps up and he glares at me. "She was at the bank last Saturday!"

"That's correct Mr. Price, she was." I pick up the photo. "Small world."

"Why on earth would you think I ever fucked *her*?!" He grimaces at the photo. "Christ on a bike! Believe me, I can do better."

I feel Vogel tense beside me. He's bracing for me to tear a strip off Price. But I count to ten, taking deep calming breaths and manage to control my temper.

"When you lived in the area, in the seventies," I begin. "Before your band became successful, I understand you lived in Ridgeway?" Price nods, his eyes narrow with suspicion.

"Everybody knows that," he says. "It's in our official biography."

"I understand you had a relationship with Rachel Weaver, that went on for a few months."

Price interrupts me with a snort of laughter. "A *relationship*?!…"

I talk right over him. "And it ended when you discovered she was only seventeen. And she was pregnant." I'm embellishing somewhat, and making up the rest, based on what Rachel had told me, but I want to see what Price will say.

Price leans back on the sofa and crosses his arms. He's clearly feeling defensive. I glance at Vogel and he steps into the good cop role while I excuse myself and pretend to take an urgent call on my phone. I step away and hold the phone to my ear while listening in on their conversation.

"It must happen a lot," I hear Vogel say in his best man-to-man tone. "Women coming onto you, claiming you had relationships with them. Even paternity claims I bet."

Price shakes his head. "It never fucking stopped," he mutters.

Vogel grins happily, urging him on. "Still, it can't have been all bad," he says. "Life of a rock star. You're a legend. I've heard the stories."

"Dude," Price throws back his head and laughs. "You have no idea. I was drowning in pussy."

What a pig. Poor Rachel. What was she thinking?

"I guess your lawyers really earned their money during that time," Vogel says.

"You better believe it," Price snorts. "About time they did some work for what I paid them. Fucking leeches."

"I'm sure you'd be willing to provide a DNA test," Vogel says. "It's just a simple oral swab and it will help us eliminate this line of inquiry," Vogel chimes in. "And put an end to the story before it gets out of control." I've got to hand it to Vogel. He's smooth.

"It'll stop the rumours," I add, returning to stand next to Vogel. I don't mention that there's no risk to him of someone demanding child support, since Ella Weaver is dead.

Price looks alarmed. "Rumours? What rumours?"

"You wouldn't want it in the media," Vogel talks right over him. "Now that your winery is just getting such good press."

Price thinks it over for a moment then agrees. "Fine, no problem."

"I suppose I need to call my lawyer," he grumbles. "I'm so sick of paying those bastards."

TEN

"Well," Vogel says as we're safely in the car and heading toward the gates. "He's certainly a jerk."

"Did you get a look at his girlfriend?"

"No," Vogel looks surprised. "Where was she?"

"In the kitchen, avoiding us. Much too young for him."

"He's a rock star." Vogel shrugs. "Par for the course I'd say."

"He's a dirty old man. She looks less than half his age."

I drive as Vogel spends the next ten minutes on the phone arranging for a technician to come out to Stan Price's home to take the DNA sample, since there's no way he'll come into the station. And, since we want to keep him onside and happy to co-operate, we do our best to comply with his request. He finally finishes the call just as I'm parking in the station lot.

There are two patrol cars heading out at the same time, which usually means something's up, but since no call has come out over the radio, I'm puzzled.

"What's going on?" I flag one of the constables as she's getting into the car.

"Funeral duty," she says. "There's a big one over at the Chapel on Killaley. Renato Rossi."

"Rossi?" I turn to Vogel. "Wasn't Price just yelling at him down the phone? Hell of a long-distance call if he's dead."

"Different Rossi," Vogel laughs and gives me a wink. "Same *family*, if you get my meaning." It comes back to me. That's why Rossi's name was familiar. He was known to have mob connections in the Niagara region that reached into New York State.

"The dead guy is Renato Rossi," the constable says. "He's a very big deal. Or he was, I guess."

"Natural causes, I assume? Nobody took him out?" The constable grins and closes the door.

Vogel and I head inside. "Renato Rossi was notorious," he continues. "Never charged though, despite the rumours. He's been a real estate broker in town, for years. And a concert promoter back in the day."

"What day would that be?"

"The sixties and seventies I guess. He also owned the radio station in Niagara Falls. And the one in Buffalo, too."

"How do you know all this? It's way before your time isn't it?"

Vogel shrugs. "My parents." Vogel's father has rich connections, thanks to his many business interests, including private helicopter and corporate jet charters. No doubt he'd been hired to fly Rossi or his business colleagues somewhere. I find it difficult to not get irritable when I talk about rich people. I don't like them, as Vogel often reminds me.

After Vogel heads in to talk with DS Agu, I do some research on Renato Rossi. The timing—the seventies—and the fact that he was a concert promoter makes me wonder if he's connected in any way to Stan Price. Interesting that Stan Price was shouting down that phone at a Rossi when we interviewed him. Small world.

The first thing the internet tells me—apart from the details of his funeral—is that Renato Rossi was a well-known realtor in the area. He ran a successful brokerage and seems to have had a large business. I scroll past the headshots of a dozen smiling real estate agents on Team Rossi, ending with the one next to his: It's Joe Rossi, his son. It's the guy from the bank on Saturday, the one I recognized from the signs all over town.

I'm over ten pages deep into the Google search before I get anywhere into Renato Rossi's past, which makes sense, given that it all pre-dates the internet. The only bits I do manage to find is from sites of superfans that document the history of rock bands or of radio stations in the area. There's even a site devoted to the Buffalo Auditorium, which was torn down fifteen years ago.

Like Vogel said, Renato Rossi had been the owner of two local radio stations—one in Niagara Falls and the other across the US border in Buffalo, NY. He was also a record and concert promoter who worked with several bands and venues across Ontario and in upstate New York. His company grossed millions of dollars annually promoting the bands that were played on his radio stations. I wonder if he worked with Running Deep? Probably, given they'd played so many times in the area. He'd have done a lot of promotion for them in the early days of their music careers.

Finally I find a few fringe blogs that refer to Renato Rossi as a *notorious music promoter.* They talk about his mob-connections and detail how he'd demanded record companies pay him to have their artists' records played on the air on his radio stations. Rossi would also heavily promote the bands that he brought into town so the concert venues sold out. He'd get kickbacks from the owners of the venues, from the recording companies, and he even took a big piece of the gate.

In the late eighties Rossi was indicted in the US in a federal payola scandal. He was up on charges of racketeering and money laundering, and he was accused of accepting bribes of cocaine and cash to play certain records on his radio stations. Luckily for Rossi, the case never came to trial because of some mysterious mishandling of the evidence, but he still got out of the record promotion business. He also sold his stake in the radio stations when the investigations started, likely to avoid charges, and then he went into real estate.

Evidently Renato Rossi died a very wealthy man, thanks to the sale of the radio stations and the success of his real estate and development companies. I'm about to research who's taking all that over when someone tosses a balled up piece of paper at my head.

"Hey Gauthier," Vogel shouts, interrupting my thoughts. "Pick up!" I glance at the phone on my desk and see it's flashing. I had it on silent, like I always do when I'm at work.

"Detective Constable Gauthier," I say when I pick up the receiver. It's Dr. Singh, the Coroner.

"I've got the results of that post-mortem for you."

"That was fast. You only got her yesterday."

"Things are quiet," he says. "And this wasn't especially challenging."

"Natural causes?"

"Heart failure," he says. "She was on beta blockers. Found trace in her blood."

"Really?! She told me she was healthy. Why'd she be on those?"

"She probably didn't think it was a big deal. They're just to regulate heartbeat and blood pressure. They're very common."

I thank Dr. Singh and hang up, but I feel uneasy. Maybe I'm being suspicious over nothing. Still, I make a note to follow up with Eleanor's doctor about her prescriptions, just to be sure.

ELEVEN

"**WHY DON'T YOU** take a coffee with you then?" Maja asks. I'm running late this morning and she's just come in after an overnight shift in Emergency. Some days are like that—we pass like ships in the night.

My phone rings as I'm pouring some coffee into a thermal takeaway cup. Maja's coffee is better than anything I'll ever get from a take away cafe and the stuff at the station is undrinkable.

"Detective Constable Gauthier" I smile my thanks at Maja who takes over pouring.

"This is Dr. Venturi, from Forensic Services. I've got the results of the autopsy on your victim…" I hear him shuffling papers. "Ella Weaver."

I put my phone on speaker then lay it down while I look for a pen.

Maja leans over my shoulder and speaks into the phone. "Hi Bill! This is Maja Kaur. How are you?"

Dr. Venturi laughs. "Maja! Wow! This is a nice surprise. Haven't spoken to you since…"

"Graduation?" Maja interrupts. "So you're a Forensic Pathologist now?"

"Yes, I've been here for a couple of years. What about you?"

"I'm working in Niagara, as a GP." I see Maja falter. "I rotate in as a Coroner, with three other doctors."

"Nice. Lots of variety."

"Yes, it's great." I see Maja's smile is forced. "Anyway, I should let you get back to your call. Nice talking to you." She turns her back as I grab my pen to start taking notes.

"Thank you, Dr. Venturi. DC Gauthier here again. What can you tell me?"

"Not much, I'm sorry to say. But I know you didn't have high expectations. After thirty years buried in a bog, there's a limited amount of forensic evidence we can get."

"Anything you've got might help." It's impossible at this point to get any useful toxicology, blood or tissue samples from the body, and even though I suspect there were drugs and alcohol in her system, there's no way to prove it.

"I can tell you the body was intact, with no evidence of fractures or blunt force trauma to her skull. No trace of any penetrating wounds, like a stab wound or from gunshot. There was no dislocation or fracture of the cervical spine or hyoid bone that would indicate she was strangled, though we can't discount it."

"No?"

"It might have been a wide, flat ligature, like a scarf. That wouldn't necessarily leave a mark."

"So…we don't have cause of death? We don't know if she'd been sexually assaulted or died of an overdose?"

"I'm sorry, no. Even the bone marrow was too degraded to give us anything viable for testing."

I thank the pathologist and hang up, cursing under my breath. So we're no closer to finding whatever happened to Ella the night she died.

I pick up my coffee and give Maja a kiss goodbye.

"Are you okay? You seem…wistful."

She gives me a sad smile. "Just tired I guess. It was a long shift."

I know Maja too well to buy that story. She's upset and she wasn't that way before she talked with Dr. Venturi. I hazard a guess. "You regret you didn't go on and become a forensic anthropologist, like him?"

Maja shrugs. "No, I don't think so. I've got my Coroner work to keep my hand in the medical/legal stuff. And honestly, I don't want to work exclusively with dead bodies. I like living people too."

"So, what you're doing is a good compromise?"

"Yes," she gives me a tight hug. "I've got the best of both worlds."

I'm not sure I believe her.

The minute I arrive at the station I find an email in my Inbox from the lab. I whoop with joy; at least something is going right today. The technician had been very efficient and had taken Price's swab within the hour when Vogel had called. I guess they weren't too busy at the lab and she'd been able to run the comparisons quickly.

"What's going on?" Vogel asks from his desk across from mine.

"It's Stan Price's DNA results," I grin, grabbing for my jacket and running for the printer. "He's definitely Ella Weaver's father. Want to come for a ride?" Vogel is already on his feet.

I regret not dragging Stan Price into the interview room to hear the news. When I see the look on his face I wish I could have preserved it for posterity on videotape.

He's stunned. He grabs at the printed sheet and studies it, though I doubt very much he can decode what it says. I barely understand lab results myself and I've seen dozens of them. Though he may have too, given how many paternity cases he's probably fought.

"Mr. Price, the results are 100% accurate. There's absolutely no room for doubt. Ella Weaver was your daughter."

Stan Price first looks horrified. Then his expression changes to one I recognize as fear.

"So it was true," he whispers. "She wasn't lying."

"Excuse me, Mr. Price," Vogel says. "What was true? Who wasn't lying?" My heart speeds up. Did Price just remember Ella had met him, that she'd told him she was his daughter?

Price quickly wipes his hand over his face. "Nothing. Sorry. I'm just…shocked." He's lying, that much is obvious, but I can't push. I pull the photo of Ella Weaver out of the file and pass it to him again.

"Please take another look at this photo Mr. Price. Now do you recognize her? Did you see her that night? Did she speak with you?"

Price just sits there with his mouth agape. "Mr. Price," I continue. "We now know that Ella Weaver did attend an after-party the night she disappeared, held backstage at the Buffalo Auditorium. She had a set list from your concert that night and she was asking the band members to autograph it. Do you remember that?"

I'm taking a shot, based on what Vogel had said. I can't prove it's from Running Deep's concert, and I'm certainly not even close to identifying the autographs, but I like a gamble.

Price rubs his hands over his face then gets up and pours himself a large drink of whiskey. He downs it in one, then tops it up and stands staring out the window.

I think I remember that," he finally says. "There was a young woman there."

"A girl, Mr. Price," I can't help correcting him. "She was only fifteen."

To his credit, he looks ashamed. "Yes. She was just a girl." He slumps back onto the sofa and looks up at me. "And she was my *daughter?*"

He drops his head into his hands, covering his face. "I never knew anything. She never told me, I'm sure of that. I'd have remembered that. I thought she was just a groupie, just some chick at the party. I remember I was so high…" He stops talking for a moment, collecting his thoughts.

The fact that he now remembers the night makes me suspicious. When we first spoke with him he implied every night was the same, some kind of drunk and stoned party, typical of the life he'd lived for years on the road. *You expect me to remember?* So what triggered his recall now? How can he be so sure Ella didn't speak to him?

"We'd done some peyote, just before the encore. It was starting to kick in…I was drinking tequila with the guys. Some of them were getting it on with the women…people were fucking… It was getting wild." His head snaps up and he looks horrified. "I didn't! No…I was too drunk." He's afraid he had sex with Ella.

"Maybe not you, but someone could have," I say. I don't feel like cutting him any slack. "One of the roadies or your band mates might have raped her that night." The truth is that probably someone he knew, one of his friends or guests at the party, had killed his daughter.

"*Rape*?! What do you mean?" Stan Price's head is spinning now. "She was at the party, she would have been willing…"

"She was fifteen, Sir," Vogel interrupts. "Sex with a minor is rape."

Price holds up his hand then pulls out his phone and punches in a number. "I'm calling my lawyer." The call is answered immediately. Price must have the lawyer's cell phone and the lawyer is paid enough to jump when called. "Ed? I need you. Now. At my house."

Price hangs up and glares at Vogel and me.

"You aren't being charged with anything," I say.

"*Yet,*" Price adds. Vogel and I exchange a look then get ready to leave.

"There's no reason for us to linger," I say. "But please, hang on to those test results. Your lawyer will want to see them I'm sure."

"We'll see ourselves out," Vogel says and we head for the door.

"Somebody killed my daughter," Price says. I turn to look back. He's staring out the window. "Some bastard killed my little girl. He's going to pay for it if I have to kill him myself."

TWELVE

VOGEL IS SHAKING his head in disgust as he turns out of the drive-way, with the gates closing behind us. "A couple of hours ago he denied having a daughter at all, now he's righteously angry and ready to avenge her death."

"Stan Price thinks he's Father of the Year," I agree. Price didn't know the young woman who'd died after his concert and he didn't care about her. She'd just been some groupie at the party to him, someone disposable, someone who didn't matter to a big rock star like him. Still, I wonder what he has now remembered about that night thirty years ago.

Price is a smug bastard who thinks his money and fame allow him a certain kind of protection and license, and I wouldn't be surprised if he knows more than he's admitted. Now I wish I had brought him into the station. Perhaps a little reminder that we're all the same under the law, at least in theory, would have helped his memory.

It's possible he never met Ella that night, despite her having been at the after party. Price may have been otherwise occupied with one of the groupies. Maybe he actually was drunk or high and has no recollection of their meeting. She may well have told him about their relationship, but who knows if he believed her story.

But she also might have told someone else about it, someone who did believe her, and who thought she needed to be silenced.

The car radio blares. ***Ten Thirty Three. Pasquale's Trattoria, 13 Lakeshore Road. Code Two.***

Vogel laughs. "That place is a little upscale for a fight, don't you think?" Pasquale's *Trattoria* is one of the most expensive restaurants in the area.

"It's probably the chef, throwing a plate at a server." I laugh and dismiss it as the radio comes to life again. ***Ten Seventy. Message to all units. Backup requested. Pasquale's Trattoria 13 Lakeshore Road. Code Two.***

Vogel hits the lights and presses the pedal to the metal. We're at Pasquale's in less than ten minutes. By the time we arrive there are three patrol cars on the scene, as well as an unmarked SUV. Most of the patrons and staff are milling around out front of the restaurant in confusion as two uniformed officers try to keep everyone calm.

"What's going on?" I ask one of them as we brush past, heading inside.

She just shakes her head. "It's a brawl. Crazy. I've never seen anything like it."

I follow Vogel inside. The front room of the restaurant is empty and several chairs have been turned over and drinks spilled, probably as patrons ran out to escape whatever had happened here. There are two servers hovering near the kitchen doors, nervously looking toward the private dining room at the back where I can hear voices shouting in English and Italian.

Vogel and I head for the private dining room and walk into complete bedlam. There's a woman screaming and trying to break free from the police constable who's restraining her. She's lunging forward and struggling with him but he's tentative about holding her, so she's able to get away, pick up a dinner plate and throw it at a man who neatly steps out of the way as the plate shatters against the wall behind him. The constable grabs her again, less gently this time and she cries out in pain, then starts screeching again.

"*Bugiardo! Ladro!*" she screams. "You changed it! I know you did. Papa told me everything. *Bastardo!*"

A young man pushes the police Constable aside and takes her into his arms. "Mama, calm down," he says. "Stop this." But she won't stop. She's howling in rage, tears streaming down her cheeks as she struggles in her son's arms.

"Who is this lunatic?" I whisper to Vogel, unsure of how to proceed. "What the hell is going on here?"

"Rosa Rossi," he says. "Rossi Real Estate. That's her son Angelo."

As if on cue, Angelo starts to curse the guy his mother missed with the plate. "You bastard," he hisses. His eyes are cold with fury. "I'm gonna kill you." It's easy to believe him.

Meanwhile, the man they are all yelling at is standing at the head of the table, a shifty smile pasted on his face. The man is Joe Rossi. Twice in a week this guy's involved in a drama—first the bank robbery and now this—whatever *this* is.

Rossi looks nervous, but he's trying to act cool. He looks at a man sitting in a chair near the exit and shrugs as if to say, *See what I have to deal with here?*

"C'mon Rosa." Rossi holds his hands out, palms open. "It's not my fault."

Angelo yells at Rossi. "Papa told me himself…"

"Prove it," Rossi snaps.

Angelo lunges at Joe Rossi, but he's intercepted by one of the constables. "I saw it with my own eyes," he shouts as he's struggling to free himself. "Last year." Someone is swearing and pounding on the table and a woman starts to scream.

I shout at the top of my lungs. "That's enough! Cool it." Rosa

Rossi ignores me. She's worked herself into a complete frenzy of rage and spittle flies from her lips as she screams.

"Ma'am—I'm speaking to you." I get into her face, but she keeps yelling and I look to Vogel who steps up and intervenes.

"Ma'am, I'm going to have to arrest you if you don't stop." She pauses for a moment then starts again, so Vogel cuffs her and orders the constables to escort her out. It takes two constables, one on either side, to get the woman out of the restaurant and into the back of a patrol car. Once she's secured the officers leave her in the car and return to the dining room.

When she's gone it's as if the air is sucked out of the room. It's so quiet, apart from the comparatively quiet wailing of an elderly Italian woman, who's sitting amidst the wreckage of the table. Plates of food have been thrown and glasses spilled. Joe Rossi has red wine all down the front of his suit.

Everyone else sits in stunned silence. Rossi sits down heavily at the head of the dining table and pours himself a large glass of red wine.

The man who was sitting by the door tries to make his escape.

"Please sit down, Sir. We have some questions." He reluctantly perches in a hard chair against the wall, distancing himself from the rest of the group as much as possible and tries to be invisible.

"Now can someone please explain what's going on here?" I ask. Nobody says anything. "No?" Everyone averts their eyes, and cringes into the corners of the room.

"Okay then," Vogel says in a loud voice. "Everyone please take a seat back at the table. We're going to be here a while." Nobody moves. "*Now!*" he yells, which finally gets them moving and they reluctantly go back to their seats.

Sometimes you've just got to make it up as you go along. These people, whoever they are, aren't co-operating and we need to get the story.

"I'm going to ask again. What happened here?" One by one they all look over to the man perched in the chair by the door.

"Sir?" I ask him as I pull out my notebook. "Can you please give me your name?"

"I'm Joseph Arturo," he sighs. "I'm the Attorney for Renato Rossi. The late Renato Rossi."

"His funeral was today," I say, remembering the two patrol cars that were needed to help with traffic control. Arturo nods.

The elderly woman starts to wail again, shaking her head.

"C'mon Mama!" Joe Rossi says. "It's what Papa wanted."

"You're a crook!" someone shouts. "Thief."

"Fuck you Tony!" Rossi shouts back.

Angelo Rossi leaps to his feet and lunges across the table. The elderly woman grabs his arm to hold him back and he tries to shake her off. I step over and get between them to try and settle the two men down.

"Sit down, Sir," I shout in his face and he stops, his eyes swivelling to meet mine. I see dark rage and hatred and my blood runs cold. He sneers at me, then slumps back into his seat.

The elderly woman throws her arms around him and he allows her to comfort him, but his eyes are still on me as I direct the constable to start taking everyone's name and contact details. I decide to let Vogel interview him, so I move to the other side of the room and start there. Something about him feels wrong and I'd just as soon keep my distance from that darkness if I can.

I notice a quiet woman sitting slightly apart from the family group. She's blonde and petite and bears no physical resemblance to either Joe Rossi or Tony—who I assume is his brother, or to the woman in the back of the patrol car. She must be an in-law. I approach her discreetly.

"Excuse me, Ma'am," I say in a quiet voice. "May I ask you what happened here?"

She looks tense but nods. "Can you give me your name please? Are you a member of the family?"

"Yes. I'm married to Tony. My name is Antonietta Rossi."

"What's going on here?" I pull out my notebook and prepare to take her statement.

She exhales dramatically. "It was just a typical Rossi family production," she says, shooting a look at her husband, who's at the opposite end of the table arguing with Vogel. "First we had the funeral, at the new chapel on Killaley. That was…fine, I guess. But there's been a lot of tension, ever since Renato was in hospital."

"Tension? What kind?"

"Family stuff. Rosa and Angelo and Joe and Tony—they're always fighting about something. Poor Nonna," she indicates the elderly woman at the table. "She's always stuck in the middle trying to make peace. It's been going on forever."

"Okay, and after the funeral?"

"We all went over in our cars to the cemetery for the burial. That's when the first fight started, once the priest finished the service at the graveside."

"What was the fight about?"

"I can't actually tell you," she says. "I didn't bother going to the grave. I stayed by the car." It's obvious Antonietta Rossi has had more than enough of the Rossi family. I glance over at her husband Tony and can't help wondering how much longer her marriage will last. He's a smaller version of his brother Joe, but something about him isn't quite right. It's like he's made out of spare parts left over from when his handsome big brother was made.

I notice her glancing toward Angelo Rossi who's now sitting quietly, holding his grandmother's hand and watching everyone around him. His aggression is gone but his lip is curled in a sneer of defiance—of both his family and the police.

"He's your nephew?" I ask her, nodding my head toward him.

I see her eyelids flicker. "Angelo. He's Rosa's son. A problem child," she scoffs.

"He's hardly a child." Though I'd say he definitely has anger management issues, like his mother.

She shrugs. "*Piccolo principe viziato.*" Then she sees my confused expression. "Spoiled little prince," she translates.

"Can you tell me what happened after the funeral? What caused the…"

"Brawl?" she smirks. "Then we all came back here for the funeral meal. There was lots of wine, toasting, music, crying, singing…" she rolls her eyes. "Then the lawyer walks in." She nods at the man in the suit perched on the chair near the door.

"The lawyer?!"

"Exactly," she says. "That's when the trouble started. Joe introduces him and announces he's here for the Reading of the Will!"

"You didn't know this was happening?"

"Are you kidding? No way!" She takes a big drink from her glass. "I mean, have you ever heard of such a thing? At the funeral?" I shake my head. It's definitely unusual, but what do I know? Maybe that's what Renato Rossi had wanted.

"Everybody started making noise, Mama started to cry, then Arturo read the Will and Rosa went crazy, screaming at Joe and throwing things….it was insane."

"I'm guessing she didn't like the Will? Didn't agree with what was left to her?"

"That's an understatement." She rolls her eyes. "*Some people* claim there was another Will. A different one from what they read just now."

Some people must mean Rosa, and maybe her son too, given his anger. "Surely the lawyer has the correct one?"

"You'd think," she laughs and takes another big drink of her wine. I can see she's planning on getting loaded. "But like I said, it's another Rossi family production."

I approach the lawyer, who's looking increasingly irritated by the minute. He keeps looking at his watch as if he's anxious to get somewhere.

"Mr. Arturo," I say. "Thank you for your patience."

"I really need to be somewhere," he says. "I don't really have anything pertinent to add about what happened here today." He waves his hand at the Rossi family, who are still bickering at the table while the constables and Vogel take their details. "I'm sure you can get whatever you need from the Rossi family."

"Well, I'm sure we could use a more objective point of view," I say. "Perhaps we could speak later, if we need to?" He nods eagerly and thrusts one of his business cards into my hand as he rises to leave.

"Yes, great. Anytime. May I leave now?"

"Of course," I accept his card and stand aside in case he bowls me over in his rush to get away. "We'll give you a call. Someone may need to visit you at your office next week for some follow-up questions."

Arturo freezes in his tracks and shakes his head. "I'm afraid that won't be possible," he says. "My office burned down on Tuesday."

THIRTEEN

AFTER A DAY like I've had I am so grateful to come home to Maja and the aroma of a delicious dinner. She's had the day off so has taken the time to prepare her mother's famous Tandoori chicken, a black lentil dahl and aloo gohbi, and my mouth is watering the whole time I'm in the shower washing off the disgusting day. Starting with slimy Stan Price and ending with the Rossi family riot I can't wait to rinse them all down the drain. By the time I join Maja downstairs I feel almost human again.

"Rough day?" she asks, as she hands me a glass of wine.

I've been keeping her up to date with texts, but will need a few glasses of wine in me before I can fully share the details of the day, and give the characters and events the descriptions they deserve.

I nod and open one of the pots on the stove to inhale the fragrance of cumin and coriander, ginger and Kaffir lime. Maja bats my hand away and closes the lid.

"Abby's due any minute," she says. I forgot we're having company. Her wife Chantal is away on a training course, so Maja invited Abby to join us for dinner. We'll be able to hear all about their house renovation and understand why we never want to undertake one ourselves.

It's been a nightmare from start to finish, with contractors not showing up, cost overruns, materials not arriving on time or correctly, structural deficiencies they only found out about once they'd opened a wall, and worst of all they'd found both a leaky foundation and that their house had knob and tube electrical wiring which made it impossible for them to get house insurance until it was rectified. So, despite their having paid very little for the house, they were already months behind and tens of thousands of dollars over budget.

At least listening to Abby will be a break from my usual habit of obsessively ruminating on whatever case I'm working on. Thinking about Ella Weaver, Stan Price and Kim Parsons would be far too depressing.

There's a knock on the door and Abby comes straight in. She's practically family, so that's perfectly fine with us. I greet her with a glass of wine.

"I'm starving!" she says. "When's dinner?"

"Now if you like," Maja calls from the kitchen and Abby heads straight for the table.

"What a day," Abby says as she drops into a chair and gulps her wine. "We've already got a full ward, most of them post-ops, and two of our private rooms are being hogged by those bank robbers from last weekend. Police are stationed outside their rooms, getting underfoot, taking up a lot of space."

Abby helps herself to some of the dahl and rice. "All thanks to you, Lucy," she laughs. "Shooting one in the leg and managing somehow to break the other one's neck."

I glance over at Maja and see her lips are tight with irritation. "It wasn't intentional," I mumble. "I just landed on him when I jumped out of the ceiling."

"I'd say shooting someone is pretty intentional." Maja says. "How are they doing?"

Abby shrugs then moans with pleasure as she tastes the chicken.

"This is soooo good," she says before answering. "Fine, guess. One's got a fractured tibia from where the bullet hit his leg. The other's got a C2 fracture. He's in traction, with metal pins in his skull and he's wearing a halo brace. It's quite the production. I've never seen one before and I've been a nurse for almost ten years." She pauses to drink some wine. "And they're both handcuffed to their beds, as if either of them is going anywhere. Certainly makes bathing and changing them an interesting exercise."

"Who are these guys anyway?" I realize DS Dudek hasn't told me who any of the robbers are, assuming he even knows by now.

"The guy with the bullet in his leg is Chris Shepherd. The other's Dillon Byrne," she says. I can't think why that sounds familiar. Probably from an arrest sheet that came across my desk at some point.

"And they're both under police guard?"

Abby nods. Her mouth is full and it's a moment before she can answer. "It's sad. No one's allowed to see them."

"Probably all their friends are in jail anyway," Maya says.

Abby laughs. "Except the guy with the broken neck. His mother was there today, poor woman. She's the only one allowed in."

I'm lying in bed, sleepless, next to a snoring Maja. My mind keeps running through the evening and our conversation over dinner. Abby and I had exchanged stories about our jobs; hers on the hospital ward and mine as a police detective, and Maja had laughed at all the right spots and asked the right questions to keep things going, but I could tell her heart wasn't in it.

Even Abby noticed eventually. "You feeling okay, Maja? You're awfully quiet tonight."

Maja smiled. "All good," she'd said, but I knew something was wrong.

After Abby left, Maja and I cleaned up the kitchen together, loading the dishwasher and putting away the leftovers. Maja was still very quiet and I tried to tell myself she was probably all talked out; an evening with Abby will do that to you. But my inner voice told me different.

"What's wrong?" I asked, pulling her into a hug. "Tell me what's bothering you."

She'd sighed. "I just feel restless. Bored, maybe." I felt my insides clench as a wave of anxiety gripped me. She's bored with our relationship. I could barely even manage to ask the question.

"Bored?" My heart sped up. "You mean with us?"

"No! Not at all," she'd insisted. "I just want to feel *more*, to feel like I've accomplished something in my life."

"But you're a doctor! You've accomplished plenty."

"You don't get it." Maja just shook her head. "Your job is full of excitement, something different every day. Action. Risk."

"I thought you didn't like me taking risks."

"Not everything is about you Lucy. I'm talking about me."

"I'm sorry," I whisper, wanting her to continue and being afraid of what she'll say.

"It feels like life is…flat, somehow. Like this is all I've got to look forward to, forever?"

She'd gone upstairs to bed and I followed twenty minutes later. I wanted to give her time to fall asleep before I joined her and now I'm lying here awake. My stomach is in knots of anxiety and I'm holding myself rigid to fight the trembling. I took a rescue Ativan as soon as she'd gone upstairs to help fight off my panic but it hasn't taken effect. I should have stayed downstairs, maybe watched some television to take my mind off what she'd said.

I hate feeling so helpless, so afraid, and especially so overcome with emotion—especially the ones I'm feeling now. I'm afraid of losing Maja again and I don't know what I can do to make things better for her.

Maja has always been the passionate one in our relationship, the exuberant one, the one who wants to go dancing until the clubs close, who weeps at movies. I'm not like that. I don't feel things as intensely as she does, I never have. That intense, raw emotion—I don't have that in me. And if I ever do feel something that intense I suppress it, afraid I'll lose control.

Part of me wonders if it's genuine when I see people acting out—big sobs and tears, wails of grief…if feels false somehow, as if they're playing to an audience.

It's taken me years of therapy, but now I've learned it's not them. It's me. I'm the one who doesn't feel *big feels*. I can't afford to. And I'm afraid of where it will take me if I do—so I learned a long time ago to shut it down.

What I want, what I need, to be even close to happy, is security, predictability, and comfort. I don't need big demonstrations of love and romance, and I get more than enough excitement. I want a quiet life. I need to feel safe, and I'm starting to fear that's not enough for Maja.

The next morning I give Joseph Arturo a call on his cell and ask if he can meet me for a coffee. His office is non-existent and I don't want to bring him into the station when I'm just on a fishing expedition, trying to find out a little more about Renato Rossi during the time he promoted concerts at the Buffalo Auditorium. It was so long ago and I'm having a difficult time getting a picture of the scene Ella Weaver had wandered into. Any insight would help.

He arrives at Phil's Green Bean coffee shop right on time and orders a double cappuccino with a *cornetto*. Since it's a Saturday, he's dressed casually and he seems relaxed, especially compared to yesterday at Pasquale's.

"Thank you for meeting me here," I say to get the social

pleasantries out of the way. "It must be difficult to conduct your business…since the fire."

"Impossible," he says. "I'm thinking of retiring. Taking up golf full time."

"Nice if you can do it," I toast him with my coffee cup. "Do you have any idea why someone would try to burn down your offices?" He shakes his head. "What was destroyed?"

"Everything. All my files, records going back decades."

"What sorts of files would those be? Without being specific."

He looks exasperated. "We were a firm that specialized in Estates, so mostly Wills and Powers of Attorney, that sort of thing. With a small amount of Family Law, mostly as a courtesy to our existing clients."

"Originals? And they're all lost?"

"Yes, we kept the originals in most cases, with notarized copies going to the client for their files. Some of the documents were stored in fireproof cabinets, but apart from them, it's all gone."

"What does that mean, in terms of people's estates? Without the original Will…

He shrugs. "A notarized copy is more than adequate, in most cases. Unless the Will is contested of course."

"None of it's backed up digitally, or stored off site?"

Arturo looks embarrassed. "We're an older firm, in a small town. I'm afraid we hadn't quite caught up with new technology, or new methodology for file storage."

I imagine that really does effectively put Arturo out of business. But he doesn't look too worried. I guess he's got the money to keep working on his golf swing.

There's not really any specific reason I want to interview Arturo. He's not material to the Ella Weaver case, and the restaurant brawl hasn't even developed into anything. Once the Rossis agreed to pay for damages and the *trattoria* refused to press charges,

Rosa Rossi was released. But something is needling me. The Rossi name keeps coming up: Rossi was involved in concert promotion at the time Ella disappeared, and we heard Stan Price threatening Rossi over the phone. And Joe Rossi was present at the bank robbery last Saturday. Sure, the connection might just be one of those that happen in a small town, but I need to satisfy my curiosity.

"I wonder if you could give me some background about Renato Rossi," I ask Arturo, getting to the point of our meeting. "It's to do with a cold case I'm working on, from 1990."

He frowns and shakes his head. "I don't mean to ask for anything that would violate your client's confidentiality," I quickly reassure him. "But, since he's dead…"

Arturo laughs. "Why don't you ask your questions, and if I feel I can answer I will. Okay?" I get it. Even though his client Renato Rossi is dead, the family members are still alive and well. He needs to be discreet and careful.

"How long was Mr. Rossi a client of yours?"

"Of mine specifically, only a few years. Just since his original lawyer retired. But he was with the firm since he first started in business. Around 1975, maybe?"

"And what was his business, exactly?" From what I'd read, Renato Rossi was notorious in the music industry. Apart from the radio stations and concert promotion, he'd made lots of money organizing major world tours for bands and got kickbacks from record companies and was even paid to play certain releases on his radio stations—before he was caught. He became even more wealthy buying up music rights and catalogues from bands and record labels who didn't know any better than to borrow money from him when they were desperate.

"Mr. Rossi was involved in the music industry before he went into real estate and property development. He also owned a few media outlets—radio and newspapers. Sold out just in time—

before the internet and conglomeration killed local media." So that's the sanitized version of Renato Rossi, leaving out the mob-connection, the drug trafficking, extortion, strip clubs and auto wrecking yards working as fronts for chop shops.

"He was influential at the time I suppose?"

"I imagine so, yes. He controlled media in the region, and was able to use that to promote certain bands and recording artists. But I don't know the nature of any arrangements he might have had with them, in terms of percentages…"

"Or kickbacks?"

Arturo smiles. "Mr. Rossi was a very successful businessman," he winks, saying everything and nothing at the same time.

I don't think I'll get much more out of Arturo about the nature of Renato Rossi's businesses, so I change the subject.

"Did Mr. Rossi have a large family?"

"He was Italian!" Arturo laughs. "Of course he did! He had a couple of legal wives and a series of live-in girlfriends, one of whom was with him when he died."

"I'm guessing she wasn't there yesterday?"

"She was not invited." *Not welcome* is what I assume he means.

"Families, eh?" I shake my head, as if I'd know anything about families.

"Some are crazier than others," Arturo agrees.

I mentally go through the guest list we took yesterday after the brawl. In addition to Joe Rossi and his wife Andrea, there was his sister Rosa who we arrested, her aggressive son Angelo and an assortment of sons, daughters and their spouses as well as seven grandchildren ranging from twenty-five to twelve years in age, most of whom have the same name. Maybe Arturo can explain that to me, as a start.

"Can you tell me why all of Rossi's grandsons have Renato as their middle name?" The only explanation I can think of that makes sense is money. "It seems like a way to suck up to grandpa Renato."

"All the boys except for Antonietta's son," Arturo laughs. "She won the race to spawn the first-born grandson. Her child is named Renato."

"I guess he was the favourite?"

Arturo shakes his head. "Not a bit. Angelo was always the apple of Renato's eye. It's unfortunate that he wasn't the first male child born so he could be namesake. But in every other way, he's just like his grandfather."

I wonder what that actually means? Ruthless? Criminal? Sociopath? Are those things inherited traits? It sure seems like it is in this case. But I'm not about to ask that of Arturo.

"He's a real credit to the Rossi legacy, then?"

Arturo rolls his eyes. "In all ways, except he's got his father's surname. Rosa's married name is Gennaro, but she goes by Rossi for the business."

"What was that scene about at the restaurant yesterday?" I ask instead. "All any of them will tell us is *it's family business*."

"That's as true as anything," Arturo says. "Joe Rossi asked me to attend the restaurant for the reading of the Will."

"Forgive me, but that seems colossally inappropriate to do at a funeral." Arturo raises his eyebrows and nods in agreement. "So it's not typical?"

"I've never done such a thing in my career. Never heard of it either."

"So…why?"

Arturo sighs. "According to Joe, that's what his father requested. He was very …insistent."

"And you had no knowledge of this? Surely, you wrote the Will? Wouldn't you know about this unusual request?"

"I didn't write it. That was done years ago, before I joined the firm. I didn't even know the contents of the document, until Joe showed me."

It takes a minute for that to sink in. "Until Joe Rossi showed you? He had the Will?"

"A copy, and it was lucky he did," Arturo says. "If it had been in my office it would have burned with everything else."

"Aren't copies of these things filed with some government office?"

Arturo smiles. "Not how it works. Wills aren't filed, or even made public, until after they've been probated. Until then they're filed with lawyers and family—as I've explained."

"So what was the fight in the restaurant about?"

"Some of the family members dispute the Will Mr. Rossi had me read. They claim there was a more recent Will."

"I assume with different disbursements?" Arturo nods. "Don't they have a copy of this *new* Will?"

"No, and I've never seen it, if it exists. If there was a new Will, it's possible the original was given back to Renato Rossi for safekeeping."

"Surely then it would have been found at his house? Or maybe a safety deposit box?"

Arturo looks a bit shifty. "Apparently it was not at the house," he says. "And the safety deposit box…" I realize immediately what he's about to say.

"It was emptied, during the robbery last week." Arturo nods.

"Interesting." I feel prickles of excitement up the back of my neck. But Renato Rossi didn't die until a few days after the bank robbery, so how does that help? Maybe it's just a case of bad timing. And of course there's the fire at Arturo's office. That really can't be a coincidence. "So what happens now that this supposed new Will can't be found?"

"Under law, when a Will cannot be found, the law assumes

the owner of the Will destroyed it intentionally, with the intent to revoke it."

"Okay…and then what?"

"If there's no Will at all, the deceased is considered to have died intestate. But in this case, we must go back and use the existing Will, the only one we have—the one Joe Rossi read after the funeral."

"Even though he only has a photocopy and the original is lost?"

"If there's only a copy of a Will—and the inheritors can agree—then a case can be made in court to allow it to be probated."

"And they couldn't agree."

Arturo shakes his head. "Understatement."

"So then what?"

"There is a clear rule in law governing how an estate is to be divided in that case. All the assets are equitably distributed among the relatives. In this case, each of Renato Rossi's children inherits an equal portion of his estate, which is what the original Will said anyway."

"So what's the big deal? Everyone's getting their share, no?"

Arturo smiles and stands to leave. "According to Rosa Rossi, the new Will—the one that I've never seen—cut Joe Rossi out completely. I guess she was expecting to get his share, on top of hers. Hope she hasn't already spent it."

FOURTEEN

AFTER ARTURO LEAVES I order two take out coffees and a cinnamon bun from the new barista at the counter then head up to Pelham Woods Retirement home to see Doreen. It's a visit I've been dreading, but ever since my conversation with Eleanor Parsons it's been weighing on me, popping into my mind when I'm not watchful, when I'm not on guard. *That Melnyk girl and her boyfriend McAlpine. A bad lot.*

I find her sitting alone in the designated smoking area next to the front entrance. I realize too late that I should have brought a box of donuts, like I do every week, for Doreen's friends. A cinnamon bun won't go far if she has to share.

"Thanks," Doreen growls as she accepts the coffee and pastry.

"Where's the rest of the smoking club?" Doreen typically holds court with five or six other elderly *pack a day* types. They're the ones who defy all statistics and insurance actuaries by living to a hundred despite heavy smoking and drinking their whole lives. My theory is that their smoking has preserved them, like herrings. Or maybe they're pickled from alcohol. Or both.

"Ah, they've all gone on the bus today, to the mall for an *outing.*"

"I'm impressed how much scorn you packed into that last word."

Doreen laughs as she lights another cigarette off the one she was just finishing. Her laugh sounds like a cement truck. Or maybe a gravel mixer. "Who the fuck wants to go to the damn mall? On a Saturday?" She shakes her head in disbelief. "On the short bus?"

I sit next to her at the table. We're sheltered by the wall and in a suntrap here, so it's warm enough for Doreen to enjoy the early spring weather without worrying about getting a chill. Even so, she's wrapped up in a winter coat and boots, with a scarf wrapped around her neck. An eighty-something year old isn't going to take chances with a draft.

"How's your arm and shoulder healing?" she asks. "I keep forgetting to ask you." I had a torn rotator cuff injury last summer that took a lot longer to heal than I'd like, especially when I'd reinjured it and had my arm broken in a fight with a murderer in January.

"Both okay. Almost normal." In truth those injuries really messed me up for months. I wasn't able to work beyond desk duty and even worse I had to modify my daily workout at the gym. My weight training has helped me manage my anxiety for years; without strenuous exercise I start to climb the walls and need to rely more on my medication. One good thing that came out of that time was my taking up running. For years I've hated doing cardio, all of it: treadmill, stair climber, elliptical trainer, whatever the gym had, I avoided like the plague.

Then I discovered running outside and my world changed. The freedom and release of running far and fast, leaving everything behind and escaping my own thoughts was a relief from an itch I could never scratch. I'm sleeping better, I haven't had a panic attack in months, not a full blown one anyway, and I've had to lie much less to my therapist about how I'm doing.

Doreen gives me a skeptical look. "So, your crawling through the ceiling at the bank last week didn't give you any trouble?"

"Damn." I drop my head. "I'd hoped you wouldn't hear about that."

She laughs. "Not much I don't hear about." That's true. Doreen has lived in the area her entire life. She knows everyone and what she doesn't know she can find out through her network of seniors and friends spread across the Niagara Region. Doreen looks at me, her sharp eyes missing nothing. "So, what's going on?"

"Eleanor Parsons is dead." I fill her in on how I found Jade nestled on her dead grandmother's lap.

Doreen was a nurse for years; death doesn't faze her. "What did she die of?"

"That's the mystery," I say. "It looked like natural causes, to me anyway. She was older, worked to death…"

"But…?"

"The coroner found traces of cardiac medication in her bloodstream. But she wasn't on any medication. Eleanor said herself she was healthy as a horse."

"She probably just didn't tell you. Why would she, it's not like it's any of your concern. Farmers keep themselves, and their business, to themselves." Doreen dismisses my suspicions. "Anyway, why'd anyone want to kill her? That farm can't be worth much."

"Her daughter has disappeared." Doreen's eyebrows rise in interest.

"The plot thickens," she says, lighting another cigarette. "That's not what brought you out here," she says. Doreen never misses a thing.

"I'm working a cold case," I begin, trying to find my way. "The disappearance of Ella Weaver, back in 1990."

"She's dead, I assume. You found her body?"

"We identified her as one of the bodies from the bog."

Doreen inhales deeply on her cigarette, watching me. "Zappa did it?"

I shake my head. "Not sure about that. But he definitely buried her, like he did the others." Doreen nods. "And now I need to figure out who he did it for."

"Any progress on that?"

"Unfortunately, no. We know that Zappa was connected to the Hamilton and Buffalo mob families back in the seventies and eighties. Probably even more recently, given what he was involved with when he died last year."

Doreen shakes her head. "I don't see how you're going to find out who he was connected to now. It was thirty years ago, and he's not talking." I know. Ella is dead. Zappa is dead. How am I supposed to tell Rachel that's where the story ends?

I tell Doreen about Rachel and Stan Price, about what Kim Parsons shared with me, and about the night Ella disappeared. "The only thing I can do is work back from that party, from her father Stan Price or maybe someone else who was there that night."

"Price doesn't remember?"

"He says not. Claims he was too high or too drunk or maybe being serviced by a groupie."

"I suppose that's possible," Doreen shrugs. "Or maybe just convenient."

"When he found out Ella was his daughter, something changed in him though. He got angry and it seemed like maybe he remembered something after all."

"And he didn't tell you?"

"No. I'm not even sure that's what I saw. He talked about someone paying for what he'd done. Could be nothing," I shrug. "Anyway, I'm looking at anyone I can find from that night..."

"Good luck with that," Doreen laughs.

"Exactly. The band members, the roadies, the people from the Buffalo Auditorium—I can't even find most of them. It's just too long ago." I shake my head. "Two of the band members are dead.

And the guy who did the concert promotion for the band just died this week too. He owned the radio station…"

"Renato Rossi?" Doreen interrupts.

"You know him?"

"Everybody knew Rossi. He was a big deal around here promoting concerts, bringing big name bands in to play in his clubs and even over at the Buffalo Auditorium. I saw Elvis there, in 1976. Rossi brought all the big acts into town…"

"But then he sold it all off, after he got indicted. Went into real estate."

"Sold it all off…" Doreen echoes, shaking her head. "Probably just took his name off the companies. These rich fuckers know how to operate…hiding their money, putting things into numbered companies, into other people's names…I wouldn't be surprised if he still owned it all."

I laugh in agreement. "If you keep things in someone else's name it can't get seized by the authorities."

Doreen thinks for a moment. "Rossi had some bars and a couple of strip clubs too—I'm sure he ran with some shady people." She shakes her head. "These are dangerous men, Lucy. Rossi was really mobbed up—not someone I want to think about your going up against."

"Relax," I say. "I'm not going to do anything dangerous."

"Yeah, you will," Doreen snorts. "You always do. You think your dead girl was involved with these guys? With Rossi and that crowd?"

"I don't think so. She was a good girl, from everything I've heard."

"Good girls can get into bad situations."

I feel a lump in my throat. "I don't want to bring this up," I begin, avoiding Doreen's eye. "But there's a connection…" I feel her tense and I start over. "When I was interviewing Kim Parsons' mother, she mentioned some names. Of people Kim got involved with, after Ella disappeared…"

I can tell Doreen knows what I'm about to say.

"Helena Melnyk and Scott McAlpine." My birth parents.

"*Fuck*," Doreen exhales. "The chickens have come home to roost."

The short bus pulls up in the turn around and the driver sounds the horn when he sees Doreen. She waves back at him as the door swings open and perky young volunteer jumps out and starts assisting a stream of elderly residents to dismount. Three of them head past us, toward the entrance.

"You missed out Doreen," one woman pushing a walker says. "I got a new pill organizer and compression socks."

"Great," I can tell Doreen is working hard to keep the sarcasm out of her voice. "Anything for me?"

"A bottle of whiskey and a carton of cigarettes," says another, pointing into her bundle buggy.

"Now you're talking," Doreen says, waving her cigarette. They all stop to chat, telling Doreen about their purchases and their adventures at the mall.

I allow myself to detach, and fall back into thinking about my mother. What do I even know about her, as a person? She died so young. How did she even come to be in the life she ended up living? She went to school in town, she had friends, she even swam at Nickel Beach in the summers, just like I used to. Her name was Helena. Mine was Tracy, before it was changed to Lucy.

I've forgotten so many things and repressed the rest. I have memories of her crooked smile and half-closed eyes tucking me in some nights, while loud music played and people laughed downstairs. But I know even a drunk can be a loving mother.

After it all ended I tried to forget all the darkness, all the bad things that happened. I forced it all out of my mind so I could find a way forward, so I could find peace. But now I'm struggling to remember, to recall some fragments of light that I can hold onto to help me get through my bad moments. But I don't have very many and no matter how deep I dig into the muck I can't uncover many bright shiny things.

I remember the house, always dark with the curtains drawn day and night so my uncles could sleep it off, or keep partying and playing cards and doing drugs. I remember being hungry sometimes. I think I remember a kitten. And I remember my mother's smile.

I can see Doreen is getting irritated, impatient for her friends to leave us alone. She's fidgeting in her seat and lights a cigarette when she's already got one burning. Finally, once they've all headed inside, she turns to me. The smile she'd put on for her friends is gone.

"Lucy, let this go. You can't risk everything to help Rachel Weaver. Her daughter is long dead. You're still alive."

"This isn't about Rachel." Doreen raises a skeptical eyebrow but I keep talking. "It's about my mother. It's about what happened to her, and what she had to do to survive, and to look after me." And it's about Kim Parsons. And her little girl. I can help her— when nobody helped me.

"She did whatever she could. You know that."

"I do. And I know those men did whatever they could get away with. Men like Rossi and Ray—the men who used her. I want them to pay."

"And you're willing to risk it all, everything you've built in this new life? For what? For revenge? On Ray? Rossi? Men who are already dead?"

"Joe Rossi's not dead," I say. "He's living a big life, money, power, politics, influence. But Ella's dead. Rachel will never get over it. And Kim Parsons…"

"What about her?"

"After it happened, she started hanging around in the East Village. Her life derailed…."

"Like you'd expect."

"She dropped out of school, started doing drugs. A friend got her work at a strip club, but it didn't work out for her. This *friend*…"

Doreen's lips tighten in anger and she cuts me off. "Your mother did what she had to do, to survive at the time. I won't hear a bad word said against her."

"I'm not judging. I'm trying to understand…trying to learn." It's been a long time since I've dared to lift the rock my past is buried under. Maybe I'm strong enough now to look.

"Would that have been the same strip club my father worked at? Is that how they met?" Doreen shakes her head.

"Your mother was a good girl. She was just in high school, living with her family, when she got pregnant. She went on social assistance after you were born. She couldn't work—there was no one to leave baby with." I nod. Her parents had kicked her out of the family home when they found out about the pregnancy. I've read about my past, in the social services files. Being a police officer allows me access to certain information, not that anyone knows I'm looking.

"She didn't work at the strip club until later, when she needed money. That's where she met your stepfather. *Ray.*" Doreen's lip curls when she says the last word.

"Was my mother an addict too? A user?" If Kim Parsons had been, then it made sense. They hung out in the same group.

Doreen shakes her head impatiently. "No! She wasn't an addict. Why would you think that?"

"I don't remember much from that time, from before…" I

trail off. I can't go into what happened. "Did my father ever find out he had a kid?" I have a hazy memory of being bounced in the sunshine on someone's knee, being hugged by a man…was that him? Or was it some random stranger coming by the house to buy drugs from my uncle?

Doreen slaps her hands down on the arms of her chair. "Stop this, Lucy. Stop this digging around in the past."

"I'm not digging around…"

Doreen shoots me a glare through the cloud of her cigarette smoke. "Yes, you are. Literally. You dug up all those bog bodies and now it's brought you here."

I take a deep breath and try a different approach. "Look. I don't want to keep burying my head," I say. "It hasn't helped…not really." I'm not even sure I'm telling the truth. Avoiding the past has served me well.

"Oh, you don't think so?" Doreen isn't buying it. "Burying your head, keeping it down and hiding your past is exactly what helped you to survive. Why do you need to know about them anyway? What's the point?"

"There's no point. Her name came up and I just started to think…"

"Let it go, Lucy. You don't want to go into the past."

"Not even if it holds a key to the present?"

FIFTEEN

"**THOUGHT YOU MIGHT** want to come along," I say as Vogel climbs into the passenger seat. "Since you're such a fan of Running Deep and all." I'd called him when I left Doreen's, on the off chance he'd have nothing else to do on a Saturday morning and he's jumped at the chance. Knowing Vogel he'd picked up a woman last night, stayed the night, woke up without his beer goggles and was desperate for a way out of her apartment, so I'm doing him a favour.

I've picked him up at home, where from the look of it, he's quickly showered and shaved and dressed just in time to meet me. His hair is still wet. I hand him a coffee, as a thank you.

"I wouldn't say I'm a fan, exactly," he says. "A bit before my time, musically-speaking. Why are we seeing Price again?"

"I met the Rossi family lawyer this morning," I begin and by the time we're pulling into Price's driveway Vogel is up to speed on my suspicions about Renato Rossi, his record promotion business and his possible mob connections.

The gate is already open and there's a red sports car parked at the far end of the driveway, near the kitchen door.

"I hope we're not interrupting anything." I point out the car to Vogel. It probably belongs to the mystery girlfriend who was here last time we visited.

Our knock on the front door is promptly answered by Stan Price, a different Stan Price from the man I've met twice before. He's in a jovial mood for a start and he invites us in and leads us back into the kitchen, where he offers us coffee.

The kitchen island is piled with boxes and a laptop is open next to one of the stools.

"No, thank you," I say. "We had one in the car just now." I hear a car door slam then the red car drives past the window. Vogel and I exchange a look. I guess we did interrupt something after all.

"What's all this?" Vogel asks while Price is pouring boiling water into the French press.

Price grins. "It's my past," he says with pride, opening one of the boxes. From what I can see it's full of memorabilia and souvenirs. He starts to pull stuff out and show it off. There are posters, bar mats, flyers advertising concerts, t-shirts, and baseball caps branded with I assume are various albums and song releases.

"You've kept all this stuff?" Vogel sounds impressed.

"I'm just a sentimental old fool," Price says. "And, I'm writing a memoir: *My Life in Running Deep*." It sounds like a terrible title for what I'm sure will be a whitewash.

He grins and starts into what is clearly a practiced pitch. "It's going to be a tell-all, about the early days of the band—an amazing time, with us touring the world, playing with other rock legends. I remember it all," he leans forward and winks. "And I know where all the bodies are buried."

I wonder how true that statement is when for a split second the smile falls from his face. He glances at me and looks ashamed as he realizes how tone-deaf his bravado sounds.

"Sorry. Bad choice of words."

"Sounds exciting," Vogel saves him.

"It's been fantastic," Price recovers with a laugh. "Getting in touch with everyone from years ago, tracking them all down.

Man…" he shakes his head. "Good times. Good people. It's funny how you lose touch…"

"How's the book coming?" I interrupt. "Is it difficult to write a memoir?"

"If Keith Richards can do it," Price shrugs, adopting a demeanor of false modesty.

"And Bruce Springsteen," Vogel adds. "Hell, even Slash from Guns and Roses did."

"There you go," Price nods at Vogel. "I'm getting asked all the time about it. Been approached I don't even know how many times, by publishers and agents." I take this with a lot of salt. At least I've heard of Springsteen and Guns and Roses. Who the hell cares about Running Deep?

"What can I do for you, Detectives?"

"It's great timing that you're writing this project. And that you have such a great memory," I begin. "Because I have some questions for you, about that time." Price looks wary. He must know he's opened himself up now.

"What do you remember about Renato Rossi? The music promoter."

"Not much," he says after a moment. "We may have met once. Working with music promoters would have been our manager's job. I didn't deal with publicity and media."

"Where's your manager these days?"

"Dead. Years ago."

"And you don't recall anything about Mr. Rossi? He owned two radio stations in the area, would have done a lot of promotion for your records and concerts. I'm sure you might have even gone into the station for on-air interviews at some point."

"I guess…don't recall really."

I'm impatient with him. The fact that he thinks he can go

from boasting about his memoir to playing dumb in a matter of minutes is irritating.

"Mr. Price, I'll be frank," Vogel says before I say something much less tactful. "It's difficult to believe you. Renato Rossi was brought up on all sorts of charges and federal indictments at the time. It was big news. It seems unlikely you wouldn't recall him."

Stan Price sits down at the bar stool and starts to put his memorabilia back into the boxes. I'm sure it's a way to avoid meeting our eyes.

"Look," he says. "We were the talent. We recorded the songs, we performed at the concerts. The record company and our managers arranged for all the promotion. They handled publicity, contests, incentivized radio stations to play our songs…"

"Incentivized?"

Price's eyes flick up to Vogel. "Cash. Drugs. Contra."

"Contra? What's that?"

"Goods exchanged. Barter," he explains. "A hundred tape players or televisions from a big retailer will get you a certain number of commercials on air—off the books. The radio station can give them away in contests, or to staff as bonuses, or…"

"Sell them?"

"Sure, if they want. And that goes for concert tickets, records, personal appearances by the band, you name it. It's all barter. That's how a lot of this stuff got paid for." He holds up a t-shirt. "Meals at restaurants, cases of wine, free use of jet or yacht…"

"…or girls?"

Price grins. "Oh yeah." Then he realizes what he's admitted to. "Not that it ever happened to us."

"No," Vogel lets him off the hook. "Of course not."

"Do you have photographs from those days," I ask, indicating the boxes. "Or is it just your recall and these mementos that you're relying on, to help you write the book?"

"Not as many as I'd like," Price admits. "I've got quite a few in here, from the record company PR reps, fans of the band, and a few from photographers who came along on tours. I'm still trying to negotiate with a couple of them for rights to more photos."

"These photographers accompanied you for the whole tour? All access? Backstage and all that?"

"Of course," Price says with pride, once again unaware he's dropped himself into it.

"Who was the photographer for the tour that brought you to the Buffalo Auditorium in 1990?" I ask. "I'd like his name."

Price flushes red and starts to stammer. "I...I don't think I know. It would have been someone hired by the concert promoter, I think."

"Think you could find out for us, Mr. Price?" I ask, dropping my voice so he hears the underlying threat. "Have a look through your copious notes and search your prodigious memory, maybe give us the name? It would be a shame if we had to get a warrant and have to remove all these items and search them ourselves. That would delay your project quite some time. Indefinitely, even."

"I'll go through these right away," Price says, understanding exactly what I mean. "I'll call you with the name." I hand him my card and Vogel and I leave.

"What kind of business has lots of cash, drugs and girls to barter with?" I say as we drive away.

"Organized crime. Strip clubs. Bikers," Vogel says.

"Exactly. And it's not a reach to connect Renato Rossi to all of this. I just need a way to tie it to the death of Ella Weaver."

By the time I drop Vogel back at his place I'm late to meet Maja. We've arranged to have an early dinner together, at the hospital cafeteria. Not the most romantic of places to eat, but she's working a twelve-hour locum shift in Emergency, so it's the best we can manage. As a new doctor in the region Maja has to wear a lot of different hats. She works in the walk-in clinic most days seeing regular patients. Since staffing is so thin at the hospital, she picks up several shifts a month as a locum in the Emergency department. She's also one of the on-call Coroners for the region, which is how we first met, years ago.

By the time she'll get home tonight, assuming she's even on time, it'll be far too late to eat. And, knowing Maja, if I don't force her to stop working and eat a meal, she'll work right through without taking a break at all. For a girl who loves food as much as she does, I can't understand it.

Even though I'm dreading it, I need to clear the air. She's been preoccupied and distracted with me ever since last night, even before that, if I'm honest. In fact, she's been distant ever since the call last week with her old classmate, the forensic pathologist. Not that the hospital cafeteria is the best place to have a private conversation, but I need to get it done.

"Maja, what's wrong?" I ask the minute we've set our trays down at a table. She just looks uncomfortable and shrugs, avoiding the question. "Seriously, I'm worried. I'm usually the broody, moody, sulky one in this relationship, not you." I'm trying to keep it light, to avoid revealing how frightened I really am. Is Maja leaving me? Has she decided she doesn't want to be in a relationship with me? The pain of that thought makes me catch my breath in fear.

"I feel like a failure," she finally says.

I'm so relieved, and astounded by her response I can't speak for a moment.

"A *failure*?! What do you mean?" She just looks away. "You're a great doctor. So many people rely on you and respect you. And you're a Coroner. How can you possibly think you're a failure?"

Maja shrugs. "After the call with Bill Venturi, I just started thinking. I was ahead of him in school." She looks embarrassed. "I'm the one who won the Medical Association Award for Young Leaders. I won the Laird Prize and the Blake Scholarship, and I'm the one who served on the Canadian Commission for UNESCO—-not Bill Venturi. But he's now this hotshot Forensic Pathologist, working at the Center of Forensic Services, giving speeches, travelling the world...."

"*Hotshot?* How do you know he's travelling the world, giving speeches?"

"I Googled him," she manages a smile. "It's all true. And here I am...in a small town. Working as a GP. It just...feels like I'm a loser. Like I didn't live up to my potential." She stares out the window for a moment. "It feels like I settled."

Settled. For me? That's all I can hear. Tears well up and start to stream down my cheeks.

"Why are you crying? Maja asks.

"You're breaking up with me."

"No, I'm not. Where'd you get that idea?"

"You're not? You promise?"

Her eyes flash with irritation. "It's not always about you Lucy," she snaps and I feel as if I've been slapped. Then she reaches across the table and squeezes my hand.

"I'm sorry," I whisper, ashamed of my insecurity.

"I love you Lucy," she says and I take a deep breath of relief.

"What do you want to do about it? About this feeling you've got?"

Maja shakes her head. "I don't know. I rushed through school, worked really hard, did my best—to please my parents. I've never travelled anywhere; I've never seen the world. Now I'm stuck here—and I'm happy with you Lucy. It's not about that. Not about us. I just...I don't know. I feel like I missed out."

"You want to take a vacation? A trip?"

She shakes her head. "That's not going to do it." I feel the anxiety flare in my chest and my hands start to tremble.

"Maybe a longer trip somewhere, like a leave of absence?" I suggest in desperation. "We could spend a few months in a villa in Italy, or maybe France. I'm sure I could take a personal leave too."

She shakes her head. "I'm thinking about Doctors Without Borders." My heart sinks. "And I'd be going alone."

"Doctors Without Borders," I echo, unable to say anything else.

"I'd be a good choice for them——I speak Hindi, Urdu, French, and English." I nod, my mind spinning. "French is what they really want—so many African countries are former French colonies."

"Africa? You're going to *Africa*?" I'm stunned. She's already done the research, has looked into it, has already started the process—without even telling me about it. I'm not part of her decision. How I feel isn't relevant to her.

She nods happily. "They currently operate in thirty-four African countries."

"Maja, it's dangerous. You're talking about going into war zones!"

Maja rolls her eyes. "Like you've never done anything dangerous in your job. Lucy, you put your life on the line all the time—in fact, more often than you need to…"

"You seriously want to put your life on the line? Because, believe me, it's not all it's cracked out to be."

"Lucy, everything isn't about you, all the time." I fall silent in the face of Maja's resentful tone. "And, it's easy for you to say, since you're the one having all the fun and excitement."

"*Fun and excitement*?! Are you kidding me?"

Suddenly there's a Code Blue—an Adult Cardiac Arrest—call over the PA system and Maja has to run out the door, leaving me with my thoughts and the remains of our lunch.

Part of me resents what Maja said. It's never been *easy for me*. Nothing is and nothing ever has been. Not with my past history, what I did and what it caused and the resulting anxiety disorder I've been hiding every waking moment.

I know I do tend to get caught up in my job. I'm often single-minded about it, to the point that even Maja takes a back seat when I'm in pursuit of an investigation.

Have I driven Maja away? Is that what this is about? The feeling in the pit of my stomach tells me that it's true.

I know Maja's going to be starving later, so I decide to wrap up her sandwich and bring it up to her on the ward. With any luck she'll have a chance to eat it at some point later this evening.

There's no sign of her when I get into the Emergency Ward, but I leave the sandwich with the nurse on the desk and head out to the parking lot. I'm about to exit through the sliding glass doors, wondering how I should spend my evening, when it occurs to me that the bank robbers are still here. I back up into the lobby and head for the elevators.

It's already been a week since they were admitted, though it feels like a lot longer. The one with the gunshot wound to the thigh should have been discharged already, but apparently he needed some reconstructive surgery, which didn't go well. The other guy, the one with a broken neck, will be in here a lot longer, from what Abby told us over dinner.

I realize I haven't had an update recently from DS Dudek recently on the status of the investigation, or into whether they've got a positive ID on the dead robber yet. It's not my case, but I feel a certain amount of entitlement around it, given my involvement. I pull out my phone and call Dudek, but it goes straight to voicemail, so I hang up without leaving a message.

When the elevator opens on the fourth floor I head for the nursing station and ask for Abby.

"She's not on shift today," one of the other nurses tells me. "Sorry."

"I'm Detective Constable Gauthier," I say, showing her my ID. "Can you please direct me to…"

"They're just down that hall," she interrupts me, knowing what I'm about to ask. "Last two rooms on the ward."

There's a uniformed constable on duty outside the rooms. She's sitting on a chair looking bored and I don't blame her. If I thought traffic duty—sitting on the side of the road for hours waiting for speeding cars was tedious, this must be a hundred times worse.

"Hi Walker," I say grateful her nametag is legible. She looks familiar but there's no way I'd remember her name without it. She looks young, like she still might be a fourth-class constable, fresh out of the academy. Walker smiles and leaps to her feet.

"There's no need for that," I laugh. I'm just a DC and this isn't the Army. "Anything new?" I ask, nodding toward the prisoners' rooms.

"Nothing," she shakes her head. "Quiet day." I imagine it would be, since it's the weekend. "One of them has a visitor though. His mother. She comes every day."

"Which one, Shepherd or Byrne?"

"Byrne," I hear her say as I peer through the window into his room. I see a man lying in the bed, his neck in a stiff brace and his head encased in one of those wire halos. This must be the guy I landed on. As I watch, a figure moves past the window, blocking my view for a moment as it heads for the bed. It's a woman, bringing him a glass of water. She holds it for him, angling the bent straw into his mouth and after he's had a sip she gently wipes his face with a washcloth before sitting down in a chair next to his bed.

I see the flash of colourful clothing in a riot of colours and patterns and the long grey hair and my breath catches in surprise. It's Rachel Weaver.

SIXTEEN

Now I remember why the name Dillon Byrne was so familiar. I pull back from the door so fast Constable Walker jumps in alarm.

"Is everything okay?" she asks, jumping to her feet.

I'm saved from answering when my phone rings and I excuse myself to answer it. I walk down the hall a few paces, keeping my eye on Byrne's door the whole time.

"Hi Gauthier," DS Dudek says. "Sorry I missed your call. I've been busy."

"No problem," I say. "How's it going? Anything turn up?"

"We've got an ID on your guy," he says. "Jason Winner. More of a loser, I suppose." He pauses for the laugh, which I provide. I'm sure Dudek has used this line a few times already. "He's a local contractor. Winner does renovations and handyman jobs in the area. Does electrical and plumbing too, apparently."

"No criminal record?"

"Nope. Nothing. His prints are on file from a job application he made at the casino, years ago, so that was a lucky break for us. I think he must have arranged for the convenient flood at the bank that required the repairs. That gave him the opportunity to cut the CCTV cameras, or to get someone in to do it for him."

"So, no clear link to anyone who hired him? To whoever set

up the job?" It doesn't seem like it would have been Jason Winner, though I suppose every criminal has to start somewhere.

"Not yet. We're pulling his bank records now. Maybe something will turn up." Dudek doesn't seem hopeful.

"Well, thanks for calling me back." I end the call just as the door to Dillon Byrne's room opens and Rachel emerges. She sees me and stops short.

"Hi." I don't know what else to say. She doesn't say anything, but walks a few feet down the hall and allows me to catch up.

"What are you doing here Lucy?" For a second I think she's angry with me for putting her son in hospital, and that's why she's being so awkward with me. Then I realize she's just embarrassed that her son is a bank robber—a failed one at that.

"How's he doing?"

Rachel shrugs. "He'll be fine," she says. "The surgery went well. There won't be any permanent damage." She presses the button for the elevator and I wait with her in silence. I've got nothing to say anyway.

"I didn't even notice him, last week in the bank." She finally says as the doors close behind us. "He was behind me in line, and when they started shouting, and told us all to get down on the floor, I thought I recognized his voice. Just for a second." She shakes her head. "He told me the other day how he'd seen me, up at the front of the line. He wasn't going to go through with it after that, he said." I'm sure that's exactly what he'd say. What guy wouldn't tell that story to his mother?

"But then it all kicked off and he went along with it. He knew they'd be wearing masks and hoped I wouldn't recognize him."

"Did he mention anything about the security cameras?"

"Only that he was told there wouldn't be any. That's why they stood in line without their masks on."

"Did he tell you anything about who he's working with? About who set the job up?"

Rachel shakes her head. "I haven't asked him anything. I don't think I want to know."

"I'm sorry for asking," I say. "Is there anything I can do for you?"

"Just find who killed Ella. Please." She sighs. "I've seen something like this coming with Dillon for a long time. I don't like it, but I've never been able to stop him doing whatever he wanted to do."

"Because of his void moon? Or his retrograde Mars?" I tease her gently.

"No. Because he's a Sagittarius," she says. "With Aries rising. Ambitious and impulsive, with no sense of consequences." The elevator doors open and we head out to the parking lot.

"Do you need a ride home?" She hesitates. "I won't ask any questions, I promise."

"Yes, please. I'd like that."

We drive for a few minutes in silence while I try and think of something to talk about that doesn't involve her son until I can't stand it any longer. But it's tough for me to just make conversation, the way other people do so naturally. I'm fine if I have a focus and a purpose to my chat. That's that kind of conversation that makes sense to me; it's also why I'm so good at interviewing people. I decide on Price since I didn't promise not to discuss him.

"When did you first know he was in town?"

"Maybe ten years ago? I had no idea he was here for ages," she says, immediately knowing who I'm talking about. "One day I was at Womyn, doing knitting circle when one of the girls came in, all excited. She put on a music CD and started telling everyone all about this rock star buying a vineyard." She stares out the window as we drive up the escarpment, past rows and rows of vines.

"It was Running Deep's biggest hit, you know the one they did for famine relief?" I nod. "I couldn't believe what I was hearing. Honestly, I almost passed out. Had to leave the room and get some air."

"I did everything I could to avoid him, not that it was difficult. We move in *different circles*," she chuckles. "Then, after he'd already been living here for over a year," she says. "I ran into him at the coffee shop downtown."

"Was that awkward?"

"He didn't even recognize me," she says after a moment.

"Well, I'm pretty sure he looked much different too. A lot of time has passed," I say diplomatically. "Did you say anything to him? Introduce yourself?"

Rachel laughs. "He said *You look familiar. Have we met?* I was speechless. What could I say? *Of course, we've met. You're my Ella's father.*"

I raise my eyebrows. "And what did you say, really?"

"I mumbled something like, *No, I don't believe so*, or *No, you must be mistaken.*" She shakes her head. "Then he put out his hand and said *I'm Stan*, and he turned his takeaway coffee cup to show me his name scribbled on the side. Playing like he's just a regular guy, not some big fucking rock star that everyone in bloody town won't stop talking about.

"I forced myself to give him a big smile and said *I'm Rachel Weaver.*

There was a moment, just a flash in his eyes, and I thought he remembered me."

"Really? What did he say?"

"How do you spell that? With one L or two?" I snort in surprise and Rachel laughs out loud at the memory. "He got out a pen, thinking I was going to ask him for an autograph!

"He started looking for something to sign. The idiot pulled a paper napkin out of his pocket and stood there with a dumb grin on his face, thinking I'm some fan. I should have punched him right in the mouth.

"My name meant nothing to him. Nothing whatsoever." She shakes her head. "I realized instantly there was absolutely no point talking to him. Seriously, what could I say? *Yes, we've met. You did your best to ruin my life? Left me pregnant while you ran off to become rich and famous?*

"That must have upset you," I mumble inadequately.

"Gee, ya think?" she laughs. "At first I was in shock, seeing him for the first time in decades. My great love. Then…after he was gone, I was surprised at the anger I felt, the sorrow."

Rachel turns to me. "I really did love him, you know. Completely." She sighs and stares out the window as we drive through the countryside. "But, time passes. Things change. The Universe spoke and said it wasn't meant to be."

Rachel seems to be keeping it in perspective, in her flaky way. I leave her to her thoughts and focus on driving.

"We did a DNA test on Stan Price," I say to break the silence after a while. "To determine if he was Ella's father."

Rachel looks offended. "I wouldn't lie."

"We need proof Rachel. Price wasn't about to take your word for it."

She doesn't ask about the results, which is interesting. There's clearly no doubt in her mind about who Ella's father was, and I'm sure she would know.

"How'd he take the news?" she asks with a chuckle.

"At first he didn't believe it. Then he got angry that someone killed his daughter."

"So now he admits it," she mutters. "Denying her…"

"*Now?*" I interrupt her, when the impact of what she said

finally gets through to me. I pull the car over to the side of the road and stop. "What do you mean *now he admits it*?" Rachel looks nervous, as she should. "What are you hiding, Rachel?"

"It's nothing," she says. "I just mis-spoke." But she won't meet my eye.

"Bullshit. You told me you'd never told Stan Price about Ella. As far as I know Vogel and I were the first ones who gave him the news." Rachel looks away. "You'd already told him? When?"

"Years ago," she admits after a moment. "I confronted him, in the street. I…I wasn't really thinking straight at the time."

"Confronted him? How?" She won't elaborate. "Well?"

Rachel is staring out the window. "I bumped into him, as he was coming out of the bank." Her voice is so low I can barely hear her. "The same bank that was robbed. I've had an account there since I was a kid." She sighs deeply. It's clear telling this story is making her miserable. "The bank had just turned down my loan application…I was upset. And then, when I saw him, Mr. Rich Rock Star without a care in the world, I just snapped.

"I went up to him and started shouting. I told him who I was…I said we had a daughter. He just looked…shocked. He stared at me for the longest time. Then…he… he…*laughed* at me. He laughed so hard tears came to his eyes. I thought he was going to piss himself."

"That's…horrible." The pieces start to fall into place. I guess that explains why Price called Rachel a loony when we showed him her photo. He remembered the way she'd accosted him in the street.

"It was humiliating. Cruel." She rubs her eyes, but she isn't crying. "He mocked me and insulted what I look like, how I was dressed. Said the idea of him *fucking me* was completely ridiculous."

"I was so angry I could have killed him, right there." She glances at me. "But of course I didn't. Obviously."

I nod. "It's tough to be angry for that many years."

Rachel raises an eyebrow. "Oh I don't know about that," she says. "I was angry for a long, long time. But I'm a pacifist. I'm still a hippie. Peace, love and understanding. I worked for years on forgiveness."

I tap my fingers on the steering wheel, thinking over what she's told me. Rachel had lied to me. Stan Price denied his daughter and shamed her. Humiliated her. What an absolute prick. She was furious and enraged, but was she capable of murdering him? And why do it so many years later, unless finding Ella's remains triggered something in her.

"Please don't say anything," Rachel pleads. "It's so…humiliating. It hurts to even remember it."

Against my better judgement, I agree. "Fine. Unless it becomes material in some way, I won't say a word." It's unlikely that Price's role in Ella's paternity factors into how she died. And it won't change what happened to her. Rachel reaches over and pats my hand in gratitude.

"Do you think Price knows what happened to Ella?" Rachel says after a moment. "Did he admit to seeing Ella that night?"

"I shouldn't be telling you any of this."

"You brought it up."

She's right, of course. I didn't have to offer Rachel a ride home. I could have turned away as soon as I saw her through the window to her son's room.

"He didn't remember seeing her that night," I say after a moment.

"Do you believe him?"

"It's tough to say. From what he told us, they'd all get pretty wasted after their concerts. He may not remember much of anything that happened for decades of his life." Rachel snorts in disgust. "But then, he's writing a memoir so I hope he can recall at least a few things from his career…"

"A *memoir*?!?!" Rachel interrupts. "The guy I knew could barely read. Who's going to write it for him?"

"Apparently he's already got a publishing deal," I shrug.

"Connections. That's what money and fame get you," she says. "Whatever you want, whether you deserve it or not."

SEVENTEEN

THE ALARM GOES off at six o'clock and I'm out of bed, into my running clothes and out the door before I talk myself out of it. I'm doing 10K this morning and the sooner I hit the road the sooner I'll be done. A raw wind blows off the lake but the air is fresh and the road is empty and I feel like I can run forever. Like I might even outrun my past.

I run and run, my feet turning over, the rhythmic pounding keeping pace with my heartbeat and I lose myself in it. My anxiety and fear, the pointless adrenaline constantly flooding through my body now has a purpose and it drives me on, further and faster until I'm done. Until I'm spent. Until I'm exhausted and satisfied, and for a brief moment, for just a heartbeat and a glimmer of time, I'll be okay. Not afraid. I'll believe there's nothing at the door or under the bed or in my mind hunting me down and keeping me in constant dread.

I'd spent yesterday at home, relaxing with Maja on our shared Sunday off. I didn't even open my laptop or glance at my phone to check email. Months ago Maja had instituted a house rule to keep, forbidding work on our days off, as a way to have some kind of balance, and it was a great thing. It gives me a few hours to feel like a normal person, and for us to be a regular couple.

We'd worked in the garden, digging the new vegetable beds we'd been planning since last year. A truckload of sheep manure and topsoil was delivered last week that we'd wheelbarrowed into the backyard and spread it around. Then we'd spent the evening stiff and sore, flaked out with exhaustion in front of the television.

Six weeks ago we started tomato and pepper seedlings under lights and now we're sowing beans, kale and salad greens, and Maja had crowed with delight about how delicious, nutritious and fresh our meals would now be.

"You do realize we've spent more on this garden—the soil, seeds, lights—than we'd have done in a year of buying fresh produce?" I teased her, not for the first time. My heart sank at the thought that I'll be tending that garden myself, if she ends up going away.

By the time I walk in the back door, sweating and smiling that I made it home in record time, beating my personal best by a minute and a half. Maja's on her way out, heading to open the clinic for eight o'clock. Monday's always the busiest day of the week.

"Your phone's been ringing non-stop," she says as she climbs into her car. "Somebody's gotta be dead."

"About time Gauthier," Vogel says when I pick up. "We've got a body. It's Stan Price."

"*What?* When?"

"Looks like he was killed sometime last night. I'll swing by and get you."

"Give me ten minutes. I need a shower."

By the time we get to Stan Price's place, the Coroner is already on the scene and the forensic team is waiting for permission to begin their investigation.

We're all waiting outside on the driveway. There's a red sports car parked by the back door.

"We've seen that before," I nudge Vogel. "The girlfriend's car."

"That's an Alfa Romeo 4C Spider," Vogel says.

"Expensive?"

"Very." I wonder what Price's girlfriend did to be able to afford a luxury sports car. Probably her sugar daddy bought it for her. Isn't that how it usually goes with rich old men and much younger women?

"How'd he die?" I ask Dr. Yun when he emerges from the house. He peels off his nitrile gloves and leaves his booties in a box by the back door, in case they've picked up any trace evidence.

"Exsanguination, caused by multiple stab wounds to his torso and abdomen. It's pretty clear. I doubt we'll find any surprises when I open him up."

"Time of death?"

"Within twelve hours, give or take."

Vogel and I pull on our booties and gloves then enter the kitchen through the back door. Stan Price's body is lying on the marble floor between the island and the sink.

"Who found him?" I ask the constable standing by the door.

"The assistant Shelley Arthur," he says, glancing first at his notebook for the name. "At eight this morning."

"*Assistant*? Is that what they're calling girlfriends these days?" I can't help myself. Vogel ignores me and heads over to the body, careful to walk only on the anti-contamination stepping plates the forensic team have already laid out across the marble floor.

Price is lying on his side, mouth agape, clutching at his abdomen. He's fully dressed, including yet another pair of expensive cowboy boots. A large pool of dried and thickening blood is under his body and has spread under the cabinets and the island. Blood has wicked up, soaking into his long grey ponytail, reminding me of Rachel's purple highlights.

"Given the amount of blood," Vogel says, "whoever stabbed

him would have a lot of blood on them. No question. It'd be on their clothes and, judging by those tracks on the floor, on their shoes." He points to several footprints left by someone wearing boots with a clear tread. SIU is already taking photos of the footprints, along with dusting for fingerprints and gathering trace evidence from the room.

"Do you suppose these footprints could be the assistant's?" I ask one of the constables. "She did find the body."

"No," she says, flipping open her notebook and reading it back. "She says she never even came this side of the island. Didn't even notice him lying here until she went to make coffee."

Vogel and I exchange a skeptical look.

"It's hard to imagine not noticing a dead body lying on the floor," he says.

"Well, the kitchen is huge," I counter. "And there's this great big island between the sink and counter. If she came in there," I point to the door, "then hung up her coat and went straight through there to the office…she might not have noticed him."

Vogel shrugs and walks it out, as I described it. "Then she comes back into the room, sees Price lying there, sees all the blood, and she runs back into the office to call 911. That fits, I guess."

I can't help but give him a smirk and Vogel shoots me an irritated look. "Okay, so the Coroner said he would have been killed last night, between seven and nine," he says. "Price was dressed. Was he alone? Was he entertaining?"

A glance around the kitchen answers that question. It's spotless. No dirty dishes or glasses or any indication that he'd had company.

"There's no sign of a break in," I say. "So I suppose he let his killer in." There's an alarm pad on the wall by the door, its light flashing. "We need to find out if that was set when this morning when the assistant came in," I snap at Vogel. "Is there security camera footage? Find out."

"Woah, Gauthier," Vogel says, putting his hand on my arm. "What's with the tone? Who do you think you're talking to?"

That stops me short. I didn't realize how I sounded, but a quick glance at the embarrassed constable makes it clear. "I'm sorry, you're right. I'm just…irritated."

"With me?"

"No, with Stan Price."

Vogel smiles. "For being murdered?"

"No…because a fresh victim will take precedence over a cold case. I know DS Agu will pull me off the Ella Weaver case and I'll need to focus on Price's death instead of hers."

"Yeah. Probably." Vogel shrugs and turns away. "She's been dead a long time. Another few weeks won't make much difference, will it?"

"But it's obvious the two cases are related," I say. "I can't be a coincidence that Stan Price was killed just a few days after our visit, and after the DNA proved Ella Weaver was his daughter."

"Obvious? I don't know about that. It could be a coincidence." He heads out of the kitchen, then turns back when he realizes I'm not with him. "A positive DNA test doesn't feel like a motive for murder. Who'd benefit? His daughter is already long dead."

The first person to come to mind is Rachel. But why would she murder Stan Price now, so many years after he'd abandoned her? *Who benefits?* Not Rachel, that's for sure. Unless something snapped in her and she killed him out of anger. Maybe she blamed him for Ella's death—since she'd died after going to his concert in Buffalo? Or is there something else Rachel hasn't told tell me?

"C'mon. Let's talk to the assistant," Vogel says, interrupting my train of thought. "She's waiting in the living room."

A police constable keeping watch over a young woman who I immediately recognize as the one who'd closed the door in my face on our first visit to Price's house, just a few days ago. Now that I'm able to get a close look at her, I see she doesn't look anything like what I'd expect of Stan Price's girlfriend. Shelley Arthur is tall and slender and blonde, which is a standard rock star girlfriend cliche. But her glasses, baggy jeans, fleece hoodie and Doc Martin boots make her look more like a graduate student.

"How are you, Ms. Arthur?" Vogel asks. "Holding up all right?"

She nods, keeping her eyes on the carpet. Her cheeks are tear-stained and her makeup smeared. No surprise, given she'd just found her boyfriend dead on the kitchen floor. Assuming that's what really happened and she's not the one who stabbed him.

"Shelley, are you able to answer some questions?" I ask. "We won't take too much of your time, then you can go home, okay?" She nods again, eyes down.

"How long have you known Mr. Price?"

"Just a few months," she mumbles.

"How did you meet?"

"At a party. His publisher introduced us."

"How did you get in this morning, Ms. Arthur?"

"I have a key."

"And you know the alarm code?" She nods. "Really? That seems fast, given you only met a few months ago."

Shelley finally looks up from the carpet. "What do you mean, *fast*?"

"You've only been seeing one another for a few months and you've got a key and the alarm code?"

"*Seeing each other*? What are you even talking about?"

Vogel raises his hand to stop me before I put my other foot in my mouth. "What was the nature of your relationship with Mr. Price?" he asks.

"I didn't have a *relationship* with him," Shelley rolls her eyes. "I don't know what you're insinuating. I worked for him. I'm his *assistant*."

"Forgive me Ms. Arthur," I try to keep the skepticism out of my tone. "Why does a retired musician need an assistant?"

"I'm helping him gather his memorabilia and catalogue it all. He's writing a memoir." She catches Vogel and I exchange a look. "Gross," she continues making her point clear. "Stan Price was an old man. Why would you assume a sexual relationship between us? What's wrong with you?"

"I'm sorry," I mumble, ashamed that I agree with her. Why did I default to the cliche explanation—old guy and young girlfriend?

"Is that your car in the driveway?" Vogel asks, pointing to the red sports car.

"You're kidding, right? I don't make that kind of money." Shelley snaps. "It belongs to a friend." I don't say anything, still embarrassed by my assumption that her sugar daddy boyfriend had bought it for her. I need to let Vogel ask the questions now, since I've clearly misread the situation and have also thoroughly pissed her off.

"It's nice," Vogel says. He's got a gift for relaxing people, getting them to talk to him, to like him. I don't have that knack. It seems like I often put peoples' back up, get off on the wrong foot. "Handles great too I bet. Your friend appreciates fast cars?" Vogel is looking longingly out the window at the car.

Shelley looks at him, her expression blank. "I suppose," she shrugs. "He's an adrenaline junkie. Loves bungee jumping, parasailing, white water rafting, all that turbo charged stuff."

"Not you?"

Shelley shakes her head. "No way. I like to live my life at normal speed, thanks."

"Me too," he says. "I like to keep my feet on the ground."

Vogel is an expert skier and he spent his last vacation cave diving in Belize, so I know he's lying to try and develop some connection with Shelley. When he sees her faint smile in response he flips out his notebook and takes over the interview.

"Still, it is a very nice car," Vogel says with a wink. "Expensive. I guess your friend isn't a police detective."

Shelley Arthur manages a laugh. "Hardly. He's got a very big toy box, full of shiny new things. A spoiled brat really." I wonder who this rich friend of Shelley's is. Maybe someone she met through Price, like a rich vintner or someone in the music industry?

Vogel gets down to business. "When was the last time you spoke with Mr. Price?" he asks, sitting across from her.

"Yesterday. He asked me to be here for eight this morning so we could get an early start. I think he had somewhere to go later today."

"He sent me an email last night to confirm the time." She holds up her phone to show us an email from Price that was sent last night at seven o'clock. So, he was alive until then, unless someone else sent the email.

"How do you normally work with Mr. Price?" I ask. "Does he have an office here in the house, or…"

"In the kitchen," she says. "At the island." She glances toward the kitchen where Stan Price's body is still lying on the tile floor.

"He'd set up his laptop on one side of the island, and I'd have mine next to him. We'd exchange notes and files." I'd print up the notes we'd taken in our meetings, and give them to him to mark up—to review. They should be here, somewhere."

"Did you keep digital documents? On a drive?"

"Price was a Luddite," she says. "We tried to share documents and have him mark them up online, but it was a disaster. So, we had to go old school in the end. The system was working okay."

"Where's his computer?" She shrugs.

"I don't know. Normally the laptop is all set up when I arrive…" I remember seeing it, among the boxes of memorabilia and files that had been stacked up the last time Vogel and I had visited Price.

"Do you know where the laptop and files are kept when you aren't working?

"I have no idea where he stored everything," Shelley says, shaking her head. "But he acted like it was the Crown Jewels. I wouldn't be surprised if he'd kept it all locked up in a safe or something."

"Any idea where a safe might be?

"Couldn't tell you," she shrugs. "I've never been beyond the kitchen and powder room."

I'm skeptical. "Really? You weren't curious? Maybe had a look around when Price went out? See how a real live rock star lived?"

She snorts. "Price never went out when I was here. Never once left me alone in his *fabulous house*." Her tone makes it very clear that he'd told her all about the house construction and design, no doubt more than once.

"Could you please give us the contact information for Mr. Price's lawyer and accountant?" I ask, handing her my card. "Actually, his entire contact list would be helpful."

Shelley hesitates for a split second then shrugs. "Sure, I guess it's not an issue now that he's dead." She goes into her phone and starts to send his contact list to me, name by name. My phone starts to ping with each received text. "But he was very careful about his privacy. *Ping.* Very," she emphasizes. *Ping.*

"Any idea why that might be?" *Ping.*

"Rock star paranoia," she says rolling her eyes. "He was so uptight about security and his papers and having people in the house." *Ping.* "I don't think he ever had anyone visit him here. *Ping.* At least not that I saw."

Why would Stan Price build this fortress, this showcase of a house that's all about showing off his wealth, his collections and his fame—and not have people in to show it off? Isn't that what it's for? I understand some collectors just want the pride of ownership and public display isn't their main goal, but Stan Price was a rock star. Public display was his whole life.

Instead, it seems he was secretive and private. But then why was he writing a memoir, especially one he hinted was sensationalistic? It makes no sense, unless Price wanted to control the narrative, to tell his side of a story before another one might come out. He referred to it as a *tell-all,* that would share *where all the bodies are buried.* I shudder at that phrase and hope that Price wasn't using it in its literal sense. Or maybe he was—using it as leverage against someone, a person who'd rather the past remains buried.

Vogel continues taking Shelley Arthur's statement while I put on a pair of gloves and begin looking through Price's house. I go room by room, starting on the main floor. By the time I get to the second floor Vogel has finished with Shelley and sent her home. With him working alongside me we're able to move that much faster and have finished our search in less than an hour. We don't find either Price's laptop or his files.

"Do you think they were stolen, maybe by whoever killed him?"

"Possibly. Could be the motive—whoever killed Price wanted to shut him up. Make sure whatever he had to say about the past stayed buried."

"So you think this is about something from Price's past?"

"Who knows at this point? Could be, I suppose. Or maybe it's the usual motive—money."

"Price certainly had a lot of that." I look around the palatial house, with the acres of vineyards stretching into the distance. "I don't understand where it's all from though. I've never even heard of him, and since he's so old I assume it's not like he's touring anymore or putting out new albums."

"Royalties, Gauthier! Vogel laughs. "Radio airplay, cover versions of his hits, commercials or even video games that license his music. It practically gave Price a license to print money."

Vogel pauses for a moment. "You know…I remember reading a while ago that one of Running Deep's songs was used in a movie. It was one of those superhero flicks…" His face is screwed up in thought as he struggles to remember. "It's just on the tip of my tongue…"

"I don't care," I interrupt.

"…one of those space ones…used retro music from the seventies…"

"It's not important Vogel."

Except it clearly is, to him at least. "C'mon Gauthier, you know the one I mean."

"Forget it Vogel," I snap. The smile drops from his face.

"What's wrong?" He sounds wounded, upset that I won't play his game. "What's going on Lucy?"

Vogel never uses my first name and hearing it makes me flinch. "Nothing." I brush him off. I honestly can't say what's wrong, but for some reason Vogel is really getting on my nerves. Maybe I just need to get used to him being back after his week away. Or maybe my worries about Maja's plans to leave are starting to affect my work. "I'm just…tired, I guess."

He's disappointed that I'm not giving him an honest answer. Vogel knows me better than I'm comfortable with. Even though I've kept my past from him, and haven't shared any of my anxiety or depression, he's not a stupid man. And he genuinely wants to be my friend, I know that. I just don't feel safe enough to have close friends—beyond Maja of course.

I change the subject. "So, all this royalty money…Price got it all? None of the other band members?"

"No, I checked. He's the only one with the songwriting credits, so he holds the copyright. The rest of the band gets nothing. Anyway, two of them are already dead, years ago."

"That must have led to some bad blood between them," I say.

"If he's rich and they were left out. I wonder how they're all doing. Worth looking into the remaining members of Running Deep."

"I guess. But if that were the motive, why'd they do it now? The band broke up decades ago."

"So where do you suppose Price hid everything, assuming it wasn't stolen? If he thought they were so valuable, it makes sense he'd do his best to keep them in a place they'd be secure."

"Do you think there's a safe in the house?"

"I'd bet on it. We'll ask SIU to do a thorough search. If there is one, they'll find it."

The boxes of memorabilia are stacked on the floor of his office and it doesn't look as if Price's killer has gone through them. Whoever took his laptop wasn't interested in the promotional t-shirts, baseball hats, posters or the piles of photos, so I close up the boxes and move on. But a moment later, I turn back and pull all the photos out. I'll take them back to the station and go through them there. Maybe there'll be something of interest after all.

One of the constable's voice is raised as he demands someone leave the property. "Turn around, immediately. This is private property." The driver hesitates and I can see someone in the back seat is holding a video camera, trying to get some footage. The constable smacks his hand hard on the hood of the car and quickly moves in front of the camera, blocking the view. "Leave, now."

The car starts to back slowly up the driveway, while the cameraman is trying to capture as much as he can.

"Looks like the word is out," I say. "Media will be all over this." I'm sure every network and cable news service will have a satellite truck parked out front within the hour, as I hear a helicopter approach overhead.

Vogel gets on the radio and I hear him instruct the patrol cars to ensure nobody gets past the front gate, no exception. "It'll be a circus," he agrees.

"Something's bugging me," I say as Price's body is finally removed and loaded into a mortuary van. "Does Stan Price strike you as a writer? As the sort of guy who could write a memoir?"

"He wrote songs," Vogel says. "Lyrics."

"Yeah…that's not the same thing as writing a whole book, is it?"

"I guess not."

"What are you saying? Shelley Arthur's lying to us? He wasn't really writing a book? Then what's she doing here, going through all his stuff?"

"I don't know. Maybe she really is just his assistant, helping him curate and catalogue all his stuff. But it just doesn't feel right."

EIGHTEEN

BACK AT THE station, I'm spinning my wheels looking through Ella's cold case files for the third time, hoping something new turns up. We're waiting for the autopsy results on Price, even though cause of death seems obvious. I'm not sure what the Coroner is likely to find, though maybe the forensic team will turn up some trace evidence that will help focus our investigation.

Who wanted Stan Price dead? He was not a nice man—that much is clear, but there are millions of unpleasant men wandering around who don't get knifed for it. Any resentment former band members might have over royalties or profit shares seem unlikely, given how long it's been since the band was together. The band members who are still alive began working and touring with other bands when Running Deep split up and it doesn't look like they're broke from what Vogel has learned.

There is still Rachel, but I try to not think of her in that way. I've been over and over it in my mind, trying to see her as a viable suspect, but unless she's nothing like the woman I've known for years—an artist, a pacifist, a psychic, a spiritualist and a flaky astrologer—I can't see it. Even if she'd lost her mind after we found Ella's remains, there's no way I can see her deciding that after all these years Stan Price needed to die.

140

That only leaves the argument Vogel and I overheard Price having, when he slammed down the phone on Rossi. Which Rossi we don't know. What it was about is a mystery, and knowing Price it might have just been loud bluster over nothing. He was a guy who liked to make a big noise.

There's a knock on the glass window of the briefing room that makes me jump. It's one of the constables and she's holding her hand to her ear. I've got a call.

"I've got someone here," a male voice says when I pick up. "She's in really bad shape. You need to come get her."

"Who is this?"

"The bartender at Aphrodite's." *Aphrodite's.* The strip club.

"Why are you calling me?" He doesn't reply. "This is Special Investigations, Homicide." I'm about to hang up, or at least switch him over to the desk sergeant so they can send over a cruiser.

"She had your card in her pocket," he says. "DC Gauthier."

"Okay…Who is she?" He puts the phone down and I can hear him talking to someone. *What's your name? C'mon lady, give me a break here. Who are you?*

He comes back on the phone. "She says her name is Kim."

Kim Parsons. "I'll be there as fast as I can. Fifteen minutes, maximum. Keep her there."

I drive as fast as I can, with lights flashing but no siren. I don't want to explain what's happening if another officer decides to join in the chase.

Why would Kim have my card? She must have taken it from her mother before she disappeared. Why is she at a strip club? And why'd the bartender do her the favour of calling me? I'd have expected them to just throw her out on her ass into the street if she was creating a problem. It's not like a strip club to give a shit about their patrons——if that's in fact what Kim was.

Then I remember that Kim used to work as a stripper, many

years ago. Maybe someone at the club knew her from that time—either management or even a patron. Maybe they were taking pity on her, being kind—if that's believable. Still, calling a Detective isn't necessarily going to keep her out of trouble. But probably she'd have better luck than if a patrol car picked her up off the street.

When I get to Aphrodite's, the parking lot is full, in the middle of day. The club is always full, with regulars, with tourists who've wandered over from the casino, with frat parties and stag nights. The strip club is a license to print money, and it's all Renato Rossi's—or at least it used to be.

I flash my ID at the burly doorman and he gives way without question. Inside the club, the lights are dim and focussed on the stage at the far end of the room. Coloured lights, music, women dancing on the pole. I avert my eyes. I've been to a few call outs here and other clubs in the area and it makes me uncomfortable. It's even worse now I know my mother used to work here.

I push my way up to the bar and call over a bartender, who gives me the side eye when he realizes I'm a cop and not a paying customer.

"Somebody called me?" I have to shout to be heard over the loud music. He just shrugs and looks confused. Then he holds up a finger and goes over to the other bartender to ask. He's a tall skinny guy with glasses, who looks like he'd be more comfortable as a barista in a hipster coffee shop. But I imagine the money's much better working here. He comes over and leans across the bar.

"You're too late," he says. "She's gone."

"When? I told you to keep her here."

"I'm not sure. It got busy and I had a lot of people at the bar. When I came back, she was gone." He looks genuinely concerned, both about Kim's welfare and whether he'll get in trouble for letting her get away. He can tell from my expression that I'm not buying it.

"Look, we had no choice," he admits after a moment. "I had to bounce her. She was making a scene."

"What kind of scene?"

"Man, she's high as a kite. She broke a glass, fell off her chair, then tried to pick a fight with one of the waitresses."

I shake my head in disgust. "Guess she was bad for business." He couldn't hold her for another few minutes?

"Bad for my job," he says, trying to placate me. "I really need to keep it." He glances over his shoulder at the door marked Office, where I guess the managers are watching everything on CCTV cameras.

I nod my thanks and rush back outside. I ask the doorman about her but he just looks irritated and plays dumb.

Kim can't have gone far if she's on foot and in bad shape, so I get into the car and drive slowly up the street, peering into the crowds on the sidewalk. I make it twenty blocks, all the way to Erie street, then turn around and come down the other side.

I'm waiting for the light to change when I see a crowd gathered around a storefront. Kim is in the middle of it, and she's shouting at them and wildly swinging what looks like a tree branch. Everyone is standing at a distance, hands out as if trying to calm her down, but it's not doing any good. Kim is obviously in a state of agitation and she flings the branch at the front window of the store, punching a big hole in the plate glass. The branch bounces back onto the sidewalk and she picks it up again and takes another wild swing at the window. This time the branch goes right through and the window shatters.

I pull over and climb out of the car, just as the light changes again so I have to wait to cross over. Kim is now standing on the side of the road, leaning on a postbox. People are passing her by on the sidewalk, giving her a wide berth. She looks unsteady and I can see the front of her shirt is stained with vomit. She's also barefoot and her feet are bleeding from walking in the broken glass.

She looks safe for the moment, so I exhale in relief as I wait for the light to change, but as I'm watching, she steps off the curb and into the street. I jump out of the car, leaving it in the street.

"Kim!" I shout. "Kim, stay there!" I can't tell if she hears me but she hesitates just for a second as I run toward her to try to stop her from walking into traffic. Car horns blare and I see a dark blue pickup truck accelerate and drive straight for her. I can hear the impact as Kim is flung back onto the sidewalk, over the screams of the other witnesses. Then I hear the squeal of tires as the truck speeds away.

When I reach Kim and crouch beside her, she's breathing and moaning in pain as she clutches her arm. "Call 911!" I see several people in the crowd already have their phones in hand. "It's okay, Kim. You'll be okay," I keep repeating as I stroke her head and try to keep her comfortable. I hope I'm right.

Two cruisers pull up, lights flashing and one of the uniformed officers tries to drag Kim up onto her feet.

"Stop! She's injured," I shout at him. "Don't move her." He looks irritated and I know he's about to argue, then he recognizes me.

"Sure thing, Detective Gauthier," he says, pasting on a smile. "Ambulance is on its way." He backs away and establishes a perimeter with the other Constable while I kneel beside Kim. She's lost consciousness, which I doubt is a good sign, but her breathing is steady. I don't dare move her, in case she has some spinal damage or internal injury and I'm relieved when the paramedics pull up with a stretcher and take over.

Kim looks like a complete mess: no jacket, dirty clothes, and feet filthy and covered in blood. Where are her shoes? Then I notice her pants are covered in blood as well, dried blood that didn't come from her feet. What happened to her?

As I'm waiting to give my witness statement to the Constables I get Dudek on the phone. The hit and run happened in his Division, so he needs to hear about it.

"Hi Gauthier," he says when he picks up. "We still don't have an ID on the fourth bank robber, but we've sent in his prints and I've got my fingers crossed he's in the system…"

"That's not why I'm calling," I interrupt him. "There's been a hit and run, on Maple Street, near Erie. It wasn't an accident. I saw the driver of the truck speed up and aim right for her."

"Don't suppose you got the plate number?"

"Sorry, no," I'm ashamed to admit. "Maybe one of the other witnesses noticed it, or we can pick it up on traffic cameras.

"How's the victim? Dead?"

"They've taken her to hospital. Want to meet me there?"

It takes me less than twenty minutes to drive over to the hospital and Dudek is already waiting when I arrive.

"She's in x-ray now," he says. "It doesn't look like the injuries are serious."

"She got lucky," I tell him. "If she hadn't hesitated that little bit when I shouted at her, the truck would have hit her full on. He was trying to kill her."

"Why? Who is she?"

"Kim Parsons. She's connected to a thirty year old cold case I'm working."

Dudek's eyebrows rise in surprise. "And someone wants her dead now?"

"I'm not sure this has anything to do with it," I say. But in my gut I know it does. Kim ran off right after I appeared at the farmhouse, after Ella's remains were identified. Something sent her off the rails.

A doctor wearing blue surgical scrubs approaches us. "X-rays don't show any broken bones or internal injuries," he says with a smile. "Which is remarkable, really."

Dudek laughs. "Because she was drunk? Isn't that always the way!" he says. "They're all relaxed so when they get hit they bounce?"

"I think that's a myth," the doctor shakes his head dismissively and checks Kim's chart. "We'll discharge her as soon as she sobers up a bit."

"Great, and then we'll *charge* her!" Dudek looks to me for approval. "Get it? Discharge, Charge?" I'm sure he'll be telling this joke all day.

"Charge her with what?" I ask.

"Disorderly conduct, public intoxication, cause disturbance, criminal damage," Dudek shrugs. "We'll figure something out."

"Why? Isn't she the victim here? Someone tried to run her down in the street."

"That's true…" he says. "But, she broke a shop window up the street. Smashed it with a tree branch. That's why the cruisers were already on their way to the scene before she was hit."

"C'mon Dudek," I plead. "Her mother just died. I don't even think she knows about it." He nods.

"I know the story," he says. "It's sad. I get it. But we can't just let it slide. The store owner will lose his mind if we let her walk."

"Shit," I mumble. Poor Kim. "What store was it?"

Dudek looks at his notes. "A real estate office. Rossi Realty."

Now that is interesting. Why would Kim decide, in her drunken state, to smash Rossi Realty's window? Was it another coincidence, or was she targeting him?

"What's that look for?" Dudek asks. "You know something I don't? Something you might want to share?"

I shake my head. "No, just remembered I have to pick something up on the way home." I don't need to let Dudek in on my suspicions. He's not part of the Ella Weaver investigation. There's nothing I can do at the moment to help Kim Parsons. She's going to jail.

Dudek glances at his watch. "I'm meeting the Public Defender at the hospital in a little while. Questioning the two bank robbers. Want to come along?"

I can tell from his expression he knows he didn't need to ask.

Dudek and I grab a coffee from the hospital cafeteria before heading up in the elevators. Apart from identifying the dead robber as Jason Winner, they've gotten nowhere in the investigation, and I can tell he's frustrated.

"Not that the bank really lost anything," he says. "I mean, they were arrested before they were able to escape."

"Have you determined that everything that should be in the safety deposit boxes is…safe?"

He laughs. "So far. But I'm thinking a lot of them are reading over their insurance policies right now to see if they can make a claim. Good luck to them."

"So, the white envelope I saw Winner put into his jacket pocket is the only thing missing."

Dudek nods. "And since nobody's claiming it was in their boxes, I'm going to assume it was something very important." Dudek isn't questioning what I saw and I'm grateful. A lot of other detectives would have just put it down to my imagination and closed the investigation when nothing was reported missing.

Dudek knocks on the door before we enter Chris Sheppard's room. I recognize the robber lying in the hospital bed. And given he's the one with his leg in cast, he's the one I shot. Abby told me that the bullet went into his thigh and shattered the femur, and the disintegrated shards of bone fragments caused a lot of vascular trauma, but missed the femoral artery. If it hadn't he would have bled out before the ambulance arrived.

A young man wearing what looks like a brand new suit is sitting next to him, his briefcase open on the patient's tray table. This must be the Public Defender who's representing him on the robbery charges.

He stands and introduces himself with a nervous smile and I can tell he's new on the job. I'm not sure what kind of defence he'll be able to present for his client, and I'm sure he'll need all the help he can get.

Dudek pulls up a chair next to the bed so he can be at eye level with Sheppard. I remain standing by the door, trying to stay out of his eye line, but it's obvious he recognizes me instantly.

"I'm not talking to you," he says. "You shot me."

"Line of duty," Dudek says. "Nothing personal."

"Feels personal to me," Sheppard mumbles, still looking away.

"What do you want to tell us about the bank robbery?" Dudek asks, with a glance at the lawyer.

"Nothing," he says. "No comment."

"You don't have anything you want to share that might help mitigate the charges? Maybe something in your defence? Or give us the name of whoever set this up?"

"No comment."

"C'mon Sheppard," Dudek cajoles. "You didn't set this up yourself. You just don't have the smarts. Who were you working for? Was it Jason Winner?"

"No comment."

This is clearly a waste of time and Dudek realizes it. He stands and glowers down on Sheppard, who meets his eye. His jaw is set in defiance, like a real tough guy he's seen in a movie once. "Last chance Sheppard. We're heading out the door. Anything you want to say?"

"No comment."

"Well that was helpful," Dudek mutters when we're back in the hospital corridor. "Not that I expected much."

"You don't want much," I laugh. "Just a motive, and who set up the job, and who paid for the job, and why Jason Winner only took that one item."

We wait for a few minutes while the public defender finishes speaking with Sheppard, then he emerges from the room and we all go across the hall into Dillon Byrne's room. Looks like the lawyer is defending both of them.

Seated next to him is Rachel. She avoids meeting my eye and that unsettles me. Is Rachel angry with me? Or is she being careful to not let Dudek know we're friends?

"I'm sorry Ms. Weaver," the lawyer says. "You'll have to step outside for a while, while these officers interview your son." Rachel quickly gets up and brushes past me as she goes out the door. She's taking care not to speak with me and I'm not sure why. Does she think she's protecting me somehow? Or more likely it's because she doesn't want Dillon to find out we know each other. I wonder if he has any idea I'm the one who broke his neck, and decide to stand back again as Dudek interviews him, just in case.

Dillon must take after his father—he looks nothing like Rachel, apart from his eye colour. He's lying in the bed with his head is completely immobilized, encased in a halo brace of metal rods, with four pins going into his skull. It looks like some kind of torture device.

Dudek pulls up a chair and sits next to Dillon. "What can you tell us about the bank robbery?" Dudek asks after he's introduced himself. He doesn't mention me, which is just as well.

Dillon just stares straight at a fixed point on the ceiling. "Dillon Byrne, Cadet, December 3, 1996."

Dudek rears back in astonishment. Then he turns to the Public Defender, his eyebrows raised. The lawyer just shrugs and looks baffled.

"Dillon, you're not a POW. You've been arrested for participating in a bank robbery."

"Dillon Byrne, Cadet, December 3, 1996."

Dudek turns to me. "Does he have brain trauma? I know he broke his neck, but…" I shake my head.

"Enough of the Geneva Convention BS," Dudek says. "This isn't the military."

"Dillon Byrne, Cadet, December 3, 1996."

Dudek takes a deep breath then goes through the same questions he just did with Chris Sheppard, but instead of *No Comment*, the replies are always name, rank and I assume birthday. Why? Because Dillon doesn't have a serial number? I have to suppress a laugh.

Dillon is trying to act tough and he never breaks his eyeline. Never does he look away from that spot on the ceiling. But he's still young and I suspect not as experienced with criminal activities as his partner Sheppard. He looks frightened and his voice quavers every time he answers Dudek.

It's possible neither Sheppard nor Dillon know who's behind the robbery, I suppose. They might have been hired by Winner, or referred by one of their mutual buddies.

"Dillon, be honest with us." Dudek says. "We know you didn't set this up yourself. Jason Winner did." For the first time Dillon's eyes flicker between Dudek and the lawyer, both of whom are in his line of sight.

"Dillon Byrne, Cadet, December 3, 1996."

"You were just hired for the job, right?" I say, speaking for the first time. "Maybe a friend put you onto it? A good score for not much risk."

Dillon's eyes slide as far as they can toward the door but he's unable to see me. I make a point of staying out of his line of sight. "I guess your friend was wrong about that. Too bad about your neck." He closes his eyes. I can see tears under his lashes, but I keep pushing.

"You'll recover in a few months. Probably," I say and his eyes fly open in terror. "It would be better for you if you didn't end up going straight to prison. Minimum sentence for robbery with a weapon is five years, but since it's your first offence, and if you co-operate with us…we might be able to shave some of that time off."

The lawyer shoots me a dirty look. He knows I'm not in a position to make that kind of offer, but he's not brave enough to challenge me.

"Why don't you tell us who's behind it all?" I press him again. "What's the name of your friend?"

Dillon's eyes close and he sighs deeply. "Dillon Byrne, Cadet, December 3, 1996."

I catch Dudek's eye and he shakes his head, signalling it's over. He leaves the room without saying anything else to Dillon and I follow him out. We're waiting for the elevator, when the doors open and Rachel steps out.

"I'll call you later," I tell Dudek. "I need to speak with Ms. Weaver—about another case." He nods as the elevator doors close behind him.

Rachel is wary, but she walks with me to the waiting area so we can chat privately.

"He won't talk to us," I tell her. "But I'm sure he's covering for someone. Maybe a friend of his. Any ideas?"

She shakes her head. "I tried to press him on it. He just clams up." Rachel slumps into one of the sofas, clearly exhausted. "Honestly, I don't even know who his friends are."

I don't know how to ask the questions I need to. Why doesn't she know her son? Where has he been living while she's been at Womyn? Rachel sees my expression and pats my hand. "It's complicated?" I say.

"Life usually is." She sighs deeply. "After Ella…disappeared…I broke, inside. I didn't feel anything anymore. Not a thing, not for years. I had to give up my psychic practice." She gives me a sad smile. "It's a cruel joke. Didn't see that coming."

"Eventually I met a new man—Sean Byrne. And we had Dillon, and were together for a while, then it broke down. Pretty sure I'm to blame for that. He was emotionally needy and sexually greedy and for a while I could feel needed. We both realized pretty quickly that he didn't love me any more than I loved him. Which was not at all."

Rachel looks up at me, tears in her eyes. "I have this empty ache inside." She thumps her chest. "The place where Ella used to live is empty. Maybe I was too afraid to love Dillon enough, to give of myself again, afraid I'd have that pain again. The pain of losing a child. And maybe that's why Dillon ended up like he did."

She manages a smile. "Or maybe it's genetic and he's just a deadbeat like his father. Sean Byrne. Stan Price. Boy I know how to pick them, eh?"

"Rachel," I begin carefully. "I've got some news. I'm not sure how you're going to take it."

"What kind of news?" She looks at me suspiciously.

"Stan Price was found this morning, dead."

"Dead!? How dead?"

"Murdered." I give her a minute to take it in. "You do understand we need to look at everyone connected with Stan Price."

She scoffs. "Connected. Don't be ridiculous."

"I believe everything you've told me about Price," I say. "But speaking objectively, the timing doesn't look good. Stan Price was killed less than a week after we identified Ella's remains. And just a few days after the DNA test proved she was his daughter."

"So? Not news to me. I've always known he was her father. Why'd I suddenly decided to kill him now, after all these years?"

I shrug. "I just need to ask you where you were on Sunday night."

"You want an alibi!" Rachel laughs. "Seriously?! I'm a suspect?"

"Just to eliminate you from our inquiries."

"I was at Womyn," she says. "Working on my loom. Like I am every night." As she turns her back on me and goes back to Dillon I feel as if I've betrayed her. I'm too ashamed to ask if anyone can confirm her alibi.

NINETEEN

THREE HOURS LATER I got a call from Dudek. "Would you like to come out and speak with Kim Parsons? She's sober now, more or less. We've got her down at Division 2."

When I arrive he brings me through security to the interview room.

"How is she?" I ask. "Does she know what happened? How close she came close to being dead?"

He nods. "We told her, not sure how much got through to her, given her state," he says as we watch Kim through the glass. "She's being charged with disorderly conduct. She was abusive and resisted arrest, but we're letting that drop, given the circumstances."

"Does she know about her mother?"

Dudek nods. "And we've told her that her little girl's in foster care and her father's in hospital."

I take a deep breath and am about to go in to speak with Kim, but Dudek puts a hand on my arm to hold me back.

"We've got that list of whose safety deposit boxes were robbed," he says, handing me a folder.

"Anyone I've heard of? Anything of interest missing?"

Dudek shrugs. "Hard to say. Some cash, some jewellery and documents. They robbed almost three dozen boxes, including Stan

Price—you know, the rock star? And Renato Rossi, the mob guy," he says, making air quotes as he says Rossi's name.

"Sounds like whoever set it up went for the boxes that could have had a lot of cash in them. Big names."

"Yeah…that makes sense." Then an idea starts nagging at me. "You know Joe Rossi was actually there, in the bank the day of the robbery." Dudek looks at me, clearly unsure what I'm getting at.

"Coincidence?" He says. "Lots of people need to go to the bank on the weekend."

"True…but his father's safety deposit box is one that was targeted. And so was Stan Price's. And they're both dead."

"Like I said," Dudek shrugs again. "Big names, rich guys, logical targets for theft." He opens the door to the interview room but doesn't come in with me. Kim Parsons is sitting at the table, head bent, and a zoned-out expression on her face.

"Hi Ms. Parsons," I begin. "I'm Detective Constable Gauthier. Do you remember me? You called me, from Aphrodite's."

She nods without raising her head. "You were at the farm," she mumbles. Then she looks up at me in confusion. "I called you? When?"

I start to explain but she just loses interest and I can tell she's not listening.

Kim Parsons looks like death warmed over. Her hair is a mess and she's wearing a pair of dark green prison overalls with short sleeves. I can clearly see fresh needle marks in her arms. Something sent Kim right off the edge and it's not hard for me to guess what that was: hearing the investigation into Ella Weaver's disappearance was being reopened.

"I'm still looking into Ella's death," I begin as gently as I can. I need to remind her but don't want her to lose it again. "Her mother Rachel is a friend of mine." I pause, looking for a response and see Kim blink. "She could really use your help. It's been a long time for her, waiting…"

Kim starts to cry. "I don't know anything," she says. "I never saw Ella after the concert." She's sticking to her original story. Maybe she honestly doesn't remember, or maybe she's told it so many times she believes it to be true. I decide to try another tack.

"I met with Ella's father. Stan Price." That gets her attention and she looks up. I'm careful not to mention Price is dead. She'll find out soon enough and she's had her fill of bad news today. There's no point risking her getting upset when I need to get some information. An idea flickers for a moment before it dies: maybe she wouldn't necessarily see Stan Price's death as bad news, especially if she blames him in some way for what happened to Ella.

"You know about that?" She asks, stealing a look at me through her stringy hair.

I nod. We sit in silence for a few more minutes. I can see she's thinking hard, trying to make a decision. Or maybe she's just feeling ashamed for what she's done. Her actions will have consequences beyond what she thought when she ran off, if she thought anything at all. If her mother were still alive, then Jade would still have a responsible adult to care for her. But now, Kim may have lost the rights to her daughter. Luckily her child was fine after two days alone, but it could have gone badly wrong.

"I'm sure you're very proud of your daughter. You only want the best for her." I say after a while. "As a mother you understand why it's so important for Rachel to know the truth about what happened to her daughter."

"Kim, something set you off, pushed you off the wagon. I know you've been clean and sober for years."

She looks up at me, her chin trembling. "Since I was pregnant with Jade."

"And the only thing I can think of that might be responsible is my visit to the farm on Tuesday. When you first heard Ella was dead." She nods. "I know there must be something you remember. Something you want to tell me. Something that could help Rachel now."

Kim takes a ragged breath. "I didn't ever believe she was dead," she says. "Not at first. I kept thinking she'd be back. But then time passed and she never wrote me. Or called. I didn't know what to think."

"And then it was too late to change your story?" I say. "You didn't want to come to the police?" She nods. "So where did you think she'd gone? What did happen that night?"

"Ella told me about Stan Price. Once Rachel told her who her father was she wouldn't let go of it. Kept talking about him, wanting to meet him. She had some idea that he'd take her on tour with the band or something, once he knew about her."

"So she got tickets to the concert?"

"I didn't even want to go, but Ella was my best friend. So…"

"In your original statement, you said you were at the concert then Ella snuck up front to get close to the stage. But you didn't go with her. You stayed in your seat and you never saw her again. Is any of that true?"

"All Ella could talk about was getting backstage, meeting the band, talking to her father. She kept pressuring me to come to the front with her."

"So you did."

"I always did what Ella wanted." She shakes her head. "We got stopped by the security guard once we made it down to the floor level. He checked our tickets spend told us to go back to our seats. But Ella managed to charm him. She flirted with him, told him Stan Price was her real father, whatever she could say to convince him." Kim shrugs. "He let us through."

"And then what?"

"We were dancing up front. People were passing joints and bottles of liquor. It was a party." Kim thinks for a minute, remembering what happened. "Ella kept flirting with one of the roadies who was running cable across the stage and changing guitars for the band. And, when the concert was over, we just kind of hung around by the stage, waiting while the audience emptied out of the stadium. One of the roadies tore the set list from where it was taped on the floor and handed it to Ella. She made a big fuss about it, begged to have it autographed." Kim looks over at me. "It was gross. Anyway, the guy caved. He invited her backstage to party with them."

"Did you go along?"

She nods. "I didn't want to, but Ella and I'd come to the concert together. I didn't know what else to do. I was scared. These guys were older and…it just wasn't cool. But Ella, she didn't see anything wrong with it. She just wanted to see Stan Price."

"So what happened backstage?"

"The guy led us into a room full of people. There was loud music playing. Everyone was drinking and smoking weed. I was so intimidated by it all I just sort of hung back in the corner. But Ella went right up to the band members and kept asking them all to autograph the set list. These pervy old guys were putting their arms around Ella, giving her drinks. I don't think really she had a clue what was going on. I know I sure didn't. I was only fifteen! There were some women there—groupies, hanging off the guys. I saw some of them having sex, giving blowjobs in the corners, on the couches. God it was so creepy."

"Did you have a drink too?"

She nods. "We were already a bit drunk and high from being out front during the concert. But I had a couple more drinks at the party. I was nervous. And I thought it would help me look cool, more grown up."

"And then what?"

Kim looks up at me. "That's it. That's all I remember, until I woke up on the beach two days later."

"Do you know if Ella ever met Stan Price? Was he at the after party?"

"I'm pretty sure he was there," Kim says. "Everyone in the band was. But I don't know if she met him or not." She shakes her head. "I spent years trying to remember what happened that night. Almost as much time as I spent years trying to forget. It's all a blank."

"I think it's likely you were drugged. The toxicology, such as it was in 1990, showed traces of chemicals in your blood. Possibly something like Rohypnol. That would explain your lack of recall. But there was no evidence of sexual assault, you know that, right?"

She nods. "They told me. To be honest, I wasn't sure I believed it. That whole scene was so…ugly. And Ella…"

I understand. "You think she may not have been so lucky."

Kim scrapes her hair back off her face. "After it happened I told myself that Ella's dream had come true. That she'd met Stan Price and that she was on tour with the band. Then after a while I didn't believe that any more. I felt so guilty, so ashamed."

"It wasn't your fault." The whole thing had been Ella's idea. Kim was just dragged along in her wake.

"Maybe not," she whispers. "But I could have said something. Maybe they'd have gone after those guys, found Ella sooner. Maybe she wouldn't have died."

Probably not, but I don't say so. Whoever killed Ella buried her body in a place it took a miracle to find. It was a one in a million chance. But at the very least we may have found her body sooner. And maybe had a shot at finding her killer.

TWENTY

BACK AT THE station I pull the photographs I took from Price's house out of the plastic evidence bag and spread them across my desk. Several are old Polaroids that have started to peel and separate. Most of them are black and white prints, probably taken by a professional photographer at one of Running Deep's concerts. They show the band members during the show, in their platform heels, bell-bottomed pants and on the lead singer, enormous belt buckles. All of them have long hair, and two are even wearing sunglasses.

I remember Stan Price was the bass player, so I can pick him out in the photos, but he looks nothing like the man I'd met. If it weren't for the bass guitar I'd never recognize him. He's lean and tall, with shoulder length dark blonde hair. His features are chiseled and he really is handsome. No wonder Rachel fell for him the way she had, before she knew what kind of a man he really was.

There are several amateur photos of young women clinging to Price. They are yellowed and definitely candid, no doubt taken by another fan. The girls' eyes look glassy, but maybe it's just the camera flash. I have no idea who they are, or where the photos were taken, but I expect there are dozens just like them, of teenage fan girls having a photograph with their rock idols. It could be innocent, but now I feel like nothing connected to the band is. I can't think why Price had them in his collection.

I come across a photo of the band members together, standing with a skinny young man who looks very much like the angry nephew at the *trattoria* brawl. This must be Joe Rossi. He looks like he's barely a teenager, with large dark eyes and long lashes. The girls must have gone nuts for him then. Now he's all filled in and portly, prosperous and smug in an expensive suit. Joe Rossi, realtor and politician, and heir to his father Renato's fortune—one of them anyway. He puts on a big front, but in this photograph I can see the fear in his eyes, the scared little man underneath all the show.

I put that photo aside and turn back to the hundreds of posed studio publicity shots, in living colour, of the band members taken individually and in the group. They are all wearing their rocker clothes: boots, jeans, t-shirts and leather jackets. The lead singer has wavy blonde hair down to his chest, and is posing at a microphone wearing a black leather vest and wristbands with fringes. The rest of the band is an indistinguishable crew of black leather, torn denim, bandanas, bleached blonde hair in layered mullets, dark sunglasses and cowboy hats. It's a strange mix of biker and cowboy theme. Most of them hold guitars. If Stan Price weren't already dead, he should die of shame seeing them. On second thought, given his ego he'd think he looked great.

Printed on the back of the photos is the name of a photography studio, just over in Niagara Falls. I'd be surprised if it's still there, but I may be able to track down the photographer who took the pictures. After quick internet search and a few phone calls I've got the name and address and I'm heading out the door to meet him. Of course he lives in the East Village, the last place I ever want to go.

William Hilson meets me at the door of his house. Technically, he's sitting on the front porch, smoking a cigarette and waiting for me to pull up. From the look of the overflowing ashtray I'd say he spends most of his day out here, regardless of who's visiting. He's whippet thin and wearing tight black jeans and t-shirt, and a fedora with a feather in the brim. Hilson is obviously fashion conscious—he's also wearing a brand new pair of expensive Belstaff biker boots. I know how much they cost because I've been coveting a pair just like them, but can't rationalize the expense.

Whatever care he lavishes on his own appearance doesn't extend to his home. Referring to Hilson's place as rundown is redundant, since that's a given as far as every house in the East Village goes. I pick my way up the steps, careful to avoid the most rotten looking ones and sit next to him on a wooden stool. There's an old sofa and upholstered chair available as well, but I'm pretty sure mice are nesting in them.

"Sure you wouldn't rather talk inside?" Hilson asks.

"No. This is perfect." Even his asking the question makes my anxiety spike. I can't stand mess and a dirty house is one of my biggest triggers. Something tells me Hilson's place would set off a panic attack if I dared to go inside.

"Mr. Hilson, I wonder if you can give me some information about these photographs?" I hand him the selection of yellowed photographs of the young women I'd pulled from Price's collection. "Did you take them?"

Hilson bursts out laughing before he even looks at them. "Are you kidding me? I was a professional photographer," he says. "I didn't take snapshots. Anyway, I always shot with a 35mm SLR. Nikon not a…Polaroid." The scorn in his voice is impossible to miss. He takes the photographs from me and studies the top for a moment, then tosses it aside. "Definitely early Polaroid instant film."

"Too bad about Price," he changes the subject. "Who killed him?"

"It's an active investigation, Mr. Hilson. I can't share any information," I demur. "And I never said he was killed."

Hilson smirks. "C'mon…a guy like Price? Of course he was killed. I'm surprised someone didn't do it years ago." He laughs so hard he starts to choke on his cigarette smoke.

"That's Price," he says once he's recovered, pointing him out in the image. "And that guy…I remember him. He was some promoter. Don't know his name." He's pointing to Rossi.

"And the women? Any of them familiar?" I pick up the Polaroid again and hand it to him. He shakes his head, without even looking at the photo.

"No idea. Every night, every concert, the parties were full of beautiful young women. Models, groupies, hookers. They were all the same." I feel an ache in the pit of my stomach. Pain for Ella and for all the women, especially for my mother.

"So you've got no idea when this might have been taken? Or where?"

He shrugs. "I've got dozens of similar photos," he says, giving me back the snapshot. "After you called, I had a look around for some of my old collection,"

"You've still got them?" I'm surprised, given how long it's been.

"When I closed down the studio I had a blowout sale. Sold all my equipment, everything. Then I just boxed up what was left and brought it here. It's all in the basement."

"There's a lot?"

"A lifetime's worth," he says, taking a deep drag off his cigarette. "I was the go-to photographer in the day. All the concert promoters and radio stations hired me to get performance shots."

"You were that good?"

"I was the best." I believe him.

I take a closer look at Hilson. He looks lean and fit and I can't guess his age. Under his hat brim I can see his hair is salt and pepper and his patchy beard hasn't been shaved in a few days.

"You don't seem old enough to retire," I say as he raises a shaky hand to his mouth and inhales his cigarette again.

"Parkinson's," he says, catching my look. "Had to retire a few years ago. Couldn't keep up the pace. Anyway," he chuckles. "I had a good run."

I try to do the math in my head. If he'd worked with Running Deep in the mid-seventies, he would have spent over fifty years photographing bands and musicians. That put him at what, seventy-five? That doesn't seem possible.

I catch him smirking at me.

"I started when I was sixteen," he says. "Used to sneak out of school and into bars with a fake press pass. Pretty soon I was getting a lot of work, mostly because I worked cheap. All the record company reps and concert promoters called me first. I had no idea what the going rate was, so didn't even know I was being exploited."

"But whatever," he laughs. "I was seeing the best bands in the world, with full backstage access to all the parties. Getting high, getting laid. It was awesome."

"I got into every concert that came through the region, and in Toronto and Detroit too. Saw all the greats, from the Stones and Zeppelin, The Who, Fleetwood Mac, Bowie, Rush, Michael Jackson, Prince, Madonna, U2, you name it."

"And you've got all the pictures to prove it."

"Of course I've got all the pictures! Are you kidding me? It's my legacy." He lights another cigarette. "Not that anyone's that interested."

"What about Stan Price?" I ask. "Was he interested?"

"As a matter of fact," he nods. "Stan Price was in touch with me, a few months ago. Wanted photos from the tours."

"For his book?"

He bursts out laughing. "Can you believe it? The fucker believed people were going to pay money for his memoirs." He's shaking his head. "He says to me *Keith Richards and Bruce Springsteen did it*. Price was delusional."

"Did you give him the photos?"

"Give?" He raises his eyebrow. "No fucking way. But he wanted me to. I said, why should I give you my work, for free, when you're planning to make money off it? Are you going to be giving your book away? He said he'd give me credit in the book."

"So did you come to an understanding?"

He shakes his head. "Not then. I told him I need cash, not credit. Look," he leans in to me. "I'm not going to be working again anytime soon. I need the money. No retirement fund for concert photographers."

"What do you mean *not then*? Did he come back?"

"He calls me on Friday and says he'll pay me what I want. I agreed to sell them all. Good price, too."

"Did he pick them up?"

"Nope. Bastard died." He shakes his head. "And I really could use that money."

"So, where are the photos now?"

"Inside," he points with his cigarette. "Boxed up and ready to go to Price."

"I'd like to borrow them," I say. "They might be material evidence in our investigation."

"Can you pay me for them?"

"Sorry, not in the budget."

"Story of my life." He shakes his head.

I give him a smile. "I guess you did okay for a time…"

"Sure, for a while," Hilson agrees. "Photography is expensive. Film, prints, cameras and equipment, studio, you name it. That's why there's such bad work out there now," he sneers. "Anyone can get into it and call themselves a photographer. " Kind of like you did, I almost say.

"Now everyone's got a cell phone, with a megapixel camera in it, taking photos all the time. The market's saturated."

"Not as good as your work though…" It's not like me to flatter anyone, but I feel sorry for the guy.

"Of course not. But it's good enough. Standards aren't what they used to be, not in journalism, not in photography. Just has to be good enough. And it's a low bar."

"People take candid snaps, post them all over their Instagram pages or whatever." He snorts and drags on his cigarette. "That's why they don't allow phones and cameras backstage or at parties. They make you check them at the door—toss them in a bowl and hope you get yours back at end."

"Why?"

"So nobody takes pictures. Make sure nothing like this happens again."

"Like this?"

He raises his eyebrows. "Cops like you showing up, looking for evidence. They don't want proof on some camera somewhere, just waiting to be exposed. It's too risky. They'll end up in jail."

"Maybe that's where they belong?" I say. "Seems to me like the real risk is in having underage women at parties and plying them with drugs and booze…but hey, what do I know?"

When he goes inside to get the photos I have to wonder how many things he'd witnessed that would put someone in jail, and how many times he'd destroyed evidence that could have done exactly that.

I leave Hilson sitting in his chair and load two bankers boxes of photographs into my car. When I get back to the station I spread out the photos across several tables in the briefing room, trying to make sense of them all. Even my untrained eye can see he was very good at his job. A few of the shots are *artsy* and I suppose Hilson was playing around with techniques and lighting but most are straight forward journalistic shots that he could sell to newspapers and music magazines. Thankfully, Hilson's record keeping is meticulous. The photos are all catalogued and dated, and I'm quickly able to locate Running Deep's concerts from the 1990's at the Buffalo Auditorium.

There are hundreds of images of people I don't recognize. They're laughing, drinking and dancing. Some are in focus, some out of focus, and some are unconscious—passed out on the beds and sofas in what I guess is the hotel suite where the after party was held. Several photos are of musicians—band members I assume—quietly playing guitars in corners, lost in their creative space, oblivious to the party whirling around them.

I recognize a photograph of Joe Rossi, in a group of young women. There are several of Stan Price as well, mostly with the other band members. Price has not aged well, which I guess is to be expected after a lifetime of hard drinking, late nights and drug use.

Finally I find several photos of Ella Weaver, posing with a friend. I try hard to find Kim Parsons in the face of the second young woman and fail. But I'm sure it's her, even though the Kim I just met looks nothing like this photo, taken before her wasted life and hard times. Both girls are grinning at the camera, blowing kisses and flirting with the camera.

These two young women, in department store jeans and UGG boots, are easy to spot in photos. They stand out, with their long, unstyled hair and barely any makeup. I bet it was easy for whoever preyed on them to pick them out as well. They were the newbies, innocent girls with fresh faces who'd appeal to anyone whose taste ran that way.

The photos aren't dated, but I know they were taken the night Ella disappeared. I'll need to match the clothing Ella's wearing in the picture with the remaining fibers that were found on her body, but I'm sure I'm right. This proves that Ella was definitely at the party after the Running Deep concert. I've struck gold and let out a whoop of triumph so loud they can hear me in the next room. Several heads turn to look and I duck in embarrassment.

With a smile of satisfaction I slowly go through the rest of the photos. Now that I've got the proof I need I can take my time. There are dozens of shots of women in low cut jeans, with bare shoulders and navels. As the night got later and the party got crazier, many of them are topless and a few nude. No wonder Hilson loved his work and didn't mind he wasn't paid enough.

I keep going through the images of that night, looking at the party guests in various stages of intoxication. In typical nineties' fashion the women are all wearing stiletto heels and heavy makeup. There are a lot of animal prints, lamé mini skirts, spaghetti straps and body glitter, very low cut jeans with thongs showing at the back, and lots of bare navels and bra tops.

I look more closely at the women's faces. A few of them seem to be Hilson's favourites and they show up at many different photos. Maybe they were groupies, or professionals, hired for the night to party with the band. Beautiful, but their eyes are glazed and vacant. Either high, lost in thought or perhaps just lost.

I pick up one of them and freeze. My pulse starts to pound and I feel my face flush. Straight blonde hair, large blue eyes, wistful smile. The same eyes that have haunted me for years. Helena Melnyk, my mother.

TWENTY ONE

VOGEL AND I decide to divide and conquer in order to get through Price's contacts more efficiently. He starts with the accountant and I get the lawyer, Ed Jorgensen. He's a partner in one of the biggest firms in Niagara Falls, which makes him a big fish in a small pond.

I'd called ahead to make an appointment, but I still have to cool my heels in the lobby for ten minutes until he's ready to see me, squeezed in at the end of the day. It's tiresome really, the power plays these men use just to let me know their time is more valuable than mine.

I decline the receptionist's offers of a coffee; I don't want anyone to think they are making my wait more comfortable. I'm irritable and tired and it's been a very long day. I'm heading home for a well-deserved and eagerly anticipated bottle of wine and frankly I don't feel like playing games. It was apparent Jorgenson was reluctant to meet with me, but it's not as if he's got a choice. His client was murdered and there'll be many more police interviews he'll have to deal with, so he might as well get used to it.

I'm still trying to figure out an explanation for Dillon's absurd responses in our interview this morning. It was laughable. Maybe he did have brain damage from my landing on him. If not, then he's living in some delusion, in some fantasy that he's obeying some military or bro-code. I've seen it before, this loyalty to someone who likely doesn't even deserve it. *Don't be a rat. Snitches get stitches.*

Who would Dillon feel this kind of loyalty to? Rachel said she doesn't even know her son's friends, so she's no help. We need to find out who he was living with, who he hung around with in the East Village. It's likely they're the ones he's covering for and it's possible that will lead us to whoever planning the bank robbery.

Exactly ten minutes after my appointment time, the receptionist escorts me into Jorgenson's empty office.

"Mr. Jorgenson will just be a moment," she says, retreating and closing the door.

A few minutes after that, long enough that I could have searched his files if I'd been so inclined, the door opens and a tall, very big man with a shaved head comes in. His thick neck makes me think of a professional wrestler, or a bodyguard, and his energy is high—as if he's full of either testosterone or steroids. Or both.

But he extends his hand and smiles, introducing himself as Ed Jorgenson, the most unlikely looking lawyer I've ever encountered. His eyes are dark and expressionless like a shark's, and I swear his teeth are pointed.

"What can I do for you Detective?"

"We're investigating one of your clients—Stan Price," I say returning his smile. "So I'll need some background on his business interests."

"You'll need a warrant," he says flashing me another shark grin. "That information is privileged."

"Mr. Jorgenson, your client is dead. He was murdered last night."

Jorgenson leans back in his chair, puffing out his cheeks as he exhales. "Wow. I did not know that. Really?"

"Really."

"Okay," he slaps his hands down on the desk. "What can I tell you?"

"As a start, I'd like you to tell me about your client's dealings with Joe Rossi."

"Why Rossi?"

"Stan Price was heard in a heated dispute with Mr. Rossi last week—on Friday."

"Oh I don't know about that…" Jorgenson demurs. "Maybe check your sources…"

"I'm the source Mr. Jorgenson. I heard the argument myself. Mr. Price was very angry. Enraged, you could say."

"Okay," Jorgenson agrees. "Stan was suing Joe Rossi for unpaid royalties."

"How much are we talking about?"

"Around three hundred thousand dollars—a lot." Jorgenson shrugs. "Not that Price was hurting, but it's the principle of the thing, you know."

"Sure, I know. Stan Price was definitely *principled*." I try not to roll my eyes. "Had Mr. Price filed a suit?"

"Not yet, no," Jorgenson says, glancing at his phone. "He was supposed to meet with me this week to get started."

"Convenient timing," I mutter under my breath, but Jorgenson catches it.

"I very much doubt Joe Rossi would have murdered Stan Price," he says with a laugh. "Anyway, did you say last night?" I nod. "Joe Rossi was with me and a few investors at the golf club. We closed the place, left after midnight." He laughs again at the memory. "It was quite a night."

"Well, thanks for this," I say on my way out. I'll certainly be confirming Rossi's alibi with the golf club.

"I can't see Rossi getting his hands dirty, can you?" Jorgenson is still laughing as I leave the office.

It's my turn to make dinner tonight. This morning I planned to make an effort to make something special, or at least up to Maja's level of quality. But the day got away from me so I've brought in two prepared meals that I'm going to serve with a tossed salad. I made up for it with a better than usual bottle of wine, not that it'll fool Maja. She knows me too well.

When I'm unpacking everything I notice some documents on the kitchen island. I can see one is a passport application. My pulse starts to race as the reality of what that means sinks in. Maja is renewing her passport so she can join Doctors Without Borders.

When she first mentioned it I'd hoped it would go away, that it would pass, like a fever. But clearly it hasn't. She still intends to go. I lean in, careful to not disturb the paperwork in case she accuses me of snooping, and study it. She has filled in the intended date of travel as three months from now, and this is the first I've heard of it.

TWENTY TWO

DC ANITA REYES is perched on Vogel's desk, chatting with him and waiting for me when I get into the station in the morning. She quickly jumps off and flips open her laptop. Her energy is alarming, especially since I've got a headache.

"We've got the security footage from Stan Price's gate camera," she says with a grin. Anita is always smiling, which is inconceivable to me, given that she spends her days as an SIU technician on the Tech Crimes Unit doing forensic examinations of technological devices like computers, cameras, cell phones, tablets and things that probably haven't even been invented yet. She's been working on extracting video from Price's security surveillance cameras, which we'd found were damaged when we tried to review the footage from the night of the murder.

"I thought there was a problem with the system. Did you fix it?"

"Not yet," she sighs. "There's an issue with the DVR we're still trying to work out. But the gate camera isn't on the network." As she's talking her fingers are flying over the keyboard. "It's motion activated and on its own SD card, which was in the camera." She spins the laptop around and presses play. "Take a look."

Vogel and I lean in and watch footage showing deliveries, cars coming and going, the gate opening and closing.

"How many days have we got?" Vogel asks.

"It goes back thirty days," Anita says.

"Thirty days of this? Does anything ever actually happen?"

Anita laughs. "Not a lot," she says. "We're getting the license plates of all the vehicles, and will produce a report by tomorrow. But, there are a few interesting bits you should take a look at." She glances at her notes then fast-forwards the footage, then hits play. "This is from Sunday afternoon."

The screen shows a clear shot of the front gate. It's closed. Nothing happens. Then a figure appears in front of the wrought iron, standing outside the gate. I recognize her immediately, with her long grey streaked hair and layers of shawls over her printed skirt and bulky frame. According to the video counter, she stands there for almost seven minutes, staring through the bars toward the house before she walks away.

"She does that, that weird standing at the gate thing, every day in the last week," Anita says. "Sometimes twice. Any idea how we can identify her?"

"I know who it is." I pick up my coat and head for the door. I hear the scrape of a chair as Vogel leaps up and follows me out.

"So who is she?" Vogel asks once we're on our way.

"Rachel Weaver."

"*Weaver*? Like Ella Weaver?" I feel Vogel's eyes on me. "The mother of your cold case?"

We find her in the barn at Womyn Collective, sorting through the shipment of alpaca yarn she just received. The multi-coloured skeins of wool are spread in front of her, in a rainbow of colours, from amethyst and turquoise to coral and fuchsia.

I regret bringing Vogel along, but I didn't exactly invite him.

Men really aren't welcome here at Womyn, since the residents of the collective are all women who've escaped domestic abuse. I just hope he'll stay quiet and let me handle the interview with Rachel. But Vogel hasn't ever shown he's capable of staying quiet, so my anxiety starts to build, in anticipation of a confrontation.

"Who's your friend, Lucy?" Rachel asks, not bothering to disguise her hostility.

I'm taken aback by her tone. "Sorry, Rachel. This is DC Vogel."

"We work together," Vogel adds, with a grin. "You might even say we're partners."

I shoot him a look. "Really?" Vogel steps back and tries to disappear.

"Rachel," I'm finding it difficult to keep my voice steady. "You need to tell us the truth. Now."

She doesn't smile. "I haven't had a chance to talk to Dillon yet," she says. "I'm sorry…I just didn't know how to bring it up." I see Vogel's eyes narrow in suspicion as he studies me. I haven't told him about Dudek or the investigation into the bank robbery. It's not my case and I'm only interested now because of Rachel's connection—and because I have a hard time letting go of things.

"We're not here about Dillon."

"You were seen on the security tapes at Stan Price's farm," Vogel says. "Several times over the past month."

Rachel takes a deep breath, then nods. "Right. Of course." She stands up with a groan and I can hear her back creak, probably from hours sitting at her loom. "And now you think I killed him."

"You don't deny being there?"

"Do you think I'd be stupid enough to get caught on video tape if I was planning on murdering him?"

"Maybe you didn't know there were security cameras," Vogel says.

Rachel rolls her eyes. "The wonderful and famous Stan Price?

Not having fucking security everywhere? Now you must really think I am stupid."

"No, I don't think you're stupid at all. In fact, I'm pretty sure you made a point of getting on that tape, just so he could see you. Why'd you do that?"

She gives me a slow smile. "I wanted to disturb him, to rattle his cage. Give him something to think about."

I hear Vogel exhale loudly and know exactly what he's thinking. That Rachel did it. "Why would you do that?" he asks.

"When I learned it was Ella's body you found in the bog," she says. "I was…upset. And enraged."

"And you wanted him upset too," he says.

She nods and I can see the rage flare in her eyes, anger I've never witnessed in her before. I've seen her sorrow, pain and grief, but never this. Rachel's knuckles are white as she grips the edge of the table. "He was so untouchable, sitting there in his castle," she spits. I wanted him to feel something…fear, maybe. He denied his daughter, never cared about her. I wanted him to sweat."

"What dates were you there?" I quickly ask, hoping Vogel hasn't caught her saying Price had denied his daughter. I've kept that piece of information out of my reports, as I promised Rachel. But I see how damning it appears. "Do you remember?"

"I've been there every day since you told me Ella's body was found in the bog," she says with a sad smile. "Including the day he died."

"Why?" Vogel asks. My heart sinks when I see the expression on Rachel's face.

"Honestly, I'm not even sure. I just felt drawn there…I'd be doing my walking meditation. Walking for hours and hours and just somehow end up there. It was unconscious." Vogel rolls his eyes and his lips narrow, as if he's trying hard not to laugh out loud.

I glare at him until he leaves the barn, pretending to step outside take a phone call.

"Did you ever go inside?" I turn to Rachel. "Knock on the door? Talk to Price?" I remember her snapping at him when we were all locked in together at the bank. Her dislike of him was obvious, and that was before I knew the circumstances. I want very much to believe her story, but can't deny it sounds ridiculous. Not to mention she's put me into a bad situation, one that I'll have a hard time explaining.

I hear a noise behind me and know that Vogel has come back in. I won't be able to keep anything Rachel says from him.

I take a deep breath and wait for her to tell me the story, in her own time. "After he left me, I had put him right out of my mind," she begins. "Until one day at Womyn someone was playing one of the band's old CDs. I felt sick when I heard it. I actually went into a panic and had to ask her to turn it off. That's when I learned he'd bought the old winery in Pelham and was moving back.

"The great Stan Price. Back to restore a vineyard and create a legacy wine. *Legacy,*" she scoffs. "Ironic, for a man who hasn't got one."

Her tone is bitter and angry, unlike the placid and spiritual Rachel I've always known. I'd never imagine for a second she could kill Stan Price. But the woman sitting in front of me now is not the same Rachel I know. What is she really capable of?

"I didn't always go to the front gate," Rachel says after a moment. "Sometimes I walked across the fields, through the vine-yards, up to the house."

"All the way to house? Isn't there a security fence?" Vogel interrupts.

Rachel laughs. "No. The property isn't even fenced all around. Even the gate's a joke. It's just to look impressive, across the front of the house for only about a hundred yards. That was Stan—all show."

"Did you ever see anything unusual, any of those times you were…"

"Stalking him?" Vogel says, his voice heavy with sarcasm. I shoot him a dirty look but he ignores me.

She shrugs. "Maybe. I'm not exactly sure."

"Rachel, I can't put that in my report," I say with a glance at Vogel. "You know Price is dead. Murdered. We've got a recording of you at his front gate on the day he was killed. I need some kind of reasonable explanation for your being there."

"I can't give you a *reasonable* explanation," she says. "I don't understand it myself. Put it down to an old woman's grief."

"When you were stalking him, did you ever notice anything? Anyone?" I can hear the irritation in Vogel's voice.

Rachel thinks it over for so long I think she may have forgotten the question.

"You know, as an artist," she finally says. "I'm always in the habit of looking, of seeing. I'm looking for pattern, shape, colour, textures. I just do it, all the time, unconsciously." I hear Vogel sigh. "So yeah, I always noticed things. The light on the long grass in the meadow. The moon through the trees. I'd see his silhouette through his blinds, going from room to room. I'd watch as he turned out the lights and the house went dark."

Rachel sounds like she's gone right over the edge as far as Price was concerned. But could she have killed him?

"I think I was going crazy," she says. "Obsessing so much I sometimes think I actually did kill him. I imagined it so often." It's as if she's reading my thoughts.

"We're going to have to take your DNA and fingerprints," Vogel says. "To eliminate you from our enquiries."

"I'm really a suspect? Is that a joke?" Rachel laughs. I shake my head and she throws up her hands. "Whatever," she says. "You know where to find me."

"You want to fill me on one what's going on?" Vogel asks the second we get back into the car. "I've never seen you cut anyone so much slack in an interview before. *Looking at the moon through the trees? Walking meditation?* What a load of crap."

"She's an artist. They see things differently," I mumble. "I don't believe she had anything to do with Price's death."

"Gauthier, I don't know who you think you're talking to. At this point, that woman is our prime suspect. She had motive. Security cameras have her on the scene and she has a strong motive…" He starts driving so fast I know he's angry.

"I wouldn't call it *strong,*" I interrupt. "Why would she kill Price thirty years after their daughter disappeared? Makes no sense."

"You know it does," he says. "And any prosecutor could easily attribute it to the timing of finding her daughter's remains. Hell, she even said it herself: she started stalking Price after the body was identified."

Now I really wish I didn't have Vogel with me during the interview. If Rachel hadn't been upfront with us, he'd never know about how she really felt about Price.

And there'd be no way Rachel's connection to Price would have come out—at least not so soon. The only link between them is the DNA evidence, which only proves Ella is Price's daughter. There's no mention of Rachel anywhere on the document, so it may not have come to light.

I catch myself wondering how I could hide that somehow, then I stop short. What am I doing? Why am I trying so hard to protect Rachel? Do I really not believe she killed Price? Or does some part of me know she did it, and that he deserved what he got?

"There's something you should know," I say. "Rachel Weaver's son is one of the bank robbers. From last week."

Vogel almost drives into the back of the car in front of us, before he slams on the brakes. "What did you just say?"

"I'm sure there's no connection between the robbery and the murder of Price." Vogel rolls his eyes. "Her son's name is Dillon Byrne," I say. "The one with the broken neck."

"Gauthier," Vogel sighs. "I don't even know where to start with this. You don't get to decide what's important or what's relevant. You're not in charge. You're supposed to bring all the information in—not just what you're willing to share—and present it to DS Agu, then we work together to build a case."

"It's not like I was withholding," I lie. "I just told you!"

"Sure. Right. And when did you know?" He shakes his head. "Last week? I get that this Rachel is somehow a friend of yours—and don't even get me started on how that's a conflict of interest right there—but if you can't be objective and fully disclose what you find, then you aren't able to do your job." He glares at me. "What do I have to do, go to DS Agu?"

"You going to report me to Dad?"

"Fuck off Gauthier. You know I'm right."

We drive on for a few minutes in silence. I'm stubborn, maybe even obstinate, and I don't need to continue this argument. I have a feeling it's one I'll lose anyway.

Then Vogel starts laughing. "If I hadn't seen the DNA results I wouldn't believe it for a second!"

"What are you talking about Vogel?"

"Rachel Weaver with Stan Price. It just doesn't fit." I give him a dirty look, but don't dare say anything in case I lose it. "C'mon Gauthier! Have you *seen* her? That obese, old, hippy witch woman? It's crazy!"

"What exactly is your fucking problem Vogel?" I snap, unable to stop myself. "She's not allowed to get old? To be overweight?" Vogel looks at me in surprise. He has no idea what I'm talking about. "What about Stan Price? He was no prize—a burned out, dried up, miserable old rock and roller. Or is he okay, because he was a man?"

Vogel shrugs. "He was a legend."

"Some *legend*. Please shut up and drive."

We don't say another word all the way back to the station.

Maybe I've been too focussed on Ella through this whole thing— probably because of Kim, and my friendship with Rachel, and how close the circumstances I'm investigating have come to my personal history. My perspective could be off. I've been caught up in the DNA, and the admittedly odd way Rachel was haunting Price. But what if I've been looking at the murder of Stan Price from the wrong direction? The motive for murder is usually money. What if the simple answer is the right one? Who inherits Price's estate?

As soon as I'm at my desk I pick up the phone and call Ed Jorgenson. His receptionist puts me through right away, which is a surprise.

"Mr. Jorgenson," I get to the point. "Did Stan Price have a Will?"

"No…he didn't. At least not one that I ever drew up for him," Jorgenson doesn't have to think about it. "Of course, he never had his own family, there were no siblings, and his parents are dead…I guess it didn't matter to him."

"Isn't that…odd?"

"Yes," he agrees. "I brought it up to him and we spoke about it several times over the years. But Stan couldn't be bothered to address it. I think he may have been superstitious. It's a pretty common fear in my experience—he thought if he made a Will he'd die."

"What, he thought he was immortal?" I laugh.

Jorgenson pauses for a moment. "Have you met Stan Price?"

He has a point. Price probably thought he was some kind of rock god. Most likely that's what the memoir was all about—his ego, not exposing any secrets. "So, what happens now?"

Jorgenson thinks it over before he replies. "I'm not an Estate lawyer, but the law is pretty clear. If no legal Will surfaces after his death, or no hand-written Will shows up somewhere, then he officially has died intestate. Best efforts will be made to trace family—however distant they may be. They'd have to be blood relations of course—a great aunt or second cousin or whatever."

"And if there's none of them?"

"His property will escheat—become the property of the government."

"Lucky government."

"Indeed."

I make a mental note to get a Will drafted when I get some time. Not that I have much money to leave anyone, but I don't need the government to get my townhouse or my modest retirement savings. I guess having a Will certainly makes things clear and speaks for you after you're gone, when you no longer have a voice.

Assuming the Will is honoured.

I end the call with Jorgenson and sit frozen, with my hand on the phone. My mind is racing. Wills. Rossi. Why does the Rossi name keep popping up? Every time I turn around, there they are. First Joe Rossi is at the bank robbery, then his family has a brawl at the *trattoria* and Vogel and I overhear Price having an argument with Rossi on the phone. And the connection to the night Ella died—that Renato Rossi was a concert promoter, and that a young Joe was in the photos taken the night she died. And Kim Parsons. Why did she smash Rossi's office windows just before she was run down in the street? What's her connection to Rossi Realty?

What's the connection in all of this to the Rossi's? Is there one?

I think of the Renato Rossi Estate mess, as his lawyer Arturo described it to me. He supposedly had a new Will that couldn't be found after he died, so the family had to use the original one—the one that shared the estate equally among his children, regardless of the story that Joe had been cut out.

Even though Rosa Rossi said she'd seen the new Will herself, she might have lied. Unless she can find a copy she'll just have to accept what she gets.

Why would Renato Rossi cut his eldest son out of his inheritance in this new Will? And apparently he'd done so decades ago, so it must be ancient family history.

Given the bad blood between Rosa and her brother Joe, I wonder if she'll tell me what she knows? I try to think of a legitimate reason to inquire as I turn the car around and head for the Rossi real estate office.

When I present myself at the reception desk there's a brief bit of confusion about whether I have an appointment and whether I'm there about a real estate listing, before Rosa Rossi is paged.

She arrives promptly in the lobby. To my relief she looks nothing like the raving lunatic I'd seen at the *trattoria* last week, though the wide artificial smile pasted on her face is disturbing in its own way. Rosa Rossi is a well-groomed woman, wearing an expensive suit and shoes, with makeup perfectly applied. But in no way could you ever describe her as attractive. In fact, there's something repellant about her. She's sharp and hard-nosed, but at least she's calm now.

"Rosa Rossi," she extends her hand and ushers me into her private office. "How can I help you Detective?"

I make up a lie and pull out my notebook. "It's about your front window. The vandalism?" Many people might wonder why a Detective is following up on such a minor incident. But the Rossis are used to special attention and going to the head of the line, so the question never crosses Rosa Rossi's mind.

"Yes," Rosa shakes her head. "Some lunatic. High as a kite, on drugs or whatever."

"Can you think of any reason your office was her target?"

"No! She was just babbling gibberish. No idea what any of it meant."

"Did you know her?"

For a brief moment Rosa Rossi hesitates and I know she's decided to lie to me. "No idea who she was. Sorry."

Now that's interesting. I have no idea why Kim Parsons had smashed the Rossi Realty window but now I have to wonder why Rosa Rossi is lying to me. But now isn't the time to push, so I change the subject.

"I'm also following up on the incident last Friday at the Pasquale's *Trattoria*."

"Okay…" Rosa puts on a contrite expression. "That was…terrible. I behaved very badly, I'm sorry to say."

"It's understandable," I lie. "You were grieving."

Rosa Rossi sits down, looking confused. "But why are you here? The *trattoria* has agreed to not press charges if I compensate them for the damages. Which of course I'm perfectly willing to do."

"Yes, that's true. I just need to fill in my report…you understand. Paperwork."

I can tell she's impatient but she wants to keep me happy, so she takes a deep breath and gives me a smile. "Whatever I can do to expedite things," she says.

"Can you please tell me what the argument was about?"

"My father's Will," she says, frowning. It's clear she doesn't want to go into it. "Family business." I give her a bland smile and wait for her to continue. After less than a minute she breaks.

She heaves a sigh. "My brother is trying to have an old version probated. I disagree with him doing that, as does my younger brother."

"Was there another Will?"

She nods emphatically. "Definitely. I saw it myself, right after my father had it drawn it up."

"And is it substantially different?"

She smiles maliciously. "My brother Joe was cut out completely."

"Really? When was this done?"

"Ages ago…maybe twenty years ago, or even more."

"Forgive my curiosity, but why would he do that?"

She snorts in disgust. "Joe was weak. He wasn't fit to run the company, and my father knew it."

"Not fit? Based on what?" Seems to me Joe Rossi's been doing all right, but then I don't have any insight into what's going on in their family businesses—the legitimate or the criminal ones.

"Youthful indiscretions, mistakes he made."

"Serious ones?" She smiles but doesn't take the bait. "Your father didn't put it down to the bad judgement of youth?"

"I wouldn't know. You'd have to ask my father about it. Or Joe," she smiles. "Good luck with that."

"So who benefits instead?"

"My son. Angelo." She sees my raised eyebrows and offers an explanation without my having to ask. "My father saw him as his true heir. They were…alike. So similar in many ways. These things skip a generation…don't you know?"

"It's so unfortunate," she's now furrowed her brow and is holding a tissue to her eyes, dabbing away at non-existent crocodile tears. "And unnecessary. That terrible scene my brother caused after the funeral." My recollection of who caused the scene is clearly different from hers.

"Unnecessary?"

"We found the new Will," she smiles. "It turned up in my father's things."

"It just…turned up?"

She gives a dramatic shrug. "We were all so upset after Papa died, then the fire at the lawyers' offices. I thought it was lost forever. But then it turned up the day after the funeral!"

"That's fortunate. And unexpected."

She gives me a big crocodile smile as she escorts me out.

TWENTY THREE

Vogel and I are both tense as we drive out to Price's house. He drives and I work on my phone to avoid speaking to him. I don't want another argument, especially since I haven't been able to get past our last one.

The main gate is open when we get arrive and the red sports car is on the driveway. We find Shelley inside, putting things back into boxes.

"You're still working?" Vogel asks.

"His lawyer and publisher asked me to tidy up what Stan was working on." She stops and looks at the piles of boxes piled next to the island. "No idea what'll happen to all this now."

"So the memoir's not being published?"

"I don't see how," she says. "It wasn't close to being finished and now he's dead…"

"It's not unheard of for books to be written by someone else," I say. There's something off about Shelley I can't quite put my finger on. Ever since I first laid eyes on her, when I'd assumed she was Price's girlfriend, I thought she was hiding something and now I think I know what it is. "They've even published new James Bond and Hercule Poirot books…"

She laughs. "Stan Price was no Ian Fleming or Agatha Christie." She tapes up a box of mementoes and carries it through to the office. "To be honest, he was a terrible writer."

"Then I don't suppose the world will miss his autobiography," Vogel says.

"No. But I'll miss my paycheque," she says over her shoulder. To his credit Vogel looks embarrassed.

She comes back into the kitchen carrying an empty box, which she starts to fill with books. She glances over, registering that we're still here, but then she proceeds to ignore us. I expect she'd like us to leave, but instead I sit down at one of the tall stools and watch her for a moment.

"How long have you worked for Mr. Price?" I finally ask. Shelley's eyes are flickering between Vogel and me as she pretends to go through more books, deciding what to pack into the open box. She's nervous and I can see she's trying to gauge how much to tell us.

"A few months," she says. "Haven't we covered this?"

"Please remind me, how did you get this job?" Vogel asks. "It must have been a plum, assisting a famous rock star."

"I was referred to the publisher. By one of Mr. Price's colleagues."

"Someone else you *assisted*?" She gives me a sharp look, her eyebrows furrowed, but doesn't say anything. "It must be interesting, working as an assistant to a celebrity. I imagine a ghostwriter would be fascinating too. Working with an author, helping them shape their book, being part of that whole process."

"I wouldn't know."

I give her a bland smile and say nothing, but turn to the pile of envelopes and parcels heaped on the countertop.

"What is all this stuff anyway?"

"It's the same as the last time you were here," she says. "I haven't gotten to any of it yet."

"Some of it's new," I say, idly leafing through the envelopes.

"This was delivered yesterday, according to the courier's sticker. From someone named Guy Laforce."

"That name sounds familiar," she says. "I remember some emails exchanged between Stan and him, I think." Shelley sighs and glances the parcel. "When Stan got the idea to write this memoir, he and I got in touch with everyone from his past, asking them to send him whatever they had. People sent all sorts of photos, song sheets, and emailed him stories they remembered from back in the day, that sort of thing."

"Sounds like a lot to go through."

"And it's still coming in. Open them if you're curious," she says. "Though I can't see what use it will all be now."

"It does seem a shame that all that effort will have gone for nothing," Vogel says.

Shelley laughs. "Another has-been celebrity memoir? Maybe it's all for the best."

"Maybe his ghostwriter can finish it," I say. "It could still be published."

Shelley drops the box of books and turns away so I can't see her expression. "I told you he didn't have a ghostwriter."

"Are you sure?" Vogel asks.

She's flustered. "I was here most days, helping with his research. I'm sure I'd know if he had one."

"You certainly would. Could you please give us the name of Mr. Price's publisher?" Shelley looks down and I can tell she's thinking of denying she knows. "You must know it…you told us you'd been introduced at a party."

"It's Harrison," she mumbles, defeated. "Judith Harrison. Her number's on the fridge."

I've already got my phone out and I half-listen as Vogel continues interviewing Shelley. When Judith Harrison picks up the call I step into the hall. I can't miss the look of dread on Shelley's face.

"How can I help you Detective?" Judith Harrison gets right to the point, once I've identified myself. "I assume this is about Stan Price's death?"

"We just have a few questions," I begin. "About Shelley Arthur."

"Shelley?!" She sounds astonished. "What about her?"

"How long has she known Stan Price?"

"I first introduced them at a party, months ago. I'd have to check my calendar for the exact date, if it's important."

"And you recruited her for the position as his assistant?"

"*Assistant*? No…I don't think so," she sounds confused. "Shelley Arthur is a writer, a very good one in fact.."

"She's a ghostwriter?"

"Well, yes," she chuckles. "Though our contracts usually say coauthor or contributor. We've used Shelley on several non-fiction titles, to polish and revise, edit and generally improve the book."

"Uncredited?"

She hesitates. "Generally, yes. Though I expect we'll need to rethink things now that Stan Price has died. Perhaps Shelley can now write the book as a biography…" I can tell she's thinking out loud. "Maybe I'll have a word with Price's heirs and see what they think."

"Are you sure Stan Price has any heirs? As far as I know he has no living relatives."

"Well…I just assumed he did. I honestly have no idea." She sounds flustered. "I hope he does and we can work something out. It would be a shame to throw out all of the work Shelley's done so far."

"Has it been a lot? How far along is she?"

"She's been working with him for months now. And, what I've read…"

"You've read it?" I interrupt.

"Of course," she laughs. "She'd send me the draft chapters as they were completed, for my editorial input."

My heart is racing. "We're going to need to see those, immediately," I say. "It could help shed some light on Stan Price's murder." I can feel her resentment through the phone. "I can get a warrant," I add, "but it would be better if you co-operate."

"Fine. Please give me your email," she sighs. "I'll send it over. But it's only gotten up to the late eighties' so far…not sure how much help it will be."

I hang up after giving her my contact info. The late eighties'…before Ella's death. I'm disappointed, but it's not like Price would have admitted any role he'd had in her death, especially not in writing.

Shelley looks nervously at me when I come back into the kitchen. She knows she's caught.

"Okay," she sighs and she sits down heavily on the kitchen stool. "Maybe I am a ghostwriter."

"Why didn't you tell us earlier?"

"There was no way! I just couldn't," she insists. "I signed an NDA. It was twelve pages long! You think I'd risk being sued by Stan's estate or whatever? You don't know these people."

"What people?"

She looks like she regrets having said anything. "Just…music industry people—the lawyers, concert promoters, agents, publicists, not to mention the musicians. It's a rough world."

And I suppose working as a ghostwriter you'd get to learn where all the bodies are buried…so to speak." God I hate that expression and can't believe it just came out of my mouth.

She shrugs. "Yeah, more than I ever wanted to, believe me."

"Can you tell us a little bit about that? Maybe some of it will shed some light on Mr. Price's death."

"I very much doubt that," she mutters. "Who'd even care? It's all ancient history. I didn't even know who Stan Price was when I took this job."

"Never heard of Running Deep?" I say with a glance at Vogel. She shakes her head.

"What's going on?" a male voice says. I'm surprised to see it's Angelo Rossi. So that's the *friend* whose car she's been using.

Shelley gives him a big smile, obviously relieved he's here to rescue her from our questioning. "Nothing much," she says. "I'm starving."

"Great," he says. "Let's go for lunch." He gives us a wave as he escorts Shelley out of the house, his arm protectively around her waist. In a minute we hear the roar of the car's engine as they drive away.

I turn to Vogel, who's flipping through the pile of parcels and envelopes. "Think he was here the whole time?"

He nods, tearing one open. "I wonder how long he was listening? And what he heard."

"He's a creep," I say as I pick up a parcel and struggle to open it. I start to look through the nearest drawers for a blade or pair of scissors to cut through the string and shipping tape.

"You just don't like him on principle," Vogel says, picking up another letter. "Because he comes from a rich family." There's certainly some truth to that.

"No, because he comes from a *mob* family. Who also happen to be rich." Vogel doesn't reply. I glance over and see him spilling the contents of the envelope onto the countertop. I go back to looking for scissors when Vogel suddenly bursts out laughing.

"What? What's so funny?" I go over to see for myself.

Spread out across the counter is a dozen or more photographs of people, all nude, except for a selection of top hats on the men. Several women are wearing flower crowns and one wears a veil. They are all posed outside in a flowery meadow, with a stream visible in the background.

"Is this…a wedding?" There are some pictures of everyone in

a circle, holding hands around the bride and groom. Others show them dancing, or sitting around a table enjoying what I assume is the wedding feast. Everyone is smiling and clearly happy. The last one is the married couple driving away on a motorbike. The bride is naked and her breasts are pressed up against the driver's back as her long blonde hair flies out behind them.

"At least he's wearing a helmet," Vogel says. I pick up the photos and peer more closely at them, trying to figure out what they might mean.

"Is there a letter in the envelope? Something to explain what these are?"

"Gauthier, take a look at this." Vogel holds out a piece of paper. His urgent tone stops me cold and I snatch the document from him.

It's a Certificate of Marriage Registration, issued in 1976 by the State of New York. For the marriage of Stan Price to Rachel Weaver.

TWENTY FOUR

RACHEL DOESN'T PICK up any of my calls, so we drive out to Womyn Collective where we find her in her studio, surrounded by piles of colourful wood and fibres.

She's sitting at an old fashioned spinning wheel, her long grey hair hanging loose, making her look exactly like a witch from a fairy tale—if that witch was wearing a colourful knit poncho and a long purple skirt over a pair of silver-tipped cowboy boots.

"Hi Lucy," she says when she sees us enter. She barely acknowledges Vogel and I can feel him bristle. "Look what I just got! It's an antique. Still works, almost as well as my new one."

"What are you doing?" Vogel asks and I see Rachel roll her eyes. "I mean, beyond the obvious…" his voice trails off.

"I'm spinning this roving," she holds up a bunch of wool.

"So, you spin this fluffy stuff….

"Roving," Rachel corrects him.

"….into yarn, then you weave it on the loom?" Vogel seems genuinely interested and Rachel softens. It's one of Vogel's gifts— his ability to disarm people and make real connections with them. Sometimes I wish I could do that, but mostly I'm happy to keep my distance from everyone.

"Or I knit with it," she explains. "Or a combination of things, depending on what I'm envisioning. I get a bit tired of making placemats and table runners—they're our big sellers at markets. So I'm making something for myself. I've been invited to contribute to a textile exhibition at the Stedelijk Museum in Amsterdam."

"That sounds like a big deal," Vogel says. "I've been there. It's…"

"Famous?" Rachel laughs. "For real artists? Not some crazy old woman from Niagara?" Vogel looks appropriately embarrassed. "I've exhibited my work in many museums and galleries Detective, all over the world. You should Google me sometime."

Vogel looks as if he like to pull out his phone that second, but thinks better of it.

"What are you working with?" I ask, looking at the piles of purple, green and blue fibres. "Is this what you had delivered the other day?"

She nods at the roving in her hand. "This is alpaca, from Peru."

Suddenly the wheel stops spinning. "I'm tired," she says. "My legs are sore." She turns to look at us directly for the first time. "I'm sure you have some good reason for coming here, but I'm busy. So, if you're going to talk to me, you'd better make yourselves useful."

Vogel starts to object but she holds up her hand. "If you'll do my treadling so I can spin, I'll answer your questions." She pushes the stool toward Vogel. "You look strong enough. Sit down here and pump your feet. It's as easy as riding a bike."

Vogel looks to me for support but Rachel won't have it. "You can't just sit around looking pretty, Detective. Around here we have to earn our keep."

He shrugs, then sits down and starts to pedal while Rachel stands behind him, holding the ball of wool and pulling out a thin strand that stretches out into the spinning wheel, before winding itself onto a large spool.

"Good," Rachel praises him. "Keep up that pace. Nice and steady."

She looks at me after a moment, with a smile. "I drew The Tower when I read my Tarot this morning. It means revelation. What are you here to tell me, Lucy?"

I hand her the marriage certificate. She stares at it and the colour rises in her cheeks. "Where did you get this?" she whispers, dropping the ball of wool.

"That's your first question…?" Vogel asks, shaking his head. He stops pedaling and Rachel doesn't even notice.

I talk right over him. "Rachel, why would you keep this from us?"

She sinks heavily onto the seat at her loom, her head shaking, still staring at the certificate. "Where did you get this?"

"Stan Price had it," Vogel says. "In the memorabilia he was gathering for his memoir."

"We found it in his mail, unopened. It was sent to him recently."

"*Sent* to him?" Rachel is pale and seems stunned in disbelief.

Vogel checks his notebook. "From a Guy LaForce, in Albany, New York."

"Guy!?!…" Rachel shakes her head. "I haven't heard that name in…years."

"Maybe 45 years?" I ask. I'm impatient and need her to focus, but there's no point in pressuring her. "What's going on Rachel? You were married to Price?" How could she not have said a word to us, let alone to Price? And how did Price manage to act so cool, as if he didn't even know Rachel, if we're to believe her story? Not knowing Ella was his daughter, when he'd gotten married to Rachel just a few months before Ella was born? It makes no sense to me.

"Is it…*legit?*" she asks, finally raising her eyes from the document. Vogel and I exchange a look. How can she not know?

Though, given the nature of the wedding photos it's maybe not an unreasonable question.

"It sure looks like it," I say, taking it back from her. "All signed and sealed by the State of New York."

"We've got a call in to Guy LaForce for more information," says Vogel.

"You're saying you don't remember getting married?" I'm dumbfounded. "That's difficult to believe."

Rachel stares off across the room, shaking her head. "It was such a long time ago. I was so young. We both were. What can I tell you?"

"How about the truth Rachel?"

"The truth," she chuckles. "They were wild times. Barefoot hippies I guess you'd call us. It was the seventies…sex, drugs and rock and roll. "

"Drugs?"

"Oh yes! Lots of drugs," she grins. "I'd been travelling around with the band for months. For a while we were all staying at a commune in upstate New York."

"The same one where you said you first met the Parsons? They're the witnesses on your marriage certificate."

Rachel laughs. "Really!? Eleanor and George?" I show her their signatures. "I have no recollection of that, but I guess it makes sense," she nods. "They were living at the commune when we were there. Funny how Eleanor was from Niagara too…small world."

"And they came back here too, like you did." Rachel nods, smiling at some memory. "What do you remember about that time?"

Rachel takes a deep breath. "I remember the wedding. We got married in a meadow full of daisies. The sun was shining…the sky was cornflower blue. All our friends around us, singing and dancing." She giggles. "We all danced naked, under Father Sun and

Mother Moon. We played tambourines and guitars. And bells, so many Tibetan bells, and chanting." She shakes her head at the memory. "It was full-on hippie stuff. Stan and I were crazy about each other. Or so I thought."

"And you never thought to mention this?" I just can't get over her keeping this a secret.

"You do know how this looks Rachel," Vogel interrupts.

"No, I don't know!" Rachel throws up her hands. "Honestly, I wasn't even sure it had happened. It feels like it might have been a dream." She winks. "We were always high. In my defence, it was the seventies! Like I said it was a crazy time."

"Do you remember where this was?"

Rachel thinks for a moment. "Not really. Maybe Eleanor will…oh. I forgot. She's dead." She glances at the Marriage Certificate. "New York State I guess. Maybe Guy will remember, when you talk to him. I guess he managed all the legal stuff…" her voice drifts off.

I see Vogel roll his eyes. "Then what happened?"

Rachel shrugs. "Then Stan left. Just like that. I found out I was pregnant a while later," she says. "I came back home to have Ella."

"You didn't think to chase him? To get him to support Ella?

"No! I was too angry. I didn't even put his name on her birth certificate. Why would I?"

Rachel catches Vogel and I exchange a look.

"Oh I know what you're thinking—money. But don't forget, at that time he didn't have a penny. The band weren't successful at all. He was just a broke-ass bass player with big aspirations. It's not like I could have sued him for any support. Assuming I could even have found him."

"How hard could it have been?"

"We're talking about over forty years ago!" she says. "There was no internet, no computers, no cell phones. And I lived here, in a small town. What was I supposed to do, hire a private investigator to track him down? As if I could afford that." Rachel sighs deeply, her expression resigned. "The money didn't start to come in for him for a long time after that, and I was already over him. I had Ella. We were enough, just the two of us."

"You neglected to mention this earlier," Vogel says. "It doesn't look good." Rachel just shrugs.

It's starting to look like Rachel's motive to kill Price isn't amounting to much. She doesn't seem angry enough to have killed Price out of bitterness.

"Anyway," Rachel shakes her head impatiently. "I don't believe for one minute that marriage certificate is even legal. Guy LaForce wasn't a real minister, I'm pretty sure."

Suddenly she laughs out loud. "But I guess if it is that means the other women Stan married and divorced over the years were never his legal wives? The big divorce settlements and all the alimony he paid them?"

Vogel clears his throat. "Technically it also makes him a bigamist."

"So if he wasn't dead he'd be in jail?" We can hear Rachel laughing all the way out to the car.

TWENTY FIVE

"You drive," Vogel says, tossing me the keys. "I've got shin splints from pedalling that damn spinning wheel." He climbs into the passenger side, glaring toward the barn where we'd left Rachel. "You never told me she's a textile artist," he says.

"Rachel's had exhibits in Rochester, Albany, at the AGO in Toronto, all over the world. She's the real deal."

Vogel looks both impressed and embarrassed. "I feel bad. With the way she looks I dismissed her as being just a crazy person." He pulls out his phone and I can see he's looking into Rachel's career. The last time I checked a Google search on her brought up almost a hundred pages.

"Oh, she's definitely crazy, I give you that. But in a good way. Totally into astrology and crystals and auras. She's psychic too."

Vogel laughs as a car speeds past us, overtaking on a bend, going at least thirty over the limit. It's a red sports car and I can see long blonde hair flying out that passenger window.

"Rossi, Jr. Should we pull him over?"

Vogel shakes his head. "Nah, I can't be bothered with the paperwork. Let's hope there's a cruiser up ahead with radar that'll get him."

I nod in agreement and we drive back to the station in companionable silence, the tension between us gone for now. Once we're back at our desks, fresh coffees in hand, I get to what's on my mind. Something's been bothering me about Angelo Rossi since the first time I laid eyes on him, especially the way he was lurking, probably eavesdropping on my conversation with Shelley.

"What do we know about Angelo Rossi anyway?"

"Nothing, offhand," Vogel says, leaning back in his chair. "But I've gotta say the kid definitely has a creepy vibe, that's for sure."

"Does he have a record? Anything on file?"

"Why don't we just have a look?" Vogel says with a smile as he logs onto his computer. Within a few keystrokes he's in, then I hear him whistle.

"Find anything interesting?" I ask, walking around to his desk so I can look over his shoulder.

"Oh yeah. Lots of speeding tickets. Suspended license, for stunt driving. He was caught going over 200K on the QEW."

"In his fancy red sports car?"

"Nope, in his grandfather's Audi TT. Which, according to our records, he totalled a few months later." Vogel shakes his head. "I can't even think what his vehicle insurance premiums are."

"*Insurance*? How does he even have a license?"

Vogel rolls his eyes.

"Car's not in his name," Vogel shrugs. "It's registered to his mother, Rosa Gennaro, but of course he drives it. He's also got a sealed juvenile record," Vogel says with a sly smile.

My mouth goes dry and I can barely speak. "Can we unseal it?" I ask, afraid what the answer will be. I feel sick as the past floods back. My pulse is racing and there's a yawning pit in my stomach. If my records were ever opened…what it would do to me, to my life. My juvenile record needs to stay sealed forever.

Vogel shakes his head "Doubtful. We'd need a court order," he says. "We wouldn't be able to get it without cause." The relief that washes over me is completely irrational, but I have to sit down because I feel overwhelmed with emotion.

"Okay, so let's take a different approach," I manage to say. "What school did he attend?"

"Probably expensive private ones," Vogel laughs.

"Like Ridley?" I raise my eyebrow suggestively. Ridley is Vogel's old alma mater. Maybe he still knows someone there. Vogel sighs and looks irritated. "C'mon," I urge him. "Make a call."

He sighs dramatically then picks up the phone. I return to my desk and try to get my head straight. The visceral fear that my juvenile record could be unsealed, and what the cascade of destruction that would unfold takes me time to shove back into its box and lock down.

In a few minutes Vogel puts down the phone. "You owe me a drink. No—a dinner," he says.

"Why? For doing your job?"

"That was Jane Moffat, the registrar at Ridley," he grumbles. "I used to go to school with her. We were lab partners."

"One of your conquests?"

"No, sadly. Jane and I went out a few times, but it never came to anything. Not sure why."

I bite my tongue. Looks like yet another woman has escaped Vogel's charms. The Niagara Region is thick with them.

What is it with Vogel and women? I'm starting to be concerned for him, though it's too awkward to ask him about it. He never seems to get anywhere long term with anyone and yet it seems like there's nothing he wants more. Which, I realize is probably the reason they all run away. Vogel comes on too strong, too desperate, too needy and any sane woman will run a mile when they smell that on him. Of course, that doesn't account for the crazy women. There's plenty of those around, not that I'd wish any of them on Vogel. He is my partner after all.

"Poor Vogel," I tease. "Another one who got away. What'd she tell you?"

"Angelo Rossi attended until he was eleven years old. Then he was permanently expelled, after an incident."

"An *incident*? Do tell…"

Vogel smirks. "Angelo Rossi was suspended a few times, for fighting, vandalism and cheating, and in the end he set fire to the dean's office."

"Are you serious? Why?"

"There was a history of someone setting fire to garbage bins around the school, in wastepaper baskets in the boys' washroom, that kind of thing. The fires were usually set right around mid-term or final exam time. To disrupt everything so they'd have to evacuate the school, alarm goes off, tests delayed…"

"What is he some kind of pyromaniac?"

"No, just an asshole. Typical vandal. They start out setting fires for the excitement of it. They love the drama, the hysteria. Then the one he got caught for was to conceal a crime. He'd broken into one of the offices to steal tests and set the fire to cover his tracks." Vogel gives me a superior look. "Anyway, that makes him an arsonist, not a pyromaniac."

"And the difference is…?"

"Firesetting is an antisocial behaviour. A personality disorder. Pyromania is a psychiatric diagnosis…"

"And you know this how?"

"Jane Moffat just told me. She's got a Master's Degree in Child Psychology."

"Ok, I'll buy that. So Angelo Rossi doesn't have a psychiatric diagnosis?"

"Vogel shakes his head. "Apparently not. Nothing in his school records."

"What else did you learn?"

He flips out his notebook and starts to read.

"Firesetting is often associated with alcohol and drug use, aggression and hostility, and a family history of antisocial behaviour…"

"Like having a mob family?" I interrupt. "I imagine having Renato Rossi as your grandfather would set a certain standard for antisocial behavior."

Vogel nods and continues to read. "Sensation seeking…"

"Like driving his fast cars and charges of stunt driving? Well that certainly fits. Shelley Arthur did tell us he was an adrenaline junkie."

So Angelo Rossi was what some people call a troubled youth. I'd call him an entitled rich kid. Probably used to taking what he wants, whenever he wants it, just like his grandfather.

"How'd he get caught?" I ask. "Setting the fires at school?"

"Someone ratted him out."

"Glad to hear it. Then what? Where'd he go?"

"The Rossis sent him to the military school over in Beamsville."

"Tough love?" It wouldn't be the first time I'd heard of a kid being sent to military school to straighten him out, or to avoid jail time.

"Maybe. Probably no other private school would accept him." Vogel shrugs. "He finished up there, then went to work for his father."

His cell phone rings and from the expression on Vogel's face I can easily guess it's a personal call, from a woman. I leave him to it and turn to my computer to pass the time while he arranges his social calendar.

In a few minutes I learn that a typical arsonist is white, male and young. They often will have a history of physical abuse and humiliation—perhaps by someone like a grandfather, a criminal sociopath? The arsonist will have played with matches and started fires as a child, but as he gets older he wants more sensation, more danger, and a bigger rush. Arson is one of the easiest crimes to commit. Anyone can do it, there's no weapon needed and it can be done impulsively, without much planning, which is not reassuring to me as a police detective. I wonder if Angelo Rossi's time at military school managed to cure him of his firesetting tendencies.

"Detective Gauthier?" A voice calls from the doorway. It's DC Reyes again. She must have found something on the damaged security videotape. "We've managed to clean up that footage. Want to have a look?" Vogel and I jump up and meet her down the hall in the tech suite.

The monitor is divided into quarters, each one showing the feed from a different camera. The top left one is black.

"He had multiple cameras feeding live video through a multiplexer into one monitor and one recording device. But the DVR drive he was storing the video on had a hardware failure, and that caused the entire system to stop writing and storing properly. There's lots of missing or corrupted data."

She points to the top left hand of the monitor. "And we have no feed at all from one."

"Will you be able to get that footage, once the system is fixed?"

She shakes her head. "No. Maybe if he'd had a spot monitor or dual monitor display function. Or if it was backed up to the cloud. Or if he had a built in infra red transmitter…"

"Please don't feel you have to share that level of detail," I interrupt. "Seriously. Please."

Anita rolls her eyes. "To keep it simple for you, that camera wasn't properly connected to the DVR."

"Someone disabled it?" Anita nods. "Which camera is it?"

She checks her notes. "That would be the east side of the house, along the driveway."

"So, we have no footage of cars that were parked there or that drove up to the house?"

"None. Nor of any windows and doors that open on that side."

"Is there any sign of a break in?" Vogel asks.

"None that we found," she says. "Stan Price had a security alarm, but it appears he didn't set it when he was at home. Just when he went out."

"So he cared more about protecting his property than himself."

"I imagine it never occurred to him that anyone hated him enough to kill him. Fame will do that to you."

She cues up the tape and presses play. "The resolution isn't great," she says. "They are cheap cameras, so the night vision is poor, with no automatic adjustment to correct overexposure." The security footage starts to stream in three sections of the monitor, leaving the fourth one black. "This is from Sunday, the night he was killed. It's not motion activated."

We watch for a few minutes as nothing happens. "We're not watching in real time, are we?" Vogel finally asks. "Because I feel my life passing before me."

Anita laughs. "I'm playing it back at four times speed. Any faster and you might miss something."

Vogel groans and I settle in more comfortably. This could take a while.

A few minutes later I think I see a dark shadow flicker in one of the feeds. "Can you back it up? I think I saw something in that part." I point to the monitor.

Anita presses a few buttons and the video starts to play again, but this time slower, in real time. We all lean in, watching intently as nothing happens, again. Then a figure wearing a hoodie appears walking slowly along the wall of the house. "He's keeping his head down," Vogel says. "As if he knows where the camera is."

We watch as they make their way toward the back door, hand trailing along the wall for support. "It looks more like he's keeping his eyes down, to make sure he doesn't trip and fall."

"Whoever that is, they don't look very steady on their feet," Anita says. "Possibly drunk or high."

"They're holding onto the wall so they don't fall over." As the words come out of my mouth the figure stumbles to their knees, the hood falling off revealing a mess of long, lanky dark hair. It's Kim Parsons.

TWENTY SIX

"DIDN'T YOU SAY she went missing last week?" Vogel says as we head for the car. I nod and pull out my phone to call Dudek.

"She was missing. Then someone tried to run her down on Erie Street. Now she's in custody, in District 2," I say, after speaking with the desk officer and being put on hold. "I'd say she's got an alibi."

"Depends on when they arrested her. We've got her on camera at Stan Price's on Sunday night." Vogel is thinking aloud. "She could have killed Price, then got herself arrested afterwards…"

"Lucky I called ahead," I interrupt him, putting my hand over the phone. "Parsons is no longer in custody. Someone bailed her out." I wonder who that could have been. Kim's mother is dead and her father's as good as. Who does she know with any money? And more important, where is she now?

"Head for the farm," I tell Vogel. "Let's hope she's gone home."

He turns the car around as Dudek comes on the line. I put him on speaker so Vogel can hear the conversation.

"Who put up the security?" I demand, not waiting to get through the social niceties.

I can hear Dudek on his computer for a moment before he comes back on the line. "The bond was paid by Rachel Weaver."

"Rachel Weaver!?" Vogel's eyebrows rise in surprise.

"It wasn't much, given the reduced charges," Dudek says. Still, it's surprising. I didn't think Rachel and Kim were close, based on what Rachel told me.

"What happened to Kim's clothes? When I saw her she was in green prison overalls." I know they were filthy, covered with blood from the accident and vomit and god knows what else from the days she was missing. But there may be another explanation. Whoever stabbed Stan Price would have his blood all over their clothes.

"No idea what happened to her clothes. I'm sure they'd have been given back to her with her personal effects when she was released. They're not evidence."

"They could be," I say as I hang up.

"Dammit," Vogel snaps when he hears. "If she stabbed Price, she'd definitely have his blood on her clothes. Unless she took them off first. Or her shoes, maybe we can get a match on the treads."

My mouth goes dry when I remember Kim wasn't wearing any shoes when she was hit by the car. Why wasn't she wearing any? But I don't share it with Vogel and I don't know why.

"Are you serious? You saw her on the videotape. She could barely stand up, let alone have the capacity to strip, stab him to death, then get redressed again."

"Yeah, I get that," Vogel shrugs. "Unless she was acting for the camera."

"You can't have it both ways Vogel. Either she knew the camera was there or she didn't. Anyway, what's her motive?" I push. "Why would Ella Weaver's friend kill Price, especially after all this time? Kim Parsons knew all along that Price was Ella's biological father—or at least that Ella thought so."

"Unless she snapped when she heard about what really happened to Ella," Vogel says.

"She has definitely gone over the edge," I say. "But Kim's a wreck. An addict, a runaway. I still don't see her being capable of doing that. You'll see when you meet her." I'm working hard to defend Kim—and I'm not sure why.

"Unless she wasn't working alone," Vogel says. I know what he's implying but don't argue with him.

The farm is quiet when we arrive. All the goats are gone, probably off to another farm to be cared for. There's a car in the driveway and when we knock on the kitchen door, Rachel answers.

"She's in here," she says as she ushers us into kitchen.

Kim is sitting at the table, her hair wet, in fresh clothes. It's clear she's just had a shower and I can only think of lost evidence. I can see the washing machine is running and Vogel tips his head toward it, then makes a face.

"Where are your clothes, Kim? The ones you were wearing when you were arrested?"

"I don't know," she mumbles. "I think they took them?"

"They're in the wash, Lucy," Rachel answers. "I put them there." Vogel and I exchange a look. *Too late*. A forensic examination of Kim's clothes could have proven if she'd stabbed Price.

I can tell Vogel is angry and suspicious. "Where are her shoes?" he demands.

"Dunno," Rachel shrugs. "She didn't have any when I picked her up."

"Convenient," Vogel mutters.

"It's true Vogel. She wasn't wearing any shoes when I saw her hit and run. Her feet were bare." If he doubts it he can check the arrest record. They'll have documented that fact.

Vogel looks even more suspicious and I can understand why. If Kim had blood on her shoes from killing Stan Price she'd have tossed them. But by that logic she'd also have tossed her bloody clothes and she didn't do that.

"Anything you can tell me about the clothes, Rachel?" As I meet her eye I know there's no way she'll say a word.

"They were dirty," Rachel says casually. "Like you'd expect." There's no point even asking if there was blood on them, regardless if it were Kim's or Price's. Rachel would lie to protect Kim. She's spent years protecting the women who've come to the shelter and she'll do whatever it takes to protect Kim too. "What brings you here, Lucy?" Rachel asks, her tone careful.

I address my answer to Kim. "You were seen on the security footage, at Stan Price's house."

Kim looks at me, her expression blank. "What? When?"

"The night he was killed. Sunday. Why would you be at his house?"

"I don't know…" She looks stunned and stares down at table. "Killed. Price is dead?" Rachel puts her hand on her shoulder. It feels like a warning.

"I'll make you some tea. Would you like some?" We decline and Rachel turns and busies herself with making the tea. She keeps one eye on us as Vogel and I sit down across from Kim.

"Kim, did you know Stan Price?"

"I already told you," she whispers, flinching away from Vogel and looking at him in fear. He pushes his chair farther away from the table to try and make her more comfortable.

"I mean, apart from Ella," I press. "Did you know him at another time? More recently?"

She keeps her head down, but I can see her steal a look at me out of the corner of her eye. "Kim, have you ever been to Stan Price's house?"

"I worked there for a while," she mumbles, wrapping her arms close around herself. "At the house."

"Doing what?"

"Cleaning." I flinch at the memory of how messy and dirty

her room upstairs was. I can't imagine Kim Parsons as a cleaner. "I clean when people buy a house or when a rental becomes vacant. Occasional work." I realize she's not likely to be reliable enough to do regular weekly cleaning. "By referral."

"Who refers you?"

"Rossi Realty. They own lots of rental houses."

"Is that why you smashed their office window?" Kim just looks confused.

"What window?" Oh boy. I glance up and catch Rachel's eye. She shakes her head. Looks like Kim's not going to be much help filling in the details of what happened over the past few days. Drugs and alcohol can do a lot of damage, especially when taken by an addict who's been clean for a time.

"Okay, don't worry about it. Tell me about when you worked at Stan Price's house. When was that?"

Kim hesitates and I can see she's struggling hard to remember. "Last year? Maybe?"

"So, what happened? When you got the cleaning job?"

Kim rubs her eyes. She's twitchy. "When I went to meet the owner, I…I saw it was him. Stan Price. I panicked."

"So you didn't take the job?"

She doesn't answer for a moment and I wonder if she's thinking up a lie. "I needed the money," she finally says. "So I took the job. But I only lasted a week."

I'm not surprised. From what I'd seen of Price he was fastidious. I doubt Kim could have met his standards.

"Why?" Vogel asks.

"I couldn't handle it. Having him around, in the house. Knowing about him and Ella…"

"He was always in the house?"

She nods. "Always. It was like he didn't trust anyone to be there without him." That fits with what Shelley said. "He used to follow me around, pretend to have some reason to be in whatever room I was cleaning. It was weird. He freaked me out."

"So, you had a key? And you knew the security code?"

"Yeah," she shrugs. "But I'm sure he would have changed that after I quit. You're supposed to do that, right?"

So Kim once had a key and possibly the alarm code. She could have killed Stan Price. And, given the state she was in on the videotape, it's possible she wouldn't even remember doing it.

"What do you remember about Sunday night?" I ask her.

Kim looks blank. "I don't even know what today is," she admits. "When was Sunday?"

"The night you were arrested in downtown Niagara Falls."

Kim just sits there looking bewildered as Rachel sets the mug of tea in front of her. It doesn't seem likely she'll remember anything.

There's a sound of footsteps running down the stairs and Jade bursts into the room. She stops dead when she sees us and she backs up, trying to hide behind the door. I see her lip quiver when she recognizes me. She must think I'm here to take her away into care again.

"It's okay, Jade," I say quickly. "We're just here to talk with your mother and Rachel." Rachel goes over and takes Jade by the hand.

"Why don't we go outside and play on the swing," she says. "Let them have their boring talk." Jade looks over her shoulder as she allows herself to be led out, but Kim doesn't even turn her head.

I can't think of anything I can ask Kim so we sit in silence until Rachel comes back in.

"I have something for you," Kim finally says, pushing back her chair and standing. She heads upstairs, followed by Rachel, leaving us alone in the kitchen. I give Vogel a look and a moment later he follows behind them, as a precaution.

The kitchen is a little tidier now than the day I found Eleanor dead. I suspect that's Rachel's doing. I pick up the dirty dishes and mugs from the table and stack them in the sink, to give myself something to do until Kim returns. Out the window I see Jade climbing up onto the swing and pushing herself off. She's swinging back and forth, back and forth, her feet dragging along the dusty ground.

It's nothing short of a miracle that she's back home already. Rachel must have pulled some strings with social services to have that done. As a member of the Womyn Collective she's made a lot of contacts and good friends in the system who'd help her out if she asked.

I watch Jade on the swing and for a moment I'm overcome with emotion. This little girl lived alone for two days in this falling down house, living on dry cereal. All by herself she managed to get herself dressed in the morning. She went down the driveway at the right time and got onto the school bus when it came each day. Then she came back home, hoping to find her mother there, maybe even imagining she'd find her grandmother alive again. She even tried to milk the goats. Jade knew how important it was to do that every day. But she couldn't manage it. She was just a five-year old child, alone in a house with a dead grandmother, a living corpse of a grandfather and a missing mother.

I push open the screen door and go over to her. "Would you like a push?"

She nods and I take hold of the chains and start her swinging higher. Her long hair flies out behind her as she turns her face to the sun, her eyes closed. Poor kid; I'll push her until she asks me to stop.

After a long time she's had enough. "Can I have some more ice cream?" She's a clever girl. Jade's flagged me as an easy touch.

"Sure, let's go inside and I'll get you some. With chocolate sauce?" Jade smiles and takes my hand. We walk together up the wooden steps into the house.

"Did you tell anyone about your grandmother?" I ask her gently. I don't want to upset her, but I need to know.

"I told the bus driver. And my teacher," she whispers. My blood starts to boil and I feel like sticking my head into the freezer to cool down. I quickly scoop Jade some ice cream and I'm squeezing on some chocolate sauce when Kim comes back into the kitchen, holding out an envelope to me.

"What is this?"

"It's from that night." Kim slumps onto one of the kitchen chairs, her head in her hands.

"From the concert?" I open the envelope and pull out a yellowed, Polaroid picture. It's cracked and yellowed with age, but the image is still clear. It shows Kim and Ella in the foreground, arms around one another, laughing at something. Maybe a joke the photographer told, or because they are young and happy and beautiful and high. It looks like it was taken in a hotel suite. There are people around them, dancing and smiling, and in the background I can see Stan Price and Joe Rossi sprawled out on what looks like a bed, each flanked by a pair of young women.

The outfits the girls are wearing are the same ones in the photos Hilson took. That proves this snap was taken the same night, the night Ella disappeared. My heart starts to race with excitement.

Rachel comes in, followed by Vogel. I see there are two suitcases packed at her feet.

"Going somewhere?"

"They're both coming with me back to Womyn," Rachel says. Her jaw is set and I can see it's not negotiable. "It's either that or me moving in here, and I don't like goats. Anyway, I need my loom." I don't bother to point out the goats are already gone.

"I need to look after my collateral," she says with a laugh. I know she's trying to make a joke of it, but wonder if there's any truth to it. Is Kim a flight risk? Looking at her now, hunched over and miserable, I can't see it. She looks like she's been dragged out of a well, her spirit completely broken.

"Seems like a good idea." I can't see how Kim being here alone would ever work out. Not in her condition. And Jade will be much better off at the shelter than in care—which is where she'll end up if Kim goes off the deep end again.

"Jade," Rachel says, giving me a look. "Why don't you go upstairs with your mother and make sure you've got everything you need, okay?"

The little girl narrows her eyes. "Need for what?"

"We're going to stay with Rachel for a while," Kim manages to say. She reaches out and strokes Jade's hair. "She lives on a big farm, where they grow flowers." Jade considers that for a moment, then nods and takes her mother's hand. Vogel sighs and follows them up.

Rachel sits across from me. "We've been talking, Kim and I," she shakes her head. "There's a lot to catch up on. Too many years."

"After it happened…after Ella disappeared. I didn't handle it very well."

"You were distraught."

"I blamed Kim for what happened. It wasn't fair."

"No."

"Everyone thought that Ella had run off with the band, that she was a groupie. Kim bore the blame, and the shame, of what happened because she stayed behind.

"I heard all the rumours. She was *the slut*, the *druggie*, the town bike. Then when she ended up working at the strip clubs, well, that just proved them all right, didn't it? Funny how the men who go to those clubs never get shamed. Kim was the outcast. It's no wonder she ran away to Vancouver.

"We both lost Ella that night. I should have been there for her, and I let her down. But I'm here now."

"Rachel," I begin carefully. "It's great that you are helping Kim and Jade. But I've got to tell you, this doesn't look good for Kim."

"What doesn't?"

"We've got footage on Price's security camera of Kim at the house the night he was killed…"

"But not inside," she interrupts.

"No," I admit. "But…"

"If she didn't go inside," Rachel interrupts again. "How could she have done anything?"

I can't believe she doesn't get it. I take a deep breath. "It doesn't look good. Kim says she had a key and she may even have known the alarm code." Rachel waves it off. "Not to mention she can't explain why she was even there that night."

"Well of course not! She was high as a kite."

"For that matter," I say. "Your bailing Kim out—especially given the fact that we also have footage of your being at Price's front gate—looks suspicious too." Rachel's lip twists in irritation, but she's listening. "Also," I continue, exasperated. "You're still in question yourself! For all we know you and Kim were in it together."

Rachel bursts out laughing. "That's ridiculous! I explained about why I was there. It's nothing. And as for bailing Kim out, can't I help someone in need? Is that against the law?"

I sigh. "Rachel. Think about it. You and Kim, your history, the connection to Stan Price—both when Ella first disappeared, his paternity, and now his murder. You can't just shrug it off. I know we can't."

Jade comes in with a backpack over her shoulders, with several stuffed toys peeking out the top.

"All set?" Rachel asks in a bright voice, my comments forgotten. She jumps to her feet and picks up the suitcases. "Then let's go!" She hustles them out to her car and piles the cases into the trunk, laughing and chattering the entire time.

"Don't forget to lock up," she shouts as she reverses the car and heads down the gravel driveway.

Vogel and I do as we're told, then head back to the station.

"I'm starting to have a bad feeling about this," I say on the drive. "How would Kim, in the state she was in, have managed to get in the house and kill Price? I doubt she could have even remembered the alarm code."

"Maybe she just knocked on the door…" I have to admit that idea never occurred to me. "Anyway, maybe she wasn't really high. She could have been faking it, for the camera."

"Why would she do that? It makes no sense."

"To set up a timeline. She realizes we have her on camera near the time of Price's murder, so she gets herself arrested. I can't think of a better alibi than being in jail."

"Okay…" I admit, running my hands over my face. This is exhausting and frustrating. "Seriously Vogel. You've met Kim. Does she seem like a criminal mastermind to you? She's a mess."

"Can't argue that. It's definitely not an act. Did you see the needle tracks on her arms?"

"And we still have no explanation how she got over to Niagara Falls. It's about 30 or 40 minute drive away and she doesn't even have a car."

"Maybe she had an accomplice?" I know who he's referring to. "Just playing devil's advocate here," Vogel continues. "Rachel did have good motive to kill Price: she was angry about her daughter's death, and about the way he denied her all her life. Maybe when Ella's body was finally identified, after all these years, she just snapped. Figured he deserved to die."

"And what, she got Kim to do the dirty work for her?"

"Why not? It's certainly worth considering!"

"No way. Not even remotely possible."

"Gauthier. You aren't being objective. You've already made up your mind about Rachel Weaver and Kim Parsons, and you aren't even considering the evidence."

"Of course I am! That's ridiculous! There's no evidence."

"*No evidence?!* For god's sake Gauthier, we've got them both on videotape!"

I can't argue with that, as much as I'd like to. "You're only looking at it with regard to who else it could have been—and completely ignoring what it points to: that Rachel killed Price."

"That's because she didn't do it," I'm digging my heels in. "Joe Rossi did. He killed Price to shut him up about the royalties and to stop the lawsuit. You heard him on the phone."

"You're just angry about your cold case…"

"Ella Weaver." I'm irritated that he doesn't know her name and my blood starts to boil. "Has it even occurred to you that maybe there's no connection between Ella and Price's murders? Did you ever even consider that?"

Vogel glares at me. "Why are you so hell bent on it being Joe Rossi? Obviously you want to blame Rossi—and maybe he's even responsible, I don't know…"

"*Maybe*?!?!"

"But you want to wrap it all up in a nice tidy package: Rossi killed Ella Weaver, and Stan Price too, conveniently leaving the grieving mother out of it. Face it Gauthier: Rachel Weaver and Kim Price have more motive than Rossi to kill Price."

I have to admit there's logic to what he's saying. It would have been so painful to get past the fact that Price ignored her all those years, despite what she'd told us. Especially if she saw him in town a lot—at the market or the bank, wherever. Each time it would be like a slap in the face. Who knows what that would make a person do?

Vogel gets out of the car, as he slams the door.

"It's like you're on a personal vendetta against Rossi. You aren't even listening to alternatives." I shrug off his words, but I know it's true, and I don't care. I want Joe Rossi to pay for what he did to Ella and Kim. And while he's at it he can pay for what happened to my mother.

TWENTY SEVEN

AFTER I LEAVE Vogel at the station I'm late for my appointment with Joe Rossi, but still need to make a quick stop on my way. I leave the patrol car in front of Valley View Elementary School and ask for directions to Jade's classroom. I need to speak with her teacher, now.

The school bell rings as I'm heading down the hall and the students rush out of their classrooms. I feel like I'm swimming upstream in a flood of very short people. I find Ms. Jacobs alone, tidying her classroom and I introduce myself.

"Police?" The flicker of excitement in her eyes is off-putting.

"I'd like to talk with you about Jade Parsons."

She looks surprised. "She's not been in school for the past few days," she says.

"I know." I take a deep breath and try to stay calm. "Her mother was missing."

"I'm not surprised." She gives me a sly smile. "She's in trouble? Again?" I want to wipe that smirk right off her face.

"I try to stay calm. "Were you aware there might be an issue with Jade, at her home?"

"Issue?" she scoffs. "There's always an *issue* at that home."

"Really?" I raise my eyebrows. "What kind?"

She sighs heavily. "Jade's mother, of course, I know her from school, years ago. That poor child." The sanctimonious cow, pretending to care about Jade.

"Her grandmother seemed to be doing a fine job of providing a stable home for the child."

Eye roll. "Well Eleanor had no choice, did she?"

I count to ten and try to control my temper. It wouldn't be a good idea for me to punch Ms. Jacobs, as much as I want to.

"Before she stopped coming to school, did Jade speak to you at all about what had happened at home?"

She shrugs, disinterested. "Not really." I'm not surprised. This woman hardly feels like the sort of person any child would feel comfortable confiding in. "She wasn't dressed properly, but that's not unusual. She often came in with her hair uncombed, not washed."

"What do you mean by *not properly*?"

"She wore her pyjamas. To school. For *two days*." And that never raised a red flag to her teacher. You'd think neglect would be the first thing that came to mind.

"And you didn't think to ask about it?

She rolls her eyes, then leans forward conspiratorially. "She told me *My Nana is dead*. Can you imagine such a thing? I made a note to bring it up at the next parent-teacher night."

"And you didn't think to look into it?"

Suddenly Ms. Jacobs feels something is wrong. She realizes I'm not smiling, I'm not amused by her story. "Look into it? Why would I?"

"Jade's grandmother died last Tuesday."

The teacher slumps down into one of the small student chairs. I think it might crumble under her weight. "Oh."

"I found her, curled up on her grandmother's lap. Her dead grandmother's lap." I see Ms. Jacobs go pale, which is very satisfying. "It was clear Jade had been sleeping in the bed, next to her body.

"Jade was alone in that house for two nights before she even told you about it. Two nights this little girl slept with the corpse of her dead grandmother. She'd been living on dry cereal because she couldn't manage to open the new carton of milk."

Ms. Jacob's lip is quivering, but I don't care. I'm not going to stop until she's reduced a puddle of tears on the floor. The judgmental, heartless cow doesn't deserve any pity.

"I didn't know," she whispers. "I thought she was telling stories, like she always did."

"She even tried to feed and milk the goats, but wasn't able to do it on her own. She's a five-year old child. And she was alone. She came to you for help and you did nothing."

"What are you going to do…about this?" She's not interested in Jade's welfare. She's only worried that I'll report her to the school board.

I turn and leave without replying.

Once I'm back in the safety of my car I can't hold back the tears any longer and they stream down my cheeks. I'm so angry, so frustrated, and so full of rage that I pound the steering wheel until I hurt my hand, then I hit it a few more times just to make sure. I know I'm not just angry about Jade, and about Kim, and how the system isn't set up to help anyone. I'm angry for myself. And I'm heartbroken.

I breathe deeply, in and out on a count of ten, like my therapist coached me to do. Then I slip one of my rescue Ativan tablets under my tongue to help control my overwhelming feelings of panic before they sweep me away.

It doesn't take a genius to know why this case is getting to me. The echoes of my own childhood are so loud it's hard for me to think objectively about Jade and Kim's situation. The memories surface of the times I went to school on an empty stomach, with my hair not brushed, and of the nights I spent alone in the house because my mother had to work at the club. She couldn't afford a babysitter and there was no way she'd leave me with my druggie uncles. I went to school in my pyjamas too, when I didn't have anything else that was clean. I didn't know it was wrong, but I sure learned. I also learned how much worse things could get when my stepfather moved in with us.

TWENTY EIGHT

I'M STILL FURIOUS by the time I arrive at Joe Rossi's office, but I take a deep breath and try to arrange my face into a pleasant expression. The front window has been boarded over with a sheet of plywood, after Kim's vandalism. She'll have to pay restitution and damages…hopefully Rossi won't press for more.

As I walk up the sidewalk the front door is flung open and Angelo Rossi comes out. He's waving his arms and shouting in Italian and from his tone it's clear he's cursing someone out. I watch in stunned silence as he pushes past me, climbs into his shiny red sports car and roars away. When I turn back to the door, I see Joe Rossi is standing there, watching his nephew drive off. Clearly he's the one Angelo was shouting at.

"My nephew," Rossi begins then falters, at a loss for words. "A spoiled brat who'll never amount to anything. A disappointment to the family." He suddenly realizes that's way too much information for him to be sharing with me and he abruptly stops talking.

"Detective Gauthier," he says. "Please, come inside."

From the way the receptionist averts her eyes I can tell there's been a big blow up. The air is still thick with tension, but Rossi manages to give me a big smile.

I briefly explain the reason for my visit, aware that he's barely listening. His mind is clearly elsewhere and I can't help wonder what the fight with Angelo was about.

I open my folder and pull out the faded Polaroid photo Kim gave me.

"Do you recognize anyone in this photo, Mr. Rossi?" I hand it to him and he glances at it, then shakes his head. "Please, take a closer look."

Barely concealing his irritation, Rossi holds the photo closer and studies it. I can see the exact moment he recognizes the people in it; it's clearly written across his face. It's a photo I selected carefully, making a point of finding one that would shake him up the most. It shows Stan Price and Joe Rossi, both almost unrecognizable. They are both bone thin, have long hair and are wearing bell bottomed blue jeans. Several beautiful young women are in the background. One of them is Ella Weaver.

"Wow," he whispers after a moment. "This takes me back." He hands the photo back to me. "How old is that anyway?"

"It was taken thirty years ago. The night Ella Weaver disappeared."

"Who?'"

I point to Ella in the photo. "She went to the last Running Deep concert at the Buffalo Auditorium and was never seen again. You might have read about it in the papers at the time."

"And you're asking me about this now?" He runs his hands through his hair. "I don't remember anything about those days."

"That's you in the photo, isn't it? With Stan Price and the girls?" He nods. "You're telling me you don't remember anything?"

He laughs. "It was a long time ago. I was young! A real party guy, me. Drinking, drugs, you name it. Partying with the bands when they came to town." The smile falls from his face when he realizes he's talking to a police detective. "It was different times, you understand."

Different times. I think of the countless young women he and his father took advantage of. Women like my mother, like Ella and Kim. They mean nothing to him; nothing he did during that time mattered, no price needed to be paid. *Different times.*

"I get it. And I'm not interested. That was your job? Partying with the bands? Or was it just a perk because your father was the promoter?" I'm trying not to sound snide, but I can just picture Rossi Jr., riding on his powerful father's coattails and hanging out with all the famous bands of the time.

"No, I had a job to do." He sounds defensive. "My role was to facilitate things, smooth things over for the band, enforce the riders, make sure they had what they needed to be comfortable." I can imagine what that might mean: Drugs, girls, booze.

He's holding the photo for a moment, staring at it and I hope it means that something's coming back to him. "You know, this picture could have been taken with one of those Kodak Instant cameras. We did a contra deal with the company to help promote the product launch. Kodak's headquarters was just an hour away in Rochester, and the sales guys always brought cameras to show off. They gave us a bunch to give away on air too, on the radio stations. All part of the contra and concert promotion."

"And that was all legal? Between the concerts and the radio and the contra…the boundaries feel a bit…soft."

"Of course it was legal."

"Funny…I read that your father got into some kind of trouble, with a payola scandal. Isn't that why he had to sell his radio stations?"

"No, not at all," Rossi gives me a practised smile. "I appreciate the timing of it all looks questionable, but my father chose to sell. The market forces at the time, all the media conglomeration, it demanded a change of corporate direction. He needed to pivot."

"Pivot," I echo. That sure sounds like a lot of corporate jargon to me, but I'm not going to get into it with Rossi.

"What can you tell me about the dispute you were having with Stan Price?"

Rossi looks uncomfortable. "What dispute?"

Just once I'd like to not have this dance where someone plays dumb and hopes somehow I'll just go away. Seriously, if I'm asking the question, there's a reason for it. I'm not just making this stuff up. I don't say anything, but just stare at Rossi until he breaks.

"Okay, it was nothing. Just an innocent mistake," he says. "It was some bad reporting that surfaced before my father died and we were in the process of straightening it all out. Now I'm having a hard time getting all the records and Price wasn't a patient man. Kept pushing and calling and shouting at me, like that'll speed things up." He laughs. "I think he just misses the sound of his own voice, at full volume."

"Bad reporting of what, exactly?"

"Royalties. For Running Deep's music."

"Why would your father have anything to do with that?"

"He owned a share of the music rights," Rossi explains. "Stan Price did a deal with my father, in the very early days of the band. My father fronted him some cash to record their demos, and he hooked them up with a record company, and he promoted their music."

"And for that he got a percentage of the music royalties?"

"Yes," Rossi nods. "And to be clear—my father deserved every penny of it. He helped Stan Price get very rich."

"Okay…so then what was Stan Price looking for?"

"These musicians," Rossi shakes his head. "They don't understand business. They don't get how the money flows in the industry. They can't even do basic percentages. Unrealistic expectations."

"So he thought your father owed him money?" Rossi nods. "And he was going after your father, legally? Suing him?" Rossi is still nodding, and rolling his eyes at the absurdity of it all.

"And then Price conveniently…died?"

Rossi stops nodding. "Now wait a minute. There's no way my father had anything to do with that!"

"Clearly not," I say. "He died a week before Mr. Price. But, having said that, I assume Price could have still been suing your family business. We heard him arguing on the phone a few days before he died. I believe it was with you Mr. Rossi."

Rossi leans back in his chair, red faced and exasperated. "I can explain…"

I hold up my hand to forestall him. "I'm just saying Mr. Rossi. It doesn't look good."

"I get it," he agrees after a moment. "But truthfully, the music royalties for Running Deep aren't worth much anymore, apart from that charity single that still gets a bit of airplay. Okay, maybe some of their songs have been covered by other bands, so there are composition rights still trickling in. But it doesn't add up to much." Something about what he's saying doesn't sound right, doesn't ring true. Something Vogel had said, about movies? Or maybe a video game? But I can't remember what it was.

"And Price didn't believe you?" Rossi shakes his head.

There's a knock on his office door and the receptionist peers in. She points at her watch, indicating he needs to be somewhere, or someone's waiting for him. I take my cue from Rossi, who waves her off.

"So, Mr. Rossi, back to this picture." I push the photo across his desk so he can get a better look. "What can you tell me about these cameras that took these kinds of instant pictures. The sales guys you spoke of demonstrated them at the concerts, and at the after parties, taking pictures of the guests?"

"Yes. Stan used one on stage—as promo, take a photo, then toss the pictures into audience. Hype it up, you know, get people to use them. I guess these days you'd call them influencers."

"You wouldn't have any idea who might have taken this particular picture?"

"No way. Could have been anyone. Whoever was there was having a go. Why are you so interested in this party?"

"I'm just trying to find out what happened to this girl."

"There were always lots of girls there."

"Professionals?"

"No need for anything like that. They were lined up at the doors after the concerts, waiting to meet the bands."

"Groupies?"

"Fans."

"This girl, Ella Weaver and her friend were only fifteen at the time."

Rossi shakes his head. "We never checked ID. What can I tell you? It was different times." He laughs and looks to mean for understanding, like I'm supposed to give him a pass for having sex with a minor because it happened in *different times*. He realizes I'm not amused and wipes the smile from his face and tries to look concerned.

"Is there any connection to Price?" he asks earnestly. "I mean… with what's happened to him…" I can't figure out why he's asking. Is he just playing dumb?

"She was his daughter." Rossi suddenly goes pale and I leave him sweating.

I'm not surprised he denies knowing her; he may honestly have forgotten. It was a long time ago and likely as not he'd ushered a parade of young women through hundreds of after parties during that time. But something about his face when I said Ella was Price's daughter tells me he remembered something. I feel it in my gut. Maybe that night she told him the truth about Stan Price being her father. And maybe he wanted to make sure that information never came to light, so he covered it up, by drugging and killing her.

I just have to prove it.

The minute I drop my bag at my desk, DS Agu calls me into his office.

"Gauthier!" he says, his deep voice rumbling across the open concept area. "I need to speak with you, now. Please."

It's the *please* that scares me most. I know I'm in for it now, and I'm thinking fast to try and get in front of the bollocking, but I come up empty.

When he tells me to close the door I know it's bad. Then I notice Vogel sitting at the desk and I start to see what's happening. Vogel has sold me out. Tattled to the teacher.

"Gauthier," Agu begins with a heavy sigh. He's invited me to sit down, which is better than I expected. I sit as far as I can from Vogel and don't acknowledge his presence. I intend to pretend he's not in the room. "You're killing me with this one," he says.

"Sir?"

"Rachel Weaver and Kim Parsons." He glares at me across the desk.

"I've read over your reports." Agu waves a file folder at me. "Such as they are."

"Sir?"

"You can't deny evidence."

"I'm not..."

"Here's what I want to know," Agu interrupts me. "And what I'm not getting. Why are neither Kim Parsons nor Rachel Weaver your main suspects? Why are you investigating Joe Rossi?"

I shoot a death glare at Vogel. "Sir, I believe Rossi has a connection to the cold case. To Ella Weaver's death."

"Joe Rossi?" Agu is exasperated. "Based on what evidence? Where's the motive? Gauthier, why are you not focussing on Stan

Price's murder?" He waves me off. I knew it was coming but I'm still disappointed. The investigation into Ella's death is less important.

I take a deep breath. "Sir, the evidence is indicating the two crimes are related."

Agu rolls his eyes.

"Sir," I'm begging him. "Please hear me out. I have an idea." I look to Vogel for support and he avoids meeting my eye.

"I have photographs, incriminating ones showing Rossi and Price at after parties with underage girls—including Ella Weaver. There was no shortage of underage girls, drugs at those parties—all of them facilitated by Joe Rossi. He's covering it up—has been for decades."

Agu leans back in his chair, his eyes wary. I keep pushing. "Joe Rossi is about to run for office. He doesn't need any scandal that could emerge once all of this about his past gets out. He needed it to go away."

"And you think a man of his standing in the community would kill?" Agu looks angry. "I'm not buying it. Nobody cares about thirty year old scandals."

"Okay then, what about a present day motive? I've met with his lawyer Ed Jorgenson. Price was about to sue Rossi over stolen music royalties, amounting to 300K. What do you think he'd do to make that go away?"

Agu looks irritated, but I keep pressing. "Stan Price was killed to keep the truth from coming out about the past, to stop the publication of his memoir and to prevent him suing for the missing royalties."

My heart sinks as I realize Agu doesn't believe me. Or he's not interested. It's clear he's no longer listening.

"Let's talk about a more realistic motive," Agu says. He holds up one of his huge hands and starts to count off on his fingers. "One: I understand you have both Rachel Weaver and Kim Parsons on videotape at Price's house the day he was killed. Neither has an explanation. Two: that Kim Price was found—by yourself—covered in blood and without potentially incriminating shoes. Three: the clothes she was wearing when she was arrested were laundered by Rachel Weaver before you and DC Vogel could retrieve them and log them as evidence. Four: they both obviously have a strong connection in Ella Weaver, potentially strong enough to tie them as accomplices in Stan Price's murder."

I have to admit it looks bad. And Agu and Vogel don't even know that Rachel's son is one of the bank robbers. And I have no intention of telling them.

"Parsons doesn't remember…"

"Or she's lying, and Weaver is covering for her," Agu interrupts, with a glance at Vogel. Clearly he's expecting him to chime in.

After a moment, Vogel does, reluctantly. "C'mon Gauthier," he says. "Weaver went from keeping her connection to Price a secret—even from her daughter. Then, eventually, she admits she confronted him and he humiliated her in the damn street! She must have hated him."

"Weaver's shifting her story every time some evidence comes to light," Vogel continues. "She hated Stan Price and she had motive to kill him. We've got her on videotape, and we've got Kim Parsons too."

"What about motive, Sir?" I finally get a word in. I'm addressing my comments to Agu and doing my best to ignore Vogel. "Neither of them have a reasonable one."

"Oh really?" Vogel argues. "How about this for motive? Finding Ella's remains brought it all back to Rachel. She had to admit Ella had died that night…and it had to be Price's fault. She knew Ella went to the concert, wanting to speak to him. That's all she knows for sure, but it's enough. She wants to avenge Ella—and herself, for all the years of pain, guilt and shame she's endured."

"*Vengeance* is the motive? All these years later? That's pretty lame…"

Agu cuts me off, ignoring what I just said. "It's my understanding you are friends with Rachel Weaver, which puts you in a conflict of interest—something you should have told me about as soon as I assigned you the cold case."

"I don't have a personal relationship…" He holds up his hand and I stop talking.

"I'm choosing to believe you—as otherwise I'd be required to remove you from the case." He gives me a pointed look over his glasses. "Nevertheless, I don't think you're looking at this objectively Gauthier," Agu continues. "This is how it looks to me: Weaver snapped when we found her daughter's remains and she wanted Price dead. She and Kim did it together, or she put Kim Parsons up to it, or she's setting Parsons up to take the fall. One of those scenarios fits Gauthier…make it work. Stop making things more complicated than they need to be. Close the damn case."

He tosses the folder across his desk. I'm dismissed.

Vogel comes out of the office close behind me, keeping a careful distance. He must be able to feel the rage radiating off me. I could punch him for betraying me to DS Agu, but I know I can't. I restrain myself and take some deep breaths as I pick up my bag and head for the exit.

"Lucy," Vogel calls after me. "Can we talk?"

I keep walking. "I think you've said enough Vogel."

"C'mon Gauthier! Stop pushing people away. You need all the friends you can get."

"I've got you Vogel. What other friends do I need?"

TWENTY NINE

Fear not, for I have redeemed you;
I have called you by name, you are mine.
When you pass through the waters, I will be with you;
and through the rivers, they shall not overwhelm you;
when you walk through fire you shall not be burned,
and the flame shall not set you ablaze.

I WAKE UP in the dark, my heart pounding in fear then I see a blue light and realize I've fallen asleep in front of the television. A late night evangelical minister is onscreen, stalking his stage preaching the usual fire and brimstone. This verse is Isaiah 43:2, apparently. I press the remote and the room is filled with darkness and silence.

Maja's working an overnight in Emergency, so I've had dinner alone and drank too much wine while I scrolled blindly through the channels looking for something to distract me. I realize I'll need to get used to nights like this, once Maja goes away and my heart starts to race at the prospect of being alone, again.

I drag myself up to bed but know there's no chance I'll fall back to sleep. I'm sleeping less every night lately, spending night after restless night lying next to Maja, who's always sleeping peacefully. In the darkness I watch the hours tick by on the clock. And when she's not here I'm full of dread, fearing what my life will be like without her, again. I don't want to go back to that time, to how things were when we were apart, but there's nothing I can do to stop her.

That Melnyk girl and her boyfriend McAlpine. A bad lot.

Hearing those names brings back how my whole life was destroyed and I'm struggling to keep from falling into the bottomless well of rage and fear my thoughts are pushing me toward. I've spent years being afraid, decades being angry. I can't sleep, can't even think straight some days, and it's got to end, somehow.

Seeing the photographs of my mother, even just hearing her name spoken, has opened the door to a dark place, one I've avoided visiting for years. And the way it keeps coming up, again and again, the connection between my mother and Kim, my mother and Rossi, and possibly even Stan Price makes it unavoidable. Unless it's my fault; unless I'm the one making the connection when the truth is that it's only circumstantial. My therapist would probably call it projection.

But I do know my mother wasn't like Ella or Kim. She may have partied with Rossi's bands, she may have even been paid for it, but so did possibly hundreds of young women. And it's getting to me and I can't shake it off.

Fucking Rossi. I blame him for all of it and I know he's responsible. There was no mistaking the expression on his face when I told him Ella was Price's daughter. He was horrified that the truth had finally caught up with him.

I make him the focus of my anger—and my anxiety-fuelled cortisol and adrenal. Unlike my stepfather, or even Renato Rossi— Joe Rossi is alive and he's someone I can make pay for what he's done. Make him atone for his sins, pay for his crimes. I know he's behind it. He caused all of this—he somehow disappeared Ella and he ruined Kim's life. He's the one who created the wreck of a woman living out at the goat farm.

I know Joe Rossi was just some kind of glorified gofer for his father. Even though he now says he was a music promoter, I'm sure all he did was facilitate the parties for the bands, provide drugs and girls, and do whatever else his father wanted him to. I wonder if he also cleaned up when things went wrong? Was that part of his job description?

We know it was Louis Zappa who buried the bodies in the bog, there's no question about that. I'll never forget it, since I almost lost my life finding it out. And it isn't difficult to figure out the connection between Zappa and Rossi. One was a lowlife retired mob enforcer, the other the scion of a mob family but I'm sure their paths crossed often enough, through Renato Rossi's connections, not that I can prove it.

If Zappa buried Ella in the bog, then how did Kim end up back on the beach in Canada, two days after the Running Deep concert? Maybe Zappa had a conscience after all and he just left her there when he took Ella's body back to be buried. But I know Zappa had no conscience, so I'm guessing he wasn't paid enough to kill her or to dispose of her body too, so he just left her. Lucky Kim.

I think about Joe Rossi. What do I know about him, and about his family? He's now part of the Rossi real estate team and he's got political ambitions. But he is his father's son, with all that entails. Sure the Rossi family may appear to have cleaned up their act—at least on the surface—but Renato Rossi was notorious back in the old days. He was heavily invested in strip clubs, restaurants and laundromats, all great ways to launder money for the mob. Just like his concert promotion and ticket sales.

How did it all work? How did the money flow? Back in the 70's and even later, concert tickets would have been purchased in cash. There was no digital way to pay—no debit, no online sales.

Maybe some credit cards, but probably not many used by Running Deep's audience. All cash. And cash is easy to launder and to hide and it's impossible to trace.

If Rossi's radio stations in Niagara Falls and Buffalo gave a band enough airplay, then the concert venue would sell out, as would sales of t-shirts and souvenirs. Since Rossi had shares in the venue with his friends—his fingers were in every pie—it was win/win.

I don't know how Stan Price would ever have found proof of that skimming, but there's plenty of motive to shut him up over the missing royalties. Price wasn't going to let the issue go, even though he didn't need to money. Maybe someone needed to shut Price up, to stop him. There's no question that if Price's story got out it wouldn't help Rossi's political career.

Or, maybe this isn't all about money after all. Maybe it's just about secrets, and the need to keep the past buried. Whatever was in Stan Price's memoir might be worth killing him to keep quiet. But the one thing I'm sure has nothing to do with Price's murder is his daughter's death. Ella was long forgotten, until we dug up her remains. Nobody cares, except Rachel.

We know Rossi didn't kill Price. His alibi for Sunday night checked out. He was at a dinner, with Ed Jorgenson and some investors at the golf club. There are plenty of witnesses, and not just cronies who might lie for him as a quid pro quo. Several staff members said they'd seen him at the club and they don't owe him anything—not even respect, based on their attitude toward him when they were interviewed. Nobody we spoke to had a nice word to say about Joe Rossi, but they all agreed he was there, he'd had too much to drink, left his car at the club and took a cab home. As far as Stan Price's murder goes, Rossi is in the clear.

In any case I can't quite see Joe Rossi as the kind of guy who'd get his hands dirty by killing Stan Price himself. But he wouldn't hesitate to have someone else do it for him—like he had Zappa take care of Ella all those years ago. Someone he could trust. Someone in the family. Maybe someone like his nephew Angelo?

Maybe that argument I witnessed between them was staged, to give me the impression they didn't get along, so I wouldn't make the connection. Angelo Rossi was just the sort of guy to *take care of things* —just like his grandfather would have done.

I need to get Rossi or I'll never sleep again. He needs to pay for the death of Ella, and for what happened to Kim—that's his fault. And I'll bet he's behind Stan Price's death too, in some way.

Or am I ignoring the truth about Rachel? Overlooking the obvious to make sure he takes the blame? Maybe. Agu doesn't believe me. Vogel has let me down. I'm alone.

I could take care of Rossi myself. I could get away with it; I'm a cop, I know how things work. I know how easy it can be to do. But killing Rossi won't close the book on Ella Weaver. He needs to be charged and convicted, publicly, for any hope of closure for Rachel and Kim. But the photos of him with Ella and Kim aren't enough. I need proof that Rossi is responsible for Ella's death, and the only way to do that is to walk into the fire.

THIRTY

THERE'S ONLY ONE person I know who can help me with this; only one person who knows my past, who knows what I've been through, and where the bodies are buried. Doreen.

I find her in the garden at the retirement home and the expression on her face says she knows why I'm here.

"Not just a social call," she says when I hand her a coffee. "No donut?"

"Sorry. They were out of cinnamon buns. I knew nothing else would do."

She smirks and lights a cigarette. We sit in companionable silence for a few minutes, drinking our coffees and looking out over the rooftop garden of the retirement home.

"I need to get to Rossi," I finally say. Doreen doesn't move but I can feel her tense.

"It's not going to help Ella Weaver," she says, but I know that's not who we're really talking about.

"Rossi supplied those after parties with drugs. He ran girls, out of his father's clubs." I show her the photo of my mother, partying with Rossi and Price. "Including my mother."

Doreen lights another cigarette and shakes her head. "Going after the Rossi family isn't a good idea Lucy."

"Joe Rossi's responsible and he needs to pay."

"Let sleeping dogs lie. It won't bring her back." Ella and my mother, it's all blurring together. I'm so tired.

"How do you know? Maybe it will, in some way. At least she'll get some kind of justice for the shit she had to go through in life." Doreen reaches for my hand and squeezes.

"Rossi wasn't responsible for what happened to her, not in the end. You know that."

I ignore her. "I want Rossi hurt. I want him dead."

"So this isn't about Ella Weaver anymore."

"Not for me. I feel like everything in my life is coming down to this. To what happened to my mother. And now I've got a chance to do something about it, to make somebody pay."

"Do you think Joe Rossi is responsible for what happened to your mother?"

"He ran the parties. I've seen the pictures."

Doreen snorts in disbelief. "His father Renato—now that's a man with a debt to pay. But he's already dead. And whatever he did to your mother and god knows who else you can't lay on his son."

"Can't I? It's a family business. They hand it down, from father to son, all these criminals and monsters…just keeping it going. So maybe I missed having Renato pay. But seems to me that Joe's good for the debt."

"That's not how justice works."

"Who says?"

Doreen looks frightened. "Lucy…be careful. He's powerful and connected. He's carrying a lot of people's secrets, and his father's as well. It's not in anybody's interest to lift those rocks and see what's crawling around underneath. They'll kill you as soon as look at you."

"Maybe I need to pay the price, to set things right."

"And exactly how is exposing your underbelly to these gangsters, making yourself vulnerable—how is that going to repay karma or whatever you think you're doing? It's just stupid. And you're not stupid, Lucy."

"I never paid for what I did." In the deepest, darkest part of my heart I know that I got off lightly for what happened with Ray, when I was a child.

"*Never paid?* You're still paying every damn day! You think you got off easy? You're nuts."

There's no point in arguing. I'm too tired and nothing Doreen thinks or says will change what I know I need to do.

"So who do I go after?" I ask after she's finished her cigarette. "Vice isn't my world. I know a few guys in that Division, but…"

"You want my advice? I already gave it to you: Let it go, Lucy. But, since you won't listen to that, you need to follow the money. That's all these guys care about: power and money."

"They've got plenty of both. Joe Rossi acts like he's a legitimate businessman now—just like his father tried to do."

"All these guys need to look clean," Doreen says. "They don't want whatever skeletons they've got in closets to get out. Especially when they're running for office and cozying up to government."

"So what? I threaten that clean image somehow and Rossi's suddenly no longer protected?"

Doreen shrugs. "Renato Rossi is dead. There's probably a lot going on right now in the *family*—who's taking over, who's taking control…" She thinks for a moment. "And his son Joe's vulnerable now. He's going to have to make sure his past stays buried if he's going to take the reigns from his father. His enemies would love to throw him to the dogs, if it opens the way for them to take over."

"There was a big fight after Renato Rossi's funeral. It was about his Will."

Doreen is intrigued. "Renato Rossi supposedly changed his Will to favour his grandson Angelo—at least according to his sister Rosa—a crazier bitch you'd never want to meet. She told me he thought his son Joe was weak. That he wasn't fit to take over the business."

"Left it all to his grandson? Is he ready?"

"Apparently Angelo was apple of Renato's eye. He's just like his grandfather."

"A sociopath? A criminal?"

"I'd say so, yes," I laugh. "Do you suppose these things are inherited? Passed down through the bloodline?"

Doreen chokes on her cigarette. "Let's hope not—for your sake, honey."

"I need to find out when the Will was changed." Could what Rosa said about *indiscretions* have something to do with the concert promotions? Or even what happened to Ella all those years ago? On the face of it, that doesn't seem like a big enough problem to change Renato Rossi's mind.

"Hate to say it, but one dead girl isn't even going to be a blip on his radar. Whatever happened would have had to be bigger than that. It somehow would have had to cost Renato a lot of money to make it unforgiveable."

Doreen is right. It had to be bigger than the death of Ella to have Renato cut his son out of his Will. So what could it be? What made Renato Rossi suddenly get out of the concert promotion business? And why did he suddenly *pivot* and get out of the strip clubs and related interests? Until now I'd just assumed he'd done it because of the payola scandal…but maybe not. I bet he could have ridden it out. So what could it be? Who could have forced Renato Rossi's hand? Who had a big enough stick?

"I need a way in. I need a way to get to Rossi."

"You can't just walk into the fire Lucy. You'll get burned."

But maybe the fire won't hurt me. Maybe it'll purify me.

THIRTY ONE

DUDEK'S BEEN WORKING CID in District 2 for years. I'd bet he knows people in Vice or Guns and Gangs or whatever unit I need to talk to in order to get background on Rossi. He picks up on the first ring.

"Gauthier! What's up?"

"I need information," I get right to the point. "And you're the first one on my list."

"Okay…" he sounds wary. "I'm listening."

"Who's running business now between Buffalo and Niagara Falls?"

"Business? What kind, specifically?"

"Trafficking. Drugs, sex…Is it still Italians? Bikers?"

"Primarily. Todaro, Maggadino, Musitano, Violi," he laughs. "And the Chinese. And the Russians…" He interrupts himself. "Why are you asking?"

"I need to understand who'd be moving in and taking control of whatever Renato Rossi was involved in."

"Now that the old man's dead," Dudek says. "His son Joe, I suppose, though it would be buried a hundred layers deep, what with his legitimate enterprises and his political aspirations."

"Who would likely take over?" I ask. "Say if Joe Rossi weren't around."

Dudek laughs. "Rossi's going somewhere I don't know about?

"Just speaking hypothetically."

"Uh huh. Sure. Well, I guess that could be the NY *bratva*. "

"The Russians. Where could I find them?"

"Hypothetically?"

"Yes."

"I have no idea Gauthier. Honestly, I don't. Even if I don't like the sound of what you're asking me, I'm not lying to you."

"Any suggestions?"

"I guess you could start at the bottom and work your way up. If they're interested, they'll find you."

The bottom. I know how to find my way there.

THIRTY TWO

I'M IDLING OUTSIDE Aphrodite's. The car's defrost isn't working and the windshield keeps fogging up, so I've cracked the window. A cluster of smokers stand together outside the entrance and the aroma of cigarettes and weed fills the car. I've been sitting here since ten, waiting for business to pick up, and for the manager to show up.

Aphrodite's is a dump, but since so many strip clubs in the region have been shutting down it's the only game in town, unless you want to go to one of the upscale clubs in Niagara Falls. That makes it a busy dump, at least on weekend nights.

It's been around for decades, with a series of owners, at least on paper. For all we know it's just been passed around through a series of shell companies to keep the tax man guessing and the same family has owned it since it opened in the sixties. Crime *family*, that is.

Finally at almost midnight the manager pulls up in his Yukon Denali and parks in his reserved spot. Richie Cellini climbs out— shaved head, still strong as an ox even though he's pushing sixty, with a large diamond earring and a heavy gold chain around his neck. I know him by sight, both from my online research and from the five or six calls I attended during the time I was a police constable. There was no shortage of fights and of patrons being tossed out—and beaten up—by bouncers after inappropriate touching of the dancers. None of the patrons ever pressed charges against the club though, funny thing.

I give him a few minutes to settle in before I head inside. The first thing that hits me is the smell of stale beer and cheap cologne. Aphrodite's is the sort of place that attracts stag parties and frat parties, as well as solo men who come to drink beer and look at labia. I hate it here.

So many women, working in these shitty clubs, on a road to nowhere. Taking off their clothes and dancing for a hard living. Women like my mother, and Kim Parsons. Working for bikers and criminals like Richie Cellini.

If I had a dollar for every guy who told me that the women *chose this life* or they're *working their way through law school* I'd be rich. It's a lie. They fall into it because they can—they look good enough and they don't have the option to get another job. Maybe they have kids, or no skills, or worst of all— they've been trafficked and don't have a choice. Women from Montreal—enroute from Eastern Europe.

It happens all the time.

When I was in college, it was *cool* for groups of students to go to the strip clubs. Women went along, to show how chill they were, a way to show the guys we weren't *uptight*—as if being chill with women being exploited was a good thing.

So many people talking shit about how strippers are the somehow the epitome of female sexual empowerment. The only ones who've got power in a strip club are the mobsters and bikers who run them.

"I need to speak with Richie," I tell the bouncer, flashing him my badge. He looks unimpressed, but motions for me to step inside.

"Wait here," he says, before walking over to the bartender, who picks up the phone. It's the same guy who called me the day Kim Parsons was here, but he pretends he doesn't recognize me and I play along. A minute later he motions me over and points to a door at the end of the room.

"He's in there."

Richie is sitting at a heavy carved wooden desk, in front of a gilded mirror. There's a lot of gold and chrome everywhere and I can tell a lot of money has been spent, with no taste. Shame he didn't think to spend some cash on the club itself. One of his men sits in a corner, keeping an eye on a bank of monitors that show the club's interior: the stage, the bar and the front entrance.

"What can I do for you, detective?" Richie stands and gives me his best smile, and invites me to take a seat as he pours himself some cognac in a tumbler.

"Can I offer you a drink?"

"No, thank you. I'm on duty," I say, which is laughable. As if I'd ever drink with Richie Cellini, on duty or not. He sits and waits, eyebrows raised in curiosity, but doesn't ask me what I want. Richie Cellini knows how to be patient. I bet he's a great poker player.

"I'm here working on a cold case," I break the silence. "And I'm hoping you can provide me with some information." I see a look of relief pass over his eyes, but it's gone so quickly I think I might have imagined it. "It's a young woman whose body was found in the bog. Ella Weaver."

Richie's face is blank. "Never heard of her."

"She died thirty years ago."

He shrugs. "So, what's it got to do with me?"

"Not you, specifically. With Joe Rossi. He ran this place for his father then, right?"

"So ask him." He's about to ask me to leave, then a smile breaks out. "You already did. Got nowhere?"

I shrug. "This girl disappeared after a concert at the Buffalo Auditorium. I know Rossi provided girls for parties, and I've got a photo of him with her that night. The girl she was with, her best friend, ended up working here a while later. It wasn't hard to connect the dots."

"Before my time." And above his pay grade.

"I don't think so…Pretty sure you were working the door at that time."

"How would you know that?"

"Small town. Long memories."

"So? Lots of girls work here." We could go on having this conversation for hours, and I know Richie isn't going to give me anything. Not unless I give him something first. I take a deep breath and look him in the eye.

"My mother was Helena Melnyk." He leans back in surprise, then looks me up and down, appraising me.

"You don't look much like her. But then I don't imagine you'd be coming in here telling me that if it weren't true. Guess you take after your father. Anyone I know?"

I shake my head. No point bringing that up. "I doubt it." Even though there's no doubt in my mind he knew Scott McAlpine.

"I guess I owe you a favour. For taking care of Ray Miller."

Ray Miller, my stepfather. "He killed my mother."

He makes an ugly sound that sounds something like a laugh. "And you killed him right back."

I get up to leave, tossing my card in front of him. "If you think of anything, call me. Please."

As I leave I turn to see Richie, tapping my card on the table, lost in thought.

THIRTY THREE

ON MY WAY to the station I drop by Womyn Collective to see Rachel, and find her in her usual spot, among the women teaching them needlework. Some are knitting, some crocheting. Several are seated at a large table, assembling a quilt under her supervision. Her face drops when she sees me. She knows why I'm here.

"How's it going?" I'm keeping it vague in the hope she'll steer the conversation in a direction she's comfortable with. I can get to my questions once we've broken the ice.

"Fine." She's wary. "You here to arrest me?"

I shake my head. "I know you didn't have anything to do with Price's death. Neither did Kim." Rachel doesn't need to know about the pressure DS Agu put on me to close the case. It's not her problem, yet.

"Any idea who did it?" As much as I'm tempted to tell her about Rossi, I hold back. Rachel doesn't need to know what I've done and there's nothing she can do to help, so why give her the additional stress that knowledge will bring.

"Yeah, I know. I just have to prove it."

She doesn't press but I can tell she's curious. But she's still cool. I guess whatever trust we shared is damaged. "So, what brings you here?"

"I thought I'd just have a coffee…see how you're doing."

Rachel's expression changes from suspicion to something like relief. "I'm sorry," she says, ushering me away from the rest of the women in the knitting circle. "I'm just…so tired. This whole mess has taken a lot out of me. It's taken everything, actually. Feels like there's nothing left."

"I get it, believe me."

She pats my arm. "I know you do Lucy. I know."

We take a seat in the cafe and she pours us both a coffee.

"I just came back from the hospital," she says once she's had a sip. "Dillon wouldn't tell me anything about who put him up to the robbery."

"What did he say?"

"He played dumb, like he didn't know who set it up. But I know my son. He's lying." She puts down her coffee cup and meets my eye. "I've seen him lie to me since he was born."

"He's going to prison, Rachel. It'll help reduce his sentence if he gives us a name."

Rachel shakes her head. "He just kept repeating that Cadet Dillon Byrne garbage. It's all from that idiotic *code of honour* and lot of other crap he learned at that school."

"What school?"

"Ellesmere Academy."

I almost spit out my coffee. "What! The *military school*? Are you kidding me?" I think my brain is going to short circuit. Rachel is a hippie, a mystic, a psychic and an artist. How is that even possible? "*You* sent your son to *Military School*? You exposed your boy to the military industrial complex?"

Rachel rolls her eyes. "His father—who had custody at the time—did it. It was not my idea."

"You didn't raise Dillon?"

"When we divorced, he got custody of Dillon. He had a job, money, was seen a *stable influence*," she say, making air quotes.

"I was not seen in that light by the court. He made me look like a flake and a phoney and a lunatic. Plus, he could afford a good lawyer. I couldn't."

"How did you feel about that—the whole military school thing?"

"I hated it. Obviously," she sighs. "Supposedly their *structured environment* was going to remediate his math and literacy problems, and help with Dillon's ADHD and his lack of focus. "

"And did they? Help with that?"

"No," Rachel laughs. "But he can climb a rope, run ten miles, and field strip a rifle in less than three minutes. His shoes are always shiny and you could bounce a quarter off his bed. But no, he's not focussed."

"Yeah, I remember. His void moon in Capricorn or whatever." Rachel smiles and I feel her thawing. "What was your husband, Dillon's father, like? How'd you meet?"

"His name was Sean. He was in a band." She catches my look. "I know I know," she laughs. "Always with the musicians."

"He played in a folk rock band that used to gig around the area." She stares off into the middle distance. "His accent was… dreamy." She does a mock shiver. "Irish. His voice sent shivers through me. How could I resist?"

"Where'd the military thing come from? Seems weird for a musician, no?"

Rachel hesitates. "Sean came here, from Ireland, in the 80's. To get avoid arrest by the British security forces."

"Arrest?"

"He'd been recruited into one of their republican paramilitary groups…."

"…like the IRA?"

"The INLA. Same difference. You couldn't really avoid it if you lived in Belfast. So he said anyway."

"The military school seems…"

"…Ironic?" She laughs. "He ran away from Ireland to avoid the military conflict and look where our son ended up."

"When Dillon was a boy he and his father used to play war games all the time. Pretend battles and manoeuvres with toy soldiers all over the dining room table." She shakes her head. "Dillon became an Army Cadet, down at the Armoury as soon as he turned twelve, before he went away to the military school…"

"How long was your son there?"

"Just a couple of years," she laughs. "So not too much damage done. There was no money. Sean couldn't pay for the tuition in the end and I wasn't going to contribute to it, you can bet on that."

"And where is Sean now?"

"Back in Ireland, as far as I know. Haven't heard from him in years."

"What about Dillon? Is he still in touch with his father?"

"Doubt it. Sean's moved on again I'm sure. He was never one to let the grass grow under his feet."

As I'm getting up to leave Rachel rushes over and wraps me in a big hug, squeezing so tight I can barely breathe. I feel her breath on the back of my neck as she's whispering something I can't understand.

"It's a prayer," she says as she pulls away. "Of thanks and protection, for you." Rachel's eyes are full of tears and she brushes them away with her shawl. "Thank you Lucy. I'm grateful to you for what you're doing. For Ella."

"I haven't really done anything, Rachel. Not yet anyway." We haven't arrested anyone for Ella's death and I'm not sure I'll ever be able to without more evidence.

"But you have! You have no idea."

"What am I missing?"

"I got a call from Shelley Arthur," she says. "The young

woman who's writing the book about Stan Price. I'm going to meet with her."

"Sorry…what? She's writing the book now?"

Rachel laughs. "Stan can't exactly do it himself now, being dead and all."

"She knows about you and Stan? And Ella?" Rachel nods.

"She does now! Shelley is a resourceful girl," Rachel laughs. "She told me she'd called Price's publisher and pitched the idea as soon as she learned about me."

"And how'd that happen?"

Rachel shrugs. "I'm pretty sure she'd read the marriage license. She told me she'd called Guy LaForce herself for details. Then she tracked me down."

That would have been easy enough to do. Rachel is well known in the area.

"So she got the go ahead to finish the memoir? Good for her, I guess."

"I hope she's being well-paid," Rachel says. "There's no way the book could be finished without her."

"Where are you meeting her?" Rachel gives me a sly smile. "Not at Price's house!?"

"I'm curious," she admits. "God knows I've seen the exterior of his mansion enough. Time I saw the inside, no?"

"Well you know where curiosity gets you." I shake my head in disapproval.

"Dead, if you're a cat," she laughs. "I'm pretty sure I'll be okay."

"But why Rachel? Why stir up the past?…" I catch myself and stop. *Hypocrite.* Who am I to say anything about her digging up the past when that's all I've been focussed on since this all began?

THIRTY FOUR

WHEN I LEAVE Rachel all I want is to get home to safety and to Maja. She called in a takeout food order that'll be ready after I make a quick stop to get the wine. Maja and I need some time together, so I can try to understand why she needs to go away. And I desperately need a break from work—from Agu and Vogel, from Ella Weaver and Stan Price, and Joe Rossi and Kim Parsons.

I know I've been obsessing, and I admit I've lost perspective, not that I'll ever say as much to Vogel. But finding out who killed Ella, and helping Rachel and Kim, is something I can't let go of. It's personal. It became that way when I first understood that Joe Rossi was involved somehow in my mother's life.

There's a connection between my mother and Kim, and it's Rossi and his strip clubs, and the gangs, and the drugs—all of which changed the course of my life when I was still a child.

Helping Kim and Jade, and finding out what happened to Ella, feels like I'm helping myself. My therapist would dismiss it as projection, but that doesn't make it wrong. I can't change my past, but I can change Kim and Jade's future. I'm looking after Jade because no one looked after me.

Old sins cast long shadows I've often been told and I can tell you it's true. Those sins may be dead and buried, but their shadows live forever. And they have claws that will tear the heart right out of you.

When I walked into the fire I knew it was dangerous, but I hoped I wouldn't be burned. After all, when you sell your soul, when you've made a deal with the devil, the flames won't set you ablaze. But there's always a cost. I knew it would have to be paid at some point, but I didn't know the price. And it didn't matter. I had no choice.

When Pandora opened the box she released all the evils upon the world. Her curiosity brought misfortune. But I didn't open the box because I was curious. I knew what I'd find there. I knew exactly what it would unleash but I hoped I could handle it. I still hope so.

At least tonight I won't have to think about it. Nothing is going to happen, not yet. I've got two chilled bottles of wine in the backseat calling my name and the bag of takeout Thai food I place carefully into the hatch smells so delicious I'm tempted to grab a spring roll right now, but I resist.

I slam the door shut and I'm going around the back of the car when pair of strong hands grabs me. A black hood is pulled over my head and I put up a good fight until a second pair of hands restrains me and I'm thrown into the back of a car. There's no point in fighting two assailants I can't even see.

My heart is pounding and my mind racing. *Keep it together. Stay calm.* I guess they aren't going to kill me—they could easily have done that by now. So this is something else. The devil wants his due.

One of them gets in on either side of me and I do my best to stay calm. I breathe deeply, trying to stay focussed, to notice anything that might help me identify my kidnappers. We drive for about ten minutes in silence. I try for a while to guess if I'm turning left or right or going over bridges but it's futile. I have no idea where they are taking me or how far we've been going. We may have been going in circles for all I know. It feels like ten minutes, could be more or less. It's impossible to tell. Time feels elastic.

It smells like expensive men's cologne: woody with sandalwood. The scent is coming from the guy next to me. I catch the aroma of cigarettes as well, but realize that's not very helpful. I can't hear anything outside the vehicle. It's an expensive car, luxurious leather seats, quiet. I remember the windows were tinted.

What's the plan? Are they going to shoot me? Dump my body somewhere out in the country? Why?

Finally we stop and I can feel the breeze as the back doors are both opened. The nice smelling guy gets out and pulls me out of the back seat. He's firm but not rough, and I'm taken by both arms and led into what smells like a restaurant kitchen. I can smell meat being grilled and feel the steam from an industrial dishwasher, but nobody says a word. Whoever these cooks are, I guess they know enough not to notice people being escorted through their dinner service wearing hoods.

A door swings closed behind us and I'm walking on thick carpet. Classical music is playing. The men let go of my arms and I'm pushed down into an upholstered chair, then the hood is pulled off.

Sitting across from me is a well-groomed man, with a neatly trimmed beard and moustache. He's wearing an expensive suit and toying with a glass of red wine that sits on the white tablecloth in front of him. I've never seen him before; he's not the kind of man you'd forget. The table is set for one. I guess I'm not staying for dinner, which I hope is a good sign.

I steal a glance around the room as my eyes adjust to the light. We're in a private dining room, in a fancy restaurant. It's definitely no place I've ever been in.

"Who are you?" I ask.

"That's not important." He smiles. "Call me Nikolai, if you like." I nod. His voice has no trace of an accent. Russian, maybe. Mobster, probably.

"I understand you've been asking for me," he says. "What is your interest?"

"I'm a police detective. It's my job."

"Is it your job to expose yourself in this way, just to get information about someone no longer alive?" So he knows.

"She was my friend's daughter…"

"I have no interest in the girl. I ask you about Renato Rossi."

"I'm not interested in him. I want his son, Joe."

"Vengeance?"

"Accountability. Consequences."

He chuckles. "You believe in a world where actions and consequences still have some kind of connection. Interesting." He swirls his wine, then takes a drink. "I'm not sure Joe Rossi lives in that world."

"But you do. And I do." I have to assume he has some kind of justice in his organization, something to keep order, to keep the peace.

Nikolai nods. "And the consequences of your actions, Detective Gauthier? Have you considered them?"

I just look at him. I don't need to ask what he means. "I've thought about nothing but the consequences of my actions my entire life." And I've been paying that price.

"I'm not referring to your past, fascinating though it is. I'm talking about your debt to me, if I accede to your request. A debt will be owed."

"I know." Is it worth the price I'll pay? I think it is.

Nikolai drinks his wine and considers for a moment.

"We are considering closing down some of our businesses, clubs like Aphrodite's," he finally says. "Times are changing. We need to pivot, to move some of our enterprises into different industries."

"Sounds like a good idea, if you're asking me." He raises his eyebrows and laughs. "Joe Rossi is a liability for you," I press. "I'm investigating the death of a fifteen-year old girl, a death connected to Rossi. You need him gone. We'll be turning over everything connected to Rossi to get to the truth. And it'll be very public.

"The story of the bog bodies have been all over the media for months. There's even a movie being made about the story." Nikolai's lips turn down in disapproval and he shakes his head. "I don't know how comfortable you'll be with the scrutiny. Joe Rossi is bad for business."

He nods in agreement. "His father Renato had style. Yes, he was in and out of jail, and too often in the press, but he was a leader. Joe…he's weak. But he is Renato's son…" He shrugs. "So we respected him on principle."

"But Renato's gone. Maybe it's time for a change."

"I'll take it under advisement," he says. "What is it you want?"

"I want Joe Rossi."

"Tell me more."

"He killed a young girl—Ella Weaver, thirty years ago. And he had Louis Zappa dispose of her body in the bog." He watches me, expressionless, eyes steady, never leaving my face. "But I don't have proof."

He shrugs. "Thirty years is a long time."

"Not to her mother."

He nods. "And what's it to you? Just another case?"

"I have a personal interest." From the smirk on his face I know Richie has told him about my mother. And about my past.

I know I'm taking a huge risk. But I can't think of another way to get to Rossi.

Whatever he did all those years ago must have cost his father dearly. And made Renato Rossi angry enough to cut his son out of the Will. Someone had something on Joe, something huge that forced Renato Rossi to give up his strip clubs and get out of the drug business. Maybe that someone helped cover up what Joe did, and just maybe they have evidence of what it was. I know I'd hang onto it, for as long as it was useful. But now that Renato Rossi's dead, things are different. And maybe I can take advantage of it. Maybe it'll give me a lever I can use to shift the heavy rock that's burying Joe Rossi's crimes.

"We may have some mutual interests," he says. "If I help you in this, assuming I'm in a position to do so, what will you do for me Detective Gauthier?"

"What do you want?"

"We'll see." He smiles.

THIRTY FIVE

"Two weeks ago I was skiing down Mount Rundle," Vogel says, sipping his coffee and making a face. "It feels like a year ago."

"Poor you. Two weeks ago I was in the middle of a bank robbery. And it feels like yesterday."

Vogel gives me a dirty look. "You win," he says. "You have all the fun."

Vogel is trying to make nice with me, to patch up our falling out. I want to get over it, but all of his efforts just make me more irritated with him. I don't even know why. My therapist would tell me I'm deflecting, that I'm angry about something else. It doesn't take a genius to figure out I'm upset with Maja.

Last night all she could talk about was Doctors Without Borders. She didn't even notice the takeout food was cold by the time I got home after my meeting with Nikolai, which was a both a relief and a disappointment since I'd spent the entire ride home working out a plausible explanation. She's excited and happy and stimulated in a way I don't remember seeing in a long time, which makes me upset and angry, then I get angry with myself for feeling that way. It's a mess. I try to shine it on for her, to say the right things and appear supportive, but I keep hoping it will all go away. That she'll change her mind or that she'll be rejected for some reason. But so far, no luck.

"What's the status on that bank robbery anyway?" Vogel asks after a moment.

"It's not my case," I brush him off. "Division 2 is on it." I can tell from the look in his eye that he's disappointed, but I can't bring myself to care. I know I'm being mean and withholding the information Dudek has shared. I could tell Vogel, if I wanted to. But I guess I just don't want to.

I force myself to smile. "Two of the robbers are in still hospital and they aren't talking." The pathetic look of gratitude on Vogel's face makes me feel ashamed.

"It's almost a week since Price was killed," I say. "And that's not exactly moving fast either."

As soon as the conversation comes around to the Price case I can tell Vogel is uncomfortable. Maybe he regrets going to Agu, or maybe he just dreads the inevitable conversation we need to have. He's saved when his phone rings and he has to return to his desk to answer it.

A few minutes later I'm staring out the window when the officer on desk duty walks past and tosses a brown padded envelope onto my desk.

"What's this?"

She shrugs. "It was delivered a while ago. Courier."

My heart starts to race and I'm about to tear it open when Vogel appears at my side. He grabs my hand.

"Woah! Slow down Gauthier. You don't know what's in there!"

"Vogel, relax." I roll my eyes. "It's not a bomb. Or anthrax." He hands me a pair of scissors and backs away as I cautiously slice the end open and let the contents slide out onto my desktop. It's a USB stick.

I pick it up and insert it into my laptop. "Don't you want to check that for prints?"

"I know who it's from." *Nikolai. It has to be.*

As I'm waiting for the file to open my phone rings.

"Did you receive my gift?" Nikolai's voice slips into my ear.

"Yes, just now."

"I hope it fits."

I glance at Vogel who's straining to listen in, his brow furrowed. "What is it?"

"I believe it's known as *kompromat*?" Nikolai laughs. "I'll be in touch Detective Gauthier." He hangs up the phone.

"How did you get this?" Vogel asks, his eyes narrowed suspiciously.

"It's a gift, from an anonymous concerned citizen," I say. "Who wants to see justice done." A chill runs through me as I do my best to act casual.

"What did you have to do to get this *gift*? Sell your soul?"

I force a laugh and don't reply.

I open the folder that appears on the screen and start to quickly look through the documents and photographs. It looks like enough evidence to put Rossi away for a long time. There's also an audio file.

I wave Vogel over and hit play. We're sitting close together, huddled over my computer listening as a man's voice comes through the speaker. He's slurring his words and sounds panicky.

She's dead! The girl. The one who said she's Price's daughter.

"I'm sure it's Joe Rossi," I whisper to Vogel.

Cretino! Pezzo di merda! The other voice starts shouting down the phone. It's an older man. *How'd she die?*

"Think that's Renato Rossi?" Vogel says. I nod and wave my hand to quiet him as I strain to listen.

I think maybe she OD'd?

What did you give her? Cretino! The other man keeps swearing in Italian. *Non sai nulla! Asino!*

We were partying, Joe Rossi whines. *Poppers. Some Ludes. Smoked some weed. Booze.*

Is she alone?

She's got a friend. Passed out.

Is she alive? The other man snorts in disgust. *Idiota!*

She's breathing. You'll take care of it?

I can't hear what the second man is saying. His voice is distorted, as if he's speaking to someone else in the room.

I look at Vogel, eyebrow raised. "Probably looking for a fixer," he says.

Zappa? Okay. I'll wait for him.

The recording ends.

And there it is. Proof Joe Rossi was responsible for Ella Weaver's death and that he'd had her body disposed of by Zappa. Proof that Kim was there, and that she was alive, and that Zappa must have *taken care* of her as well.

Vogel gives me a high five but I don't feel celebratory as I head into DS Agu's office to report. We'll get a warrant and bring Joe Rossi in. I don't even know how much that envelope will cost me, not yet. But I'm sure it's worth the price I'll pay.

THIRTY SIX

"**Do you think** the charges against Rossi will stick?" Rachel asks when I share the news. "Is there enough?" She doesn't sound hopeful.

Kim and Rachel are together in Rachel's workshop, where Kim is treadling the spinning wheel. She's doing a much better job of it than Vogel did.

"I'm not going to lie," I admit. "It's not a slam dunk. Not that I'm a lawyer." When she hears that, Kim falters and loses her rhythm. "We could use testimony, or at least a statement from you, Kim."

Kim freezes. "I can't do it." She shakes her head and clenches her hands in her lap. I can see she's trying to stop them from trembling. "Why would he kill Ella?" she whispers.

I shouldn't share the details of the investigation, I know that. Especially before Kim has given any kind of statement, in case the information I provide colours her testimony. But she and Rachel both deserve to know.

"It looks like it was an accident," I say. "An overdose of alcohol and whatever drugs she was given that night."

"But…he buried her body!" Rachel says. "That was no accident."

"He got someone to help to hide her body, and to dump

Kim, far away from the scene. I guess he hoped she wouldn't ever remember what happened that night."

"I don't," Kim says. "Not really."

"No, true," I say. "But you can make a statement about what you do remember. And everything you left out the first time. Tell us about the concert, the party, who you remember being there. And the photo you gave me."

"Will that be enough?" Rachel asks, with a glance at Kim, who's still trembling and shaking her head.

"It'll help."

"No. I can't do it," Kim insists. "I can't testify in court. It's dangerous."

Rachel stands beside her, putting a comforting hand on her shoulder.

"It's okay," she whispers. "You're both safe here."

"Rossi can't hurt you now," I say. "He's in custody."

"You don't understand," Kim says. "They'll tear me apart. They'll bring up my past, the drugs…I could lose Jade again."

Kim's right and I can't argue with her. That's exactly what Rossi's defense counsel will do, in order to discredit Kim. If they can present her as an addict, as an unreliable witness, that'll help a jury to discount her statement.

As Rachel sees me out I glance over my shoulder to see Kim, staring out the window, still trembling.

"She'll be okay," Rachel says once we're out of earshot. "I'll look after her. And Jade."

"How is Jade doing? She's been through a lot lately…"

"I think she'll be fine," Rachel says. "Kids are pretty resilient. And I think Jade is much stronger than her mother. Funny that, these things seem to skip a generation."

I wonder if she's thinking of Dillon. A weak son from such a strong mother. Maybe if he ever has children of his own, they'll take after their grandmother Rachel. God willing.

I try once more to get Rachel to help Kim to cooperate. "Can you work on her? Get her to make a statement?" I'm not ashamed to manipulate her if I have to. "It's for Ella too. To bring Joe Rossi to justice for what he did to her."

Rachel sighs. "Not justice," she echoes. "Retribution, maybe. Punishment. Justice would be having Kim and Jade live safe, happy lives. If Ella couldn't, if she wasn't given that chance, then maybe Kim and Jade can make up for that. In some way."

"Telling the truth about Ella, and about Stan Price, will help. That's a kind of justice. That's why testifying in court can help."

Rachel just gives me a sad smile. "Price is dead, so he's beyond mortal justice. And maybe Rossi will even get away with it—who knows how the court case will go. None of it will bring Ella back anyway." For a moment it sounds like she's given up, then she winks at me.

"But this book Shelley Arthur is writing will make all the difference. Even if Rossi gets off the legal charges the truth about him will stick. He'll never get it off his shoes."

"I hope you're right."

"I'm on my way there now," she says, jingling her car keys and giving me sly grin. "Going to get a tour of Price's palace, then I'll tell her all about the early days of Running Deep and the real Stan Price. I'm looking forward to it."

I'm disappointed as I head out to the car. I'd hoped to feel victorious, so validated once we arrested Joe Rossi for Ella's death. It's so rare to have any kind of success in a cold case—especially one thirty years old. And here we have it—a solid arrest of the man I know to be guilty of the crime. But it can so easily slip away, because enough evidence for a warrant and an arrest is not always enough for a conviction.

For a brief second I wonder if the deal I made with the devil was worth it, if it turns out that Rossi doesn't get charged with murder for Ella's death. But it is. I know it is, no matter what happens, it was the right thing to do. It has to be. As for pinning Price's murder on him, well I'll just have to keep digging until I come up with enough evidence to charge him with that too.

"Hey, Lucy!" Rachel calls after me as I leave Womyn. I turn to see her running toward the car flagging me down. "I forgot… to tell you. I…spoke to Dillon this morning." She's out of breath from her run.

"Did he tell you anything?" Maybe a break in the robbery case will make up for Kim's unwillingness to testify.

"He was on some heavy pain meds. I thought that might be a good time to ask him," she winks, but something about her tone doesn't sound positive. "He mumbled something about the General. The *General needed my help*. More of his military fantasy I guess. Seriously, what kind of nonsense is that?"

"I have no idea."

Another disappointment. That's the kind of day it's been. When Vogel and I arrested Rossi this morning I had a hard time keeping the smug expression off my face. There had been no issue with our getting an arrest warrant when we presented the evidence and we'd pulled up in front of Rossi Realty with two cruisers and an unmarked car. We didn't need the flashing lights, but I wanted to rub Rossi's face in it.

Reality set in when Rossi was led away, without cuffs.

"What the fuck, Vogel?" I'd hissed in his ear. "Cuff him!"

He'd just smiled at me and shaken his head. "Sorry Gauthier," he said. "Agu says no. Give him his dignity, preserve his reputation."

I saw red. "He's responsible for the death of Ella Weaver. Why would we give a shit about his *dignity and reputation*?"

Vogel had just shrugged and I'd wanted nothing more than to punch him in the mouth.

"Oh, I get it," I'd snapped. "Rich white guy syndrome."

Vogel grabbed me by the shoulders and pushed me around the corner so the uniformed constables couldn't hear us. "You need to calm the fuck down."

"After all, who was Ella?" I kept raging. "A nobody. Just another dead poor girl. She doesn't matter as much as Joe Rossi's reputation and dignity."

"I'm following orders." I struggled to pull myself free and glared at him until he let me go. He stepped back, shaking his head. "Sometimes you've got to go along to get along. You need to learn that."

We still don't have enough evidence to charge Joe Rossi for the murder of Stan Price, which is another disappointment. I know the two cases are connected somehow and my gut tells me that connection goes way back, to before the night Ella died, possibly even to the original deal Stan Price made with Renato Rossi.

Joe Rossi definitely had the motive to kill Stan Price, if only to cover up the theft of Running Deep's royalties. And it wasn't a bad idea for the Rossi family to make sure the memoir never sees the light of day. After all, what might Price reveal in it?

If Rosa Rossi is telling the truth and *youthful indiscretions* are what got Joe Rossi cut out of his father's Will, then I'd bet in his years as a concert promoter there would have been many other times he'd had to be bailed out by Papa. Times like Ella's death, where he'd had messed up badly and left a huge mess that had to be cleaned up. If Stan Price revealed the kind of stuff they'd gotten up to, and the kind of *facilitating* Rossi had done for the band, and other bands he'd promoted, Rossi's reputation would be ruined. It would put an end to Rossi's political aspirations.

As much as I might like the thought Joe Rossi is guilty of both crimes, there's nothing that ties him to Price's murder, not to mention he has a solid alibi. The evidence on the tape proves Joe Rossi was clearly responsible for Ella's death, but that he was crying and weak, just like his sister Rosa had said. He was desperate and afraid and clearly in over his head—not a take-charge kind of guy. The first thing he did after Ella's death was to call Daddy, who sent in Zappa to clean up the mess. Sure, he was younger then. And maybe he was scared, and in over his head. Possibly he's learned a lot in the last thirty years. Maybe he's now evolved to getting his hands dirty. But people don't really change and I'd bet he's the same man he was then. I can't believe he'd have what it took to kill Stan Price…he just didn't have the jam. So who did?

If Joe Rossi needed Stan Price killed, he might have turned to someone to get it done, which is risky. It could reveal his weakness and show him to be a liability. He'd be vulnerable. Calling in someone in for help would expose his belly. Unless it was someone he trusted. Someone in the family—the biological family, that is. Someone like his nephew, maybe?

Angelo Rossi seems like the kind of guy who'd be more than happy to take matters into his own hands. He's just like his grandfather, so everyone says. Ruthless.

What was it Rachel just said? *These things seem to skip a generation.* Does that mean Renato Rossi's grandson is strong enough to do what his son Joe couldn't?

Probably, but Angelo Gennaro hated his uncle. I remember seeing Angelo Rossi's face that day at the *trattoria*, and the argument I witnessed at the Rossi Realty office between him and his uncle Joe. He wasn't about to do him any favours, let alone murder Stan Price to help him out.

I pull the car over to the side of the road so I can concentrate. The family lawyer Arturo had told me Angelo Rossi was *strong* and *a natural* to take over the family business. Had Renato Rossi seen who his grandson really was, what he was capable of—unlike his son Joe? Is that why he'd changed his Will to favour Angelo and cut Joe out of it?

My heart quickens pace. Is that why the new Will disappeared in the first place? It makes sense that Joe Rossi would steal it, since he'd been cut out and wanted it destroyed. And it's certainly interesting timing that Arturo's offices were torched right after the old man died. Was that to make sure any copies would go up in smoke? Maybe Joe Rossi's got the same fire starter gene as his nephew Angelo. That might explain a few things.

What was it Arturo had said about Wills? *You keep the original in a safe, with your lawyer, or in a safe deposit box at the bank.* My heart beats faster. Was that what Jason Winner had slipped into his pocket? An envelope containing the original of Renato Rossi's Will, stolen from his safety deposit box during the robbery.

Dudek told me that Rossi's safety deposit box was definitely one of those they'd opened, though he didn't yet know what they'd reported missing—if anything. And, since the Will had suddenly just *turned up*, according to Rosa, the timing was certainly suspicious. They'd managed to find it right where it was hidden.

Is it a coincidence that Joe Rossi happened to be in the bank the day of the robbery? Did he organize it, and then kill Winner after he handed over the new Will, so he could destroy it? Joe Rossi needed that Will to disappear. That way they'd have to revert to the original Will so his assets would be divided equally among his children. That's how Joe Rossi could keep control of at least part of the Rossi family businesses and assets.

And did he set the fire at Arturo's office…to cast suspicion onto his nephew with the history of fire starting? This feels like a real possibility to me, especially if he knew Angelo was supposed to inherit in his place.

But then the new Will surfaced, so that doesn't quite fit. There's no way Joe Rossi would have masterminded the bank robbery only to get a copy of the Will that cut him out in favour of his nephew. He would have destroyed it. My heart sinks. There goes his motive.

Unless somebody else stole the Will from the bank. And I know who.

THIRTY SEVEN

I GRAB FOR my phone and press speed dial. Vogel picks up immediately.

"Vogel!" I shout into the phone. " I know who did it."

"Who did what?"

"It's Angelo Rossi…he's behind it all."

"All what? Gauthier, where are you?"

"It's the only thing that makes sense," I cut him off. "Angelo Rossi has the motive. And both the lawyer Arturo and his mother Rosa, describe him as being exactly like his grandfather. He's the natural heir to Renato Rossi. It skipped a generation. It's all connected Vogel!"

"How? How is it all connected?" He sounds exasperated. "Please, slow down. You're way ahead of me. Help me catch up to you." I'm so grateful for Vogel in that moment I forget my anger toward him, my sulking and resentment. He's a good guy. He's my partner.

"I don't know, not exactly." Then it comes to me. "Vogel, where did you say Angelo Rossi went to school after he was expelled from Ridley?"

"Ellesmere Academy. The military school over by Beamsville."

And that's where the pieces fall into place. "Ellesmere Academy is where Dillon Byrne went to school. I bet that's where he met Rossi. And that stupid military code of honour…"I'm rambling, thinking aloud and talking rapid-fire. "Angelo Rossi got Dillon to participate in the robbery. And Dillon went along with it out of loyalty to his old school friend."

"You've lost me Gauthier," Vogel says. "Who's Dillon Byrne?"

"Rachel Weaver's son. The robber with the broken neck." Vogel is silent. "Vogel, what's wrong?"

"You're telling me Rachel Weaver—our main suspect for Price's murder—is related to one of the bank robbers?" His voice is clipped and angry. "And you didn't think to share this with me?"

I feed bad for a moment. Vogel is right. I've kept things from him, more than he'll ever know. "I'm sorry," I mumble and hear Vogel's deep sigh. "But Rachel is not a suspect. She's been helping me get some information from Dillon…He won't talk to police. I thought maybe his mother could help…"

Vogel starts to argue but I interrupt him.

"*Gennaro*!" I shout down the phone. "That's what Dillon said. Not *General*!"

"What's a Gennaro?"

"It's Angelo Rossi's legal last name."

"Okay…and?"

"Dillon Byrne told his mother he was helping *The General*. He meant Gennaro—that's who set up the bank robbery, to get into the safety deposit boxes and find his grandfather's Will, before Joe Rossi was able to destroy it."

"Destroy it? Why would he do that?"

"Because the new Will cuts Joe out of it entirely, and leaves control of the businesses to Angelo. Of course Joe Rossi would want it to disappear."

"Then he set the fire in Arturo's offices, to make sure any other Wills never surfaced." Vogel sounds excited. "It's certainly convenient that it suddenly appeared the way it did right after the funeral."

"Exactly."

"We do know Angelo liked to set fires," Vogel says. "Are you saying he killed Stan Price too? Why?"

"Money. We know Price was suing the Rossis for missing royalties. If he's dead, that problem goes away."

"Stan Price was also killed to shut him up. Everyone knew he was writing a memoir. Seems to me that anyone with something to hide, a dirty secret they wanted to stay buried…"

"Like the cover up of Ella Weaver's death?" Vogel says. "But what does that have to do with Angelo? He wasn't even born when Ella disappeared."

"Think about it Vogel. He chooses to go by the last name Rossi, not Gennaro. It's family pride—and everyone says he's exactly like his grandfather."

"You're saying he was trying to protect his family name?" Vogel says. "It seems like that ship sailed a long time ago. Everybody knows about Renato Rossi and his criminal connections."

"Not necessarily. Think about it. That was a long time ago, and the old man is dead now. People have very short memories."

Vogel considers for a moment. "And with Joe Rossi trying to have a political career…he needs to make sure the family name stays clean."

"Exactly."

"Angelo Rossi had access to Price's house," Vogel says. "Through Shelley Arthur. Maybe he even used her key."

"True. That relationship never made sense to me," I say. "She's this bookish, writer type, out here from the city on a short-term contract. She doesn't seem like a party girl. Not his type at all."

"Angelo's a flash guy," Vogel agrees. "I'd expect him to be with a different woman, one wearing a skintight mini dress and stilettos, with long fake nails and hair extensions."

"Basically the opposite of Shelley Arthur."

"Do you think Angelo got close to her to find out what she knew about the book? Maybe to find out what she knows?"

"Sure…but how'd he even know what Shelley was in town for?"

"Maybe he just guessed? Price was always going on about his book. It wouldn't be difficult to put the pieces together…"

"Wait, no!" I interrupt him. "She rented a place to live… through an agency. A real estate agency! That's how Rossi learned why she was in town. They'd have had to run a credit check on her before renting, and possibly even spoken with Price's publisher and found out what her job was."

"So…Shelley Arthur moves out here and Angelo Rossi conveniently meets her in a coffee shop, trying to get close to her. Or maybe he even showed her the apartment, on behalf of the agency. That fits," Vogel says. "Do you think Angelo Rossi figured out that Price had a ghostwriter? And that Shelley was more than just an assistant?"

"No way she'd have told him. She was terrified of the NDA."

"True…but he might have figured it out. Or, he might have found out Price's documents are still coming in—like that marriage certificate…or other things that might incriminate the Rossi family."

"And he wanted to know what those might be, just in case."

"Vogel, what do you suppose Angelo Rossi would do if he found out Shelley knows everything—about what happened to Ella Weaver, and about whatever was going on with the royalties?"

"He'd make sure she never told anyone. But since Price is conveniently now dead, I guess that's no longer an issue…"

"Vogel," I cut him off. "The book is still being written! Rachel told me that Shelley negotiated a deal with the publisher." I start the car and pull onto the road.

I hear a low whistle down the phone. "Rossi isn't going to like that. He would have thought Price's death would have ended it all."

"Shelley Arthur is in danger." My heart starts to pound and I press down on the accelerator. "Rachel Weaver is out there right now. Shelley asked her to come out and tell her the whole story." I'm speeding along the country road, spraying gravel as I pass a slow moving driver. I put on the flashers and siren. "I'm only a few minutes away."

"I'll meet you there," Vogel says as I speed up, anxious that I'll be too late. Maybe it's nothing, but I don't want to take a risk with Shelley and Rachel's safety.

"I'm almost at Price's place." I drive through the gates and tear down the driveway. The security lights are off, it's dusk. Hard to see into the shrubs that line the driveway…

As I round the bend and get close to the house,

"I see Rachel's car is in the driveway. So is Rossi's," I say, my voice full of dread. "He's already here."

"Maybe not," he says, but I can hear the tension in his voice. "Shelley borrows his car, remember?"

An orange and red glow is lighting up the evening sky. At first I think it's the sunset…then I realize it's flames.

"Vogel. The house is on fire!"

THIRTY EIGHT

I CAN SEE the kitchen is in flames and the back door completely impassable.

Are Rachel and Shelley still in there? Are they even alive? The searing heat from the fire drives me back and I know they won't be for long if I don't do something, fast. I can't wait for emergency services. Every second counts as the fire is spreading through the house.

I run around to the French doors by the terrace, pick up a heavy concrete planter and heave it through the glass. Pulling my jacket up over my face, I climb in through the broken door, relieved to find the smoke isn't too heavy yet in the dining room. But there's enough to make me start to cough and choke.

"Rachel!" I shout at the door to the kitchen. "Shelley!" There's no response, and the noise of fire is so loud I'm afraid I won't hear them anyway over the crackling and snapping of flame.

I know how quickly fire will consume wooden kitchen cabinets stocked with plastic containers and cardboard boxes of cereal and dry goods. There's already a dense smoke cloud filling the room to just a few feet above the floor. I see hot flame licking the kitchen cupboards as a spark shoots out of the undercabinet lights. Dancing angels of flame roll across the kitchen ceiling and I feel the intense heat radiating down on me. I'm instantly dripping with sweat and it's so hot I can barely draw breath.

There's no sign of Shelley or Rachel in the kitchen but I can clearly see a trail of what must be accelerant running along the marble floor, a line of fire leading down the hall toward the stairwell. For a moment I'm thankful to Stan Price. Stone doesn't burn and the fire isn't able to take hold on the floor even though the cabinets and the island are in flame and burning red-hot.

If Price's boasts about his house construction were true, the smoke won't contain the usual toxic chemicals found in a house fire. Typical construction materials give off deadly gasses like hydrogen cyanide as they burn.

Thank you Price, I whisper. Even though I'm choking on the smoke, I'm not dead. I fall to my hands and knees and crawl forward, trying to stay under the layer of smoke.

I close the door to the kitchen to try and buy Shelly and Rachel—and myself—some time, but the smoke and superheated air is already streaming out of the room. The stairwell is already full of black smoke, steam and embers —it's billowing out of kitchen now, filling the hallway and rising to fill the second floor.

I run desperately across the stone floor toward the living room. It's empty. Where are they?

"Rachel! Shelley!" I shout, praying they aren't upstairs. I'll never be able to help them if they are.

It's getting harder to think straight. Everything is black and hot and the noise is so loud and deafening…I'm suddenly overcome with terror so intense my knees buckle. I know I'm going to die if I don't get out of this house, now.

But I need to find them. I can't just let them die so I force myself to focus. I know can't check every room. There's no time and I don't think I can last much longer.

Logically Rossi would want them both to burn, and to make

it look like an accident—so he'd want them to be found close to the source of the fire. Most house fires start in the kitchen. So they must be on main floor, near the kitchen. The office. They have to be in there.

Doubling back I head back toward the hallway and stop dead. Waves of flame are rolling across the ceiling and flames are fingering the paintings and tapestries hanging on the walls. I can't get through. In the few seconds it's taken me to get through the hallway to check the living room it's filled with noise and smoke so dark I can't see anything. My only option is to get out of the house through the living room windows and save myself.

But I can't do that.

I pull one of the textile hangings off the wall and drape it over my head to protect myself from the heat, then take a deep breath, get low and crawl on my belly to stay under the thick layer of smoke. As I pass the kitchen I glance at the closed door. It's glowing red, as the inferno rages behind it. Again, I'm grateful for Price's ego and that thick oak door, but I know that at a certain temperature flashover will occur; objects will spontaneously burst into flames—even if they aren't touched by the fire. And I know that time is coming.

The office door is open, so the room is heavy with thick smoke, but I crawl in and close the door behind me to slow the fire. Coughing and gagging on the smoke,

I manage to find the window and I use one of Price's Grammys statuettes to smash it open. Immediately the smoke starts to vent and billow out the window. The room clears slightly, enough for me to see Rachel's long gray hair spread across the floor. I crawl over——and find she's still alive, her pulse is strong, but she's unconscious.

Pushing aside the boxes of memorabilia stacked on the floor, I see Shelley's legs sticking out from under the desk. I scramble across the carpet and grab for her, checking to see if she's still breathing. I exhale in relief when I find a pulse. She's alive.

Smoke is filling the room…I need to get them both out now. The flame has spread behind me and I can see the orange glow under the office door and hear the roar of fire as it devours the house. I can barely breathe through the heavy smoke and searing heat. There's no time left.

I'm strong, but I don't think I can pick Rachel up. I roll her body up in the wall hanging and heave her out the window, helped by the adrenaline rushing through my body. I hear her land in the shrubs outside and hope the wall hanging cushioned her fall. Then I crawl back for Shelley. I'm just dropping her out when I see the fire engines coming up the driveway.

I heave her up onto the ledge and out of the window, and hear a thump as she lands on the ground outside. I climb out after her, coughing and hacking so hard I vomit from the smoke.

I'm dizzy and confused but I have to get them away from the house. I grab Shelley's arm and start to drag her, staggering and desperate to escape when the firefighters arrive and take over, carrying both Rachel and Shelley to safety.

As I crumple from exhaustion on the lawn I see a figure at the back of the garden, watching the fire, half-hidden in the shrubs. It's Angelo Rossi. I see the flames dancing in his eyes.

Suddenly I hear an eruption as there's a flashover. The house windows shatter and balls of flame shoot out of the door as everything in the kitchen bursts into flame. Then I pass out.

When I come to, Vogel is cradling my head.

"It's okay," he's saying. "You'll be okay."

"Rachel? Shelley?" I whisper, my voice hoarse.

"They're both in the ambulance. They're safe. Alive."

I fall back onto the grass in relief. "Did you catch Rossi?"

"I tried," Vogel says. "I saw him hiding in the bushes, but he got away. Don't worry, he won't get far."

A paramedic takes over from Vogel. She slips an oxygen mask over my face and I lay back on the lawn. As if in slow motion the paramedics and firefighters are running toward the house, the hose is spraying from the pumper, and flames are shooting out of the second floor windows as the house is engulfed in flame.

Vogel is talking to the Fire Marshall, then he's on his phone. Thank God for Vogel I think as I allow myself to pass out again.

THIRTY NINE

"HOW ARE YOU doing?" Vogel asks me a few days later as he hands me a coffee. "Not sure you should be in this morning."

"All good. Just cut my hand on the broken window." I show him my bandaged hand.

Vogel laughs. "Given your history, that's impressive."

"Angelo Rossi in custody?"

"Yeah. We caught up with him near Toronto. His car's not exactly inconspicuous."

"Charged?"

"Murder of Stan Price. Attempted murder of Shelley Arthur and Rachel Weaver. Two counts of Arson. Bank robbery."

"Don't suppose he's confessed? I guess that would be too much to hope for."

"It's over for him. We've got him on the security camera," Vogel shrugs. "And there were witnesses."

"So Angelo Rossi burned the family lawyer's office too?"

"Looks like it. He wanted to destroy any other Wills, in case there was a dispute with his uncle Joe. That's what the bank robbery was all about—to get the new original out of the safety deposit box."

"The one that leaves the family business to Angelo?" Vogel nods.

"Exactly. He had to make sure there was no way Joe would try and take control."

"And he set fire to Arturo's office to make sure no other Will showed up?"

"I don't think so…"I'm pretty sure Joe Rossi set that one, and hoped his nephew the firebug would be blamed for it."

"Why?"

"He assumed that the copy of his father's Will was kept there, as it in fact was. He didn't count on there being one in the safety deposit box."

"Why did Angelo Rossi try to burn down Price's house? Just because he liked setting fires?"

"He wanted to eliminate any trace of tainted Rossi family history—and I'm sure he knew all of it. Probably even more than his uncle Joe, given how close he was with his grandfather. If the book died, and conveniently Price too, then the stories about the past indiscretions would die too. As would the lawsuit Price was going to file against Rossi for the missing royalties."

"So that's why he tried to kill Shelley, since he found out she was the ghostwriter. We found her apartment had been turned over, by the way. I'm guessing Rossi was looking for any notes or data drive that might have copies of the book on them. Her laptop was found it in Rossi's car when he was arrested."

"Poor Rachel," I say. "I doubt he even knew who she was. She just happened to be there when he arrived to murder Shelley. How's she doing?"

"She's got a fractured skull," Vogel says, "and she's suffering from smoke inhalation. But she'll be okay, in time. Looks like Rossi knocked her unconscious before he set the fire."

"And Rachel?"

"She's already discharged," he says. "They had her on oxygen overnight, but she was released in the morning. Said she had to get home and look after Jade and Kim."

"Is it all gone?" I ask. "All of Price's memorabilia? His notes?"

"Looks like it. Fire investigators say most of the damage was to the kitchen and his office. Angelo Rossi wanted to make sure he destroyed all traces of the Rossi family past misdeeds."

"So I guess the book will never see the light of day. The story dies with him?

Maybe it's just as well. It was all a very long time ago. Do we need another faded rock star's autobiography? Not as if it's going to make the world a better place."

"I wouldn't bet on that. Remember, the publisher had a lot of it already, and they've got Shelley to finish it. They'd be crazy to not take advantage of all the publicity in the media around this case: Price's murder, Rossi's arrest, the fire…"

"You're right. They'll sell millions of copies."

I finish my coffee and slowly get up. I'm aching and bruised all over, but no way I'll let Vogel know that. "Want to come along? I've got some news for Rachel."

Vogel grins in agreement and grabs for his coat.

When we arrive at Womyn, I see Jade is out in the flower fields with her mother, picking a bouquet. They look okay, which is the most I can hope for. Okay is pretty good, really. More than most of us get.

Rachel is in her usual spot, in her studio, struggling with something on the table, her right arm in a sling.

"Did I do that?" I point at her arm.

"Yes," she laughs, with a shadow of her usual vibrant self. "It's just a sprain, and you did save my life, so…" She points to the heap of yarn and fibre in front of her. "Do you recognize this?"

"No…should I? What is it?" Vogel picks it up and I see it's charred and burned black in places.

"It's the wall hanging you wrapped yourself in, to protect yourself from the fire," Vogel says.

"And the one you wrapped me in, before you shoved me out the window," Rachel adds with a laugh. "It's one of my pieces." Rachel fingers the textile thoughtfully. "Price had it in his collection."

"That's ironic," Vogel says. "Given everything that happened between you."

Rachel nods. "It saved my life."

"Speaking of irony," I say. Vogel and Rachel fall silent. "I've got some more news."

"Good news, please," Rachel says. "That's the only kind I'm interested in now."

"I've heard back from the Crown Attorney and she says it's clear you'll inherit Stan Price's estate. All of it." I do my best to suppress a grin at the expression on Rachel's face. "Is that good enough for you?"

"Are you serious?" she gasps. "You're not joking?"

"It's all legal. Guy Laforce, who actually was once a Reverend, filed and registered the marriage certificate with the government records office. It was witnessed by two people, and it's all perfectly in order."

"But…aren't you supposed to apply for a license or something? We never did that, I'm sure of it…"

"Guy LaForce explained it all to me. It was a religious ceremony…"

Rachel interrupts with a hoot of laughter. "That's ridiculous!"

"And in that case the minister just has to announce the banns during services for three weeks in a row prior to the ceremony. And, both the bride and groom must be members of the church."

Rachel looks confused. "*Members of the church?* I mean, that's stretching it…from what I remember. He must be senile…"

"Reverend LaForce is ninety years old now, but he's still sharp," I interrupt her. "He remembers speaking with Stan Price, and sending him the certificate, and he even remembered the day of your wedding—daisies, naked dancing, all of it."

"Anyway, it doesn't matter what you remember," I continue. "He says he did it and we're not in a position to argue. He legally registered the marriage afterwards, so it's all above board.

"And it's legal…?"

"Stan Price had no other family left who might make a claim on his estate. His only heir was Ella, who predeceased him. And you two were legally married. Even though he married—and divorced several other women—you and he were never divorced. You're his next of kin."

FORTY

I'VE FILED ALL the paperwork on the Ella Weaver case, and even got a nod from DS Agu for a job well done, which is high praise. Closing a cold case, especially one that's thirty years old, is a rare privilege. And even though Rossi hasn't confessed it's a decisive conclusion, given all the evidence. I'll just have to let the court decide his punishment.

Homicide cases never end with people happy. How could they? Sometimes there's a feeling of satisfaction, or a sense of justice being served when we're able to arrest and charge someone. But that's not exactly happy.

Vogel and I are out for a beer, down at the bar by the harbour. They have the most uncomfortable seats, but the view's the best in town. We're both looking out across the water, sharing a basket of fries and watching the sun fall slowly into the lake.

"Vogel," I start to say after a minute. "I…" I stop. I have no idea what I want to say. I don't know how to patch it up between us. I'm not great with words, or with feelings. "I was out of line…"

"Don't sweat it Gauthier. We're good."

"Are we? Are you sure?"

He meets my eye and raises his beer. "I'm sure."

"Okay," I take a drink. "Good."

It didn't take Rachel very long to accept the news about her inheritance, and she immediately began to make plans, starting with assessing the fire damage to Price's house. She'll probably sell it and the rest of the estate, and use the money to help Sophie with Womyn, as well as helping Kim and Jade get back on their feet. And Dillon, of course. Once he's out of prison maybe she can find a way to help her astrologically challenged son get a fresh start.

Rachel doesn't need much money and now she has lots of it, more than she's ever dreamed of—not that Rachel ever did think of money. Between Price's assets and investments, the winery, the house and the music publishing rights to all of Running Deep's song catalogue, there's enough to keep Womyn running forever.

Kim still refuses to testify against Rossi. She just can't face it, and I'm not sure it's a good idea anyway.

"He'll go to prison anyway, won't he?" she'd asked. "Just leave me out of it."

"But your story needs to be told Kim. It's not just Ella's—your life was ruined too. You deserve to be…avenged somehow." Kim just looked away. "For Jade's sake?"

The best I can do is to get her to say she'll think about it, but I know she won't.

Kim is afraid of what might happen if she speaks out. I know what that's like. I've been afraid my whole life. And lately I'm always waiting for the other shoe to drop.

When I contacted Nikolai I know I opened Pandora's box and released misfortune into my world, though it hasn't quite found me yet. I didn't open it because I was curious; I knew exactly what I'd find there. I knew what it would unleash, but I hoped I could handle it. I still hope so.

It's dark when I finish my beer. The sun has fully set and the water has become a dark mirror, reflecting the pale sliver of new moon. Maja and I are having Thai to celebrate, with a bottle or two of wine, and I need to get home. I leave Vogel at the harbour and head for my car.

As I walk through the dusk I feel an unfamiliar sensation, something new and a little worrying. I'm not anxious. I'm not full of dread. I'm possibly even happy, if that's possible.

Then a long black SUV pulls up in front of me, blocking the sidewalk and the back door opens.

ABOUT THE AUTHOR

Liza Drozdov is the author of the Niagara Noir series, including Blood Relative, Dark Water, The One That Got Away and In The Weeds. She worked as a bookseller and book publicist, as a garden designer and a college professor, and as a producer of lifestyle television, before settling down to writing full-time. She lives in Oakville, Ontario.

www.lizadrozdov.com

twitter.com/lizadrozdov

instagram.com/lizadrozdov